T0132453

Echo of a Dream

Echo of a Dream

Book One in the Choosing Love Series

SHIRLEY G. WEBB AND JANET M. MORELAND

iUniverse, Inc.
New York Bloomington

The central characters in this novel are all products of the authors' imaginations. Any similarity they might bear to real people, living or dead, is entirely coincidental. Names of the characters are likewise the authors' choices and do not represent real people. Where reference is made to historical people who now live or are deceased, it is by design, and their characterization, as reported, is historically accurate.

iUniverse books may be ordered through booksellers or by contacting:

iUniverse
1663 Liberty Drive
Bloomington, IN 47403
www.iuniverse.com
1-800-Authors (1-800-288-4677)

ISBN: 978-1-4401-8332-4 (sc)
ISBN: 978-1-4401-8330-0 (hc)
ISBN: 978-1-4401-8331-7 (ebook)

New York City Cover Model: Tracy Levey

Printed in the United States of America

iUniverse rev. date: 11/23/2009

To Tracy, who inspired us with her smile

A Word from the Authors

We are pleased to present the first book in the "Choosing Love" series, *Echo of a Dream*. This series will be a collection of stories with inspiration, romance, and suspense suitable for teenagers and adults.

If you are a fan of our three historical fiction novels in "The Howell Women Saga," you will also enjoy *Echo of a Dream*. You already know and fell in love with many of the characters during the reading of *Cherokee Love*, *Dance in the Rain*, and *Song of Love*. The characters were so strong and so captivating we could not let them go and have brought the family members up to 1974 through 1976. We added a few new characters, more exciting drama, page-turning suspense, and as always, the love.

We hope you enjoy reading *Echo of a Dream* as much as we enjoyed writing it.

Shirley and Janet

Prologue

Where am I? This place is unknown to me.

The lake in front of me looks like liquid silver. Mysterious swirls of white mist appear on the surface of the water like a congregation of moonbeams. The moon fades, surrendering to the sun rising behind the mountain.

In the early morning light, I see a figure standing below the mountain. With slow and deliberate steps, she (yes, the figure must be a woman) proceeds toward the edge of the lake. I move closer, my heart beating frantically.

Barefoot, she steps into the shallow water. Flutes play softly, accompanied by drums beating in unison. She wears a headband with white feathers that contrast with her long flowing black hair. She lifts the hem of her tan garment, and with the toes of her left foot skimming the water, she begins to sway back and forth to the mysterious music. She moves in the dance the way an artist uses a brush, and her gracefulness takes my breath.

As if on cue the music and dancing stop, and I see her lovely, solemn face. The anticipation she creates inside me is like the ripples of water where she stands tall and straight. Look at her, so cool and solitary and perfect. She was made for sunlight, or perhaps it was made for her. The breeze flutters the layers of her garment and the ends of her hair as she stands poised like a statue on a rock beside the lake.

She turns at the sound of my footsteps and looks into my eyes. Irritation flickers in her eyes, and then it is smoothed away, coated over with a thin sheen of cool politeness.

An urge deep within me makes me walk toward her. I cannot resist the impulse to reach out for her hand and lift it. My eyes are fixed on hers. I press my lips on the palm of her hand. Her eyes soften, and a slight smile graces the edges of her mouth.

Suddenly she is gone.

One

*A*drian Ashley awoke in a sweat. Staring up at the ceiling, he blinked, then dragged in a couple of calming breaths. The dream was over, a haunting dream he had experienced for weeks now.

This dream is driving me crazy, he thought. Throwing back the covers, he came off the bed and stood before the window, gazing absentmindedly at the rivulets of rain blurring the images below. Adrian believed his dream took place in a Native American village. But how would he know, he wondered; he had never been in one.

He smiled, closed his eyes, and inhaled deeply as the music from his dream still played in his head. A man can only hold onto a woman in a dream, he mused, if he accepts the world she lives in as reality. And this dream, although intense, was only a dream, not the real thing. It was Monday, September 23, 1974, and he was in his fourth floor suite at the Strand Palace Hotel in London. That was reality, yet Adrian wished somehow he possessed the will to cross over to her world, anything to have her, to touch her as he had in his dream.

The dream was so real that the face of the woman who appeared nightly also haunted him each and every day. Every evening when he went to bed, he prayed desperately for the dream to return, so anxious was he for just one more look at her.

At twenty-eight, Adrian was handsome and successful, but he was also a solitary man. There were fourteen years between his older sister, Roxie, and Adrian. His brother, Peter, was twenty years older than Adrian. During Adrian's youth, his parents traveled extensively, leaving him in the care of first a nanny, then a governess.

When he was seventeen, his mother died. Before her death, her great-uncle had come to live at Red Oaks, the family estate south of London. This old man told Adrian many stories about his mother and said their family was of Cherokee descent. He loved listening to the old man's enchanting tales, but never put much faith in the stories about a Native American heritage.

Adrian was certain that his financial connection with the ballet and the old tales about his mother having Native American ancestors were the reasons for his dream. His recent investment in a New York ballet, *Moonglow Fascination*, was an afterthought at the request of his friend, Ned Blanchent, the ballet's choreographer. Adrian never expected it to make a great deal of money, but after all, the troupe did need the funding, and he considered it a worthy cultural investment. He made a mental note to attend the ballet performance in London on Saturday. Ned had asked him to attend ballets previously, but Adrian declined and would now see his first ballet as a patron of the arts.

After a brief exercise workout, Adrian quickly showered and dressed. He decided to go to the Royal Opera House down the street from his hotel and find a piano. He would attempt to play the music he had heard in his dream, that haunting, mysterious music which had become so familiar to him. He had taken seven years of piano under the stern direction of his mother, and for the first time, he was glad he had been a willing student.

Luckily, the doors were open, and Adrian found a piano in the orchestra pit. He sat down on the piano bench. Almost magically, the music in his dream drifted softly and dreamily through the auditorium as he played. It was a mesmerizing refrain, and he wished he knew how to write the notation before he forgot it.

He glanced up to see a man in baggy pants and a sweat shirt who stood listening at the door to the auditorium. After Adrian attempted to play the song three times, the man walked down the aisle toward him.

"Hey, that's a different tune. What's it from? Anything I'd know?"

"Probably not." Adrian felt embarrassed for all the mistakes he had made. "I'm just playing around. It's a tune I once heard, and I was trying to remember it all. It seems I've lost my touch at the piano."

"Would you like for me to try? I'm with the orchestra. I play several instruments, but piano is my forte."

"I'd appreciate it very much." Adrian stood and stepped back from the piano.

The musician played the tune with much more agitato and crescendo than Adrian could ever play. He was clearly adept at songs with strong movement.

"That's beautiful, and you filled in my missing notes perfectly. Would you know how to write the notation?" Adrian asked the musician.

"Sure, I could do it."

"I'll be happy to pay you if you'd write it down for me."

"No problem. I'd like doing it. I'll work on it right now."

Before he turned to leave, Adrian offered his hand to the musician. "Thank you. Please leave it at the Strand Palace for me, Adrian Ashley."

"Mr. Ashley?" The musician's lifted eyebrows hinted at his recognition of Adrian's name. "Mr. Ashley, sir, it would be my pleasure. If it doesn't sound right in any place, you can always contact me here, and we'll go over it until I get it right."

"Thank you again. That's very good of you." Adrian walked up the aisle from the orchestra pit while the musician played on and on.

The day was already blooming with a harsh blue hue as soft hazy fingers of morning light crawled along the ceiling, down the mirrored walls, and along the shiny wooden floor in one of the practice studios of the Royal Opera House in London. The morning would soon stream through the windows Kaitlyn Rose Johnson opened for cross-ventilation and for the simple pleasure of feeling the early morning breeze in the studio she was using.

Katie, as her friends and family called her, heard a piano playing softly. She thought it was probably another dancer going over a routine at the far end of the building. The unfamiliar music was strange and haunting.

She went into the dressing room and put on her long sleeved white leotard and white handkerchief skirt. Today she must give her earnest concentration to her moves in the third act. This part, even though small, was her first chance to perform solo on stage.

She could not conceive of the effort and dedication it had taken her mother, professionally composing music, working hard at their family ranch in Virginia, and being a loving wife and mother. Much easier, Katie had decided, to concentrate on one thing at a time.

For her, that one thing was the ballet, and she was giving it her very best. One day she would be prima ballerina, the principal female dancer in her company, and have devoted fans all over the world. She was born for the ballet. She had known this since she was a small girl. She shied away from intimate relationships. An involvement with a man would just complicate things in her well-chosen life. Nothing would ever stand in her way again.

She slipped on her white pointe shoes and tied the satin ribbons snugly around her ankles while the music grew into a deep, dark, sensuous beat. She walked again into the mirrored practice studio, not bothering to wind her long black hair into a chignon. She felt strangely free and smiled brightly, the music enchanting her as she began her first hour-long practice of the day.

As she approached the barre to begin her warm-up exercises, her knees trembled. Then she could feel the power of a will not her own gathering like a storm within her. When the music moved to allegro, she raised her arms and twirled across the floor as light as a feather. She began moves not familiar to the routine in the third act, letting her body keep pace with the tempo of the music. An arabesque, a soubresaut, and a quick, light series of pirouettes. She could sense that her moves were beautiful, and she found a new inner strength as her body arched and swayed to the music like a swan in flight. Finally, she pirouetted, jumping high and then down, her body dipping low at her waist, with the fingers of one hand almost touching the floor.

Outside the practice studio, Adrian stopped walking in the hallway and was grounded on the spot. His feet would not move, even if he willed them to. There he was, standing in the hall of the ballet theatre, when through the window of a studio he saw a young woman dancing to the music coming from the auditorium—the music from his dream. She had a thick mane of long hair, black as midnight and straight as rain, which fell almost down to her waist. Her slim face turned to the window where he stood, which was a mirror on the studio side of the glass. She had dark dramatic brows, deep brown expressive eyes that were astonishingly clear. Not an English face, but a face such as one might meet in Greece or Rome. Or in a dream? Adrian felt a flush of embarrassment when it seemed her gaze met his. Although he knew she could not see him, he placed his fingers on the glass as if he might touch her. Hers were the eyes that haunted his dreams.

She stopped dancing, picked up a towel, and wiped her brow. She was smiling with a happiness he could clearly see but could not share.

He was breathless, but not in the same way and not for the same reasons as when he saw the woman in his dreams. His heart pounded, his throat constricted, his lungs starved for oxygen, his mind flooded with anticipation. This was an anticipation that made him aware of himself and this woman in a way he did not recall ever feeling before.

He continued walking down the hall almost in a trance when he saw the familiar presence of the stage manager coming toward him.

"Good morning, Mr. Ashley."

"Ben, do you know the young dancer with the long black hair in the practice studio?"

"Oh, yes. Her professional name is Kaitlyn Rose, but she's Katie Johnson to her close friends. She's one of the regulars from the United States and always the first one here for practice in the mornings. She's a dedicated dancer. It's a wonder you haven't met her. The entire cast and crew are staying at the Strand Palace, which I understand, is your London home. You can read about her in the programme. Her mother is the talented pianist, Rilla Johnson. You might have heard of her. She wrote the score to several American films."

"Yes, of course. I'm a fan of Mrs. Johnson's work. I met her and her husband in New York last year at a film premier. She's quite an impressive pianist, and beautiful, also. I had no idea she had a daughter in the ballet."

The stage manager nodded. "The whole family's talented. Kaitlyn's grandmother was a famous artist in Paris and throughout America. I'll introduce you after the performance, but not before. I don't want any of the girls to get close to you before curtain call. They're trained to keep their minds off men and concentrate on the ballet." He gave Adrian a friendly wink.

Katie looked forward to a visit with her family in Penzance on the following Monday. Just before noon on Wednesday, she walked quickly as she carried her suitcase toward the side exit door of the Strand Palace Hotel, near where her rental car was parked. Because of her busy schedule, she decided it was better to put her luggage in her car now. She had spent two one-hour sessions that morning going over and over the complicated movements in the third act of the ballet. Her feet ached and her toes smarted from the morning's strenuous practice. Even the tennis shoes she now wore gave little relief, but she had promised the other cast members to meet them for lunch.

At the same time, Adrian, who had just completed a business meeting, returned to the hotel and parked his car. He approached the side door looking for his friend, Ned Blanchent. He knew Ned could tell him more about this dancer who looked so very much like the woman in his dream. Adrian would be as thorough in his search for the meaning of his dream as he was in his work, which was successful enough to make him a very rich man on his own without depending on the trust fund left him by his mother.

He yanked the handle as someone took hold of it from the inside. The force of the door being pulled by Adrian caused a young woman to come bursting out and almost brought her to her knees.

Adrian's eyes widened in surprise at seeing the very woman he wished to know more about, the dancer who had been in the ballet practice studio earlier, Kaitlyn Rose. He could tell she was unnerved and embarrassed by the near accident.

"Thank goodness, you're a bellman. Put this in my trunk, please." She thrust her suitcase at him. "And watch out in the future," she chastised him. "You might hurt someone." She was cool, her chin in the air as she made an effort to regain her balance.

I guess I could pass for a bellman, he thought, looking down at his navy blue shirt and pants. "Yes, miss." He took the suitcase and followed her as she walked regally in front of him. So, he thought in disappointment, my ballerina is a prima donna. "But it's called a boot, not a trunk, miss." He purposely lowered his voice just enough so that he seemed to be mumbling. "You Yanks certainly speak strangely."

6

"I beg your pardon?" Katie turned her eyes, flashing red hot, toward him.

"Nothing, miss. Just clearing my throat," he replied in feigned earnestness.

Katie shook her head and walked on.

When they got to her rental car, she dropped the keys into his palm and tapped her foot.

He placed her suitcase inside, closed the boot, and returned the keys to her.

Katie handed him three American dollar bills. "Thank you," she said, not looking at him.

"You're welcome, miss." He bowed with a deliberate flourish and stuffed the bills into his pocket.

Adrian watched her walk down London's busy street as he put his hand in his pocket and tightly clutched the bills she had given him. *What do you know*, he mused, *little Kaitlyn Rose gave me a tip.*

$\mathcal{T}wo$

$\mathcal{F}$ar to the south of London, Brad and Olivia Johnson, Katie's grandparents, attempted to read, in spite of the afternoon rain that seemingly would go on forever. September in Penzance, England, was usually a lovely time of year. In the fall, the roses pretended that June was only just past, the trees began to shed their vibrant multi-colored drapery, and the flower beds delighted both eye and nose with their extravagant array. Days grew a bit shorter, true, but twilight lingered long in sweet, gentle melancholy, and when night came, the air was still soft. But for the past week, it had not been soft and sweet, and the raindrops pounded incessantly at the window pane.

"If it rains another minute, I'm going to go stark, raving mad!" Olivia tossed the book she was browsing and her reading glasses onto the couch beside her, her shoulder-length brown hair bouncing from the movement.

Brad looked over his newspaper to study his wife's beautiful but unhappy face. "Darlin'," he said placidly, shifting in his easy chair and turning a page of the Evening Standard, "in that case, I'd best ring up the asylum and arrange for you to be admitted as soon as possible. The Standard says rain for another day at least."

He smiled behind the paper. Once used to hard work in Virginia, their leisurely lifestyle in this cottage seemed to be stifling Olivia. His announcement brought a predictable response from her.

Brown eyes snapping, Olivia demanded, "Brad, for pity sake, put down that paper and talk to me. If I sit here any longer listening to that miserable rain, I'll go stir-crazy. A week of steady rain is just too much."

"Anything you say, darlin'." Brad lowered the paper and looked at his wife. "What would you like to talk about?"

He knew full well the temper of Olivia's youth had been dissipated by years of being a loving wife, mother, and grandmother, but he understood her restlessness. He was restless, too. However, Brad knew their predicament would be short lived.

Olivia sighed and pointed to the paper. "Isn't there anything in that newspaper besides the weather?"

"Strange you should mention it." Brad kept a serious look on his face, as though he were about to announce some world event. "Here's an article of interest. I'll read it to you. It might just bring a little sunshine to your day."

The talk of London is the new ballet, Moonglow Fascination, in which the talented New York ballet troupe, Hudson Ballet Company, will appear on stage at the Royal Opera House for a limited engagement, September 28 and October 4. A full house is anticipated for both performances.

Moonglow Fascination was in financial difficulty until an unknown benefactor invested enough funds to keep the production afloat through early into next year. Ned Blanchent, the world famous choreographer, composed for this ballet. Today, partly thanks to Blanchent, ballet is one of the most well-preserved dances in the world. Blanchent has re-choreographed many of the classic ballets, and he is particularly enthused about Moonglow Fascination.

The troupe plans to travel back to New York in early October, to Houston in December, and then on to Chicago in early 1975.

Dimitri Petrov, a native of New York City who was appointed Principal Dancer and Ballet Master for the Ballet du Grand Theatre in Geneva, Switzerland in 1970, will conduct the performance of this ballet, an irresistible mixture of dramatic music and seductive movements.

Even before he finished the article, Brad was grinning at Olivia's expression, which changed from slight boredom to amazement to indignation.

"But that's Katie's ballet troupe," Olivia pouted. "I wonder why Will and Rilla didn't tell us. Do you think these modern thinking parents just assumed we wouldn't want to be bothered traveling to London to see our granddaughter's performance?"

"No, darlin', that's not the case at all. I was going to keep it a secret from you until the last minute. I've planned a surprise trip to London this weekend for an overnight and to attend the ballet. Will and Rilla will fly into Heathrow from New York and meet us there. On Sunday, we'll all come back here to Penzance."

Olivia's soft voice betrayed her love for her granddaughter. "Katie? Do you think Katie will come, too? Oh, Will, I want her to come here, to come to Penzance. She's been so busy with her dancing, she hasn't been here since she was a young girl."

"Of course Katie will come. Her mother made all the arrangements. She can come after the first London performance. That's a Saturday performance we'll all attend. The final performance isn't until the following Friday night, so she can come for at least a day or two and visit with the family. This will be a very special time for all of us."

Brad slowly nodded his head. "I've missed her, too, Olivia. I remember her, just a little bitty thing, dancing for us back in Virginia. That child's feet must have danced over every inch of the house, the porch, and most of the front yard." He chuckled at the pleasant memories. "It's hard to realize she's twenty-one. She grew up so quickly."

"Yes. I remember her childhood well." Olivia had a far off look in her eyes and wiped a sentimental tear from her cheek. She looked at her husband and patted him on the arm. "Well, you old rascal, you barely left me time to make plans for next week's house guests."

"Are you up to it, darlin'?"

"Try to stop me." She gave him a teasing smile, and all at once she seemed alive with excitement. "I can air out the guest rooms tomorrow. I'll get Martha to come and do some baking for me ahead of time. I don't know what I'd do without help around the house." She tilted her head and frowned slightly. "Brad, do you realize we haven't been to London since last summer?"

"Yes, I know. Will the long car ride bother your rheumatism?"

"No, I don't think so. It will be wonderful to go to London again, and then have all the family here. I just can't wait." She suddenly patted her head. "Oh, I need to get my color touched up tomorrow. I don't want a single gray hair showing."

What a woman, Brad thought admiringly. He put down the paper and his eye glasses. "Rilla says the grapevine has it that Adrian Ashley from London is the unknown benefactor of the ballet, and she expects him to attend the performance. She and Will met him last year when they were in New York at a film premiere."

"My, my. So he's funding the ballet. Perhaps Rilla should invite him to Penzance for dinner while the family is here, maybe on Monday."

"That's a great idea, Olivia. I'll do you the favor of calling Will and Rilla myself, since you'll have plenty of other chores to take care of."

"We should probably have the piano tuned before Rilla arrives. I love to hear her play, and Mr. Ashley will also."

"Okay, let's do that. If I remember correctly, Adrian Ashley's family is some type of royalty, related to a Lord Wasserman or someone in the Queen's family. Adrian is in his late twenties." Brad now gave Olivia a look of playful mischief. "I understand he's quite a handsome bachelor."

"Now don't be getting any ideas about matching him with Katie. You know she feels that romance is just a distraction from the ballet." Olivia stood and paced the room. "Oh, dear, there's so much I need to do before the weekend. There's the menu to plan, groceries to bring in, and herbs to gather, flower vases to fill …." She stopped short and reached down to kiss her husband's forehead. "Brad, I'm so excited."

"Yes, my darlin'." He continued to read his paper. Boredom gone in a flash, he thought as he smiled after his retreating wife.

Olivia's happiness brought nostalgia floating around her in a golden haze. The rain unexpectedly stopped as though Olivia's brighter spirits had given the heavens a respite, and the autumn sun peeked out behind clouds that danced across the sky. She could hear the sea gulls calling and the waves washing up against the rocks as she stood looking out her window in the drawing room. A thin layer of colored autumn leaves covered the ground and gardens.

Olivia and Brad had moved here from Virginia once he felt confident in turning the management of their ranch over to their son, Will. They had lived in this cottage, left to Olivia by her mother, for over fifteen years now. She looked down at her hands and the wide gold wedding band she always wore. It still startled her to see the hands of an older woman. They were once talented, useful, and graceful hands. Now they were knotted with rheumatism and could no longer hold a paint brush or stroke a canvas at her bidding. That was fine with Olivia; she had painted all the images that were in her heart.

It felt good that her son turned to her often enough so she still felt important to him. Even after all these years, with all of the family grown, there was always a thrill of excitement to see their smiling faces, to listen to their tales, and to get involved in their problems. Katie had experienced an unfortunate situation three years ago, but she had risen above it. Olivia still worried about her family and cherished them as she always had, even though they lived so far from England. She talked to them frequently by telephone and retained her fondness for writing them letters, as difficult a task as it was with her aching hands and fingers.

She walked slowly away from the window and past the white marble fireplace where she often sat on long afternoons, thinking of her family. Looking up at her art work in frames hung all around the room, she saw her father, Hawk; the one of the brave dancing in the rain; and Deborah Howell, her grandmother, smiling almost shyly. Olivia always liked the portrait. She knew well enough that lady had not been a bit shy.

Olivia was all at once content and walked into the kitchen to prepare lunch. She began her long list of chores for the trip to London and the guests who would arrive after.

On Saturday evening, Olivia and her family arrived at The Royal Opera House early so they could visit Katie before the performance began. Olivia noticed that the dressing room contained all the messy paraphernalia of the ballet dancers: wigs, jars of makeup, a dressing table and costumes, large glittering mirrors, and walls covered with reviews and programmes of this and other ballets—some framed, some simply tacked up hurriedly. A few well-used chairs and ashtrays indicated that Katie and the other dancers who shared this dressing room were used to visitors. The contagious excitement of the ballet was evident in everyone as they showered her with red roses and white lilies. Then Katie's family left her with kisses and hugs to find their seats.

Brad passed out programmes to each member of the family. "Look at the write-up about our girl in the programme."

"Yes, Dad, she sent us one," Will said. "Isn't it marvelous? I'm so proud of her."

"This is exciting. We're all proud of her, Will." Olivia fidgeted in her seat from the thrill of being able see her granddaughter dance in the ballet.

Rilla spoke up. "Katie's been faithful to her routine. I'm certain she'll perform at her very best, but I can't help being nervous for her. This ballet could be a hallmark of Kaitlyn Rose's career as a ballerina." Her voice was tight and strained. "I'm anxious to see her maneuver the grand Pas de Chat. By the way, that means 'step-of-the-cat,' and it requires a long, high jump."

"Why, Rilla, you know so much about the language of the ballet." Olivia was both proud of and surprised by her daughter-in-law's knowledge.

"That's because I took her to ballet class and sat through the practice sessions during the fourth through twelfth grades. I learned the lingo after all that time. Remember, Olivia, how we rubbed her aching legs at night, and I told her how happy she would be one day as a famous ballerina?"

Olivia laughed at that. She did remember when she and Brad still lived at the ranch and how young Katie had complained of her legs aching time after time when returning home from her first few ballet lessons. Yet, she would not hear any suggestions about giving up her dream of becoming a prima ballerina. She had been a sweet but stubborn little girl when it came to her one passion—dancing.

Muted voices in the auditorium came to a sudden halt when the orchestra struck the first note of "The Dance of the Fairies."

Adrian, sitting in the fifth row center, had never been so impressed by anything he had ever seen. The set was made up as a forest, and the dancers flitted through flowers and among trees. Katie danced in unison with the other girls, but it was evident that she was outshining all of them with the perfection of her moves. *Kaitlyn Rose is good*, he thought as he watched her gliding across the stage. She's very good. In fact, she's brilliant. He sat up stiffly in his seat, looking only at Katie as she turned and leaped gracefully.

The third act also used the forest set, but now it was night. The forest and flowers were hidden in the darkness. Adrian looked among the dancers for Katie, but could not see her. Suddenly, blue moonlight shone through the top of the set, and gracefully, almost as if she were floating down from the stars above, Katie appeared like an angel in white. When her feet touched the stage floor, one of the male dancers lifted her effortlessly at her waist and twirled her around, as though she weighed nothing.

Then Katie was all alone on the stage. This was her debut as a solo dancer, and it seemed to Adrian she defied gravity. She was suspended in space for a moment as both feet were in the air at the same time. He read earlier in the programme that this maneuver was called the grand jeté, one that Katie was well known for. The applause was deafening as she danced and twirled around the stage. Adrian sat glued in his seat throughout the third act.

When it was all over, the cast lined up for the curtain call, and the audience rose to their feet. Adrian got up slowly. The applause was long and real, and most of it was for Katie. The cast moved back, pointing and bowing toward her. She stood there in the stage lights, such a lovely image, as patrons brought bouquets of flowers to the front of the stage and laid them at her feet. She accepted them graciously and bowed as the audience applauded even louder.

Adrian was deep in thought. Is this the woman in my dream? It seems so, yet there's one difference between Kaitlyn Rose and the dream woman. There's something different in Kaitlyn Rose's eyes—a lightness, an ease that dissolves the sadness that always appeared in the eyes of the woman in my dreams. Is it possible to fall in love in a matter of moments? Have I fallen in love with Kaitlyn Rose Johnson as she performed in the practice studio, on stage, or maybe as she appeared in my dream? He did not know when the sensation had arrived, but he was almost certain it was there now.

Adrian knew Katie was not aware of his attraction to her, and she certainly had no idea that their paths were about to cross again on Monday.

Three

Katie's family left London on Sunday to return to Penzance after an early breakfast with her. She was delayed by interviews with the press and would arrive in Penzance on Monday afternoon.

During her long drive to her grandparents' cottage, Katie's thoughts flew back to her family and her life growing up on the ranch in Virginia. She missed her dog, Gretchen, who always welcomed her home with gusto whenever she returned from a tour. She thought of her little Scottie dog as her best friend, since the ballet left little time for a social life.

The sun glinted off the elegant mansard roof of the cottage as she drove around the last bend in the seemingly endless road. It was a spectacular home, and she regretted that she had only been here a few times during her childhood. She compared it to a French chateau which she had seen pictures of in a travel magazine. It was beautiful, exquisite in every aspect of its design.

After parking her car, Katie ran to the terrace and gave her mother a loving kiss.

Rilla was wearing a winter-white wool skirt and red sweater set. She was tall and slender, and her dark straight hair was pulled back from her face. A lovely face, Katie's father always said.

"Katie, please hurry and get ready for dinner. We have a guest arriving any moment. Jeans and a turtle neck just won't do. Oh, you're staying in the same bedroom you always stayed in, dear."

"What guest, Mother?" Katie was looking forward to a quiet dinner with her family without having to conjure up conversation with a boring guest. But then, Katie knew her grandmother loved entertaining.

"Adrian Ashley, the man who's financially responsible for keeping your ballet afloat, is coming here for dinner. Have you met him yet?" Her mother stepped closer and hugged Katie again.

"No, I haven't. Why is he coming to …?"

Rilla cut her off. "Well, hurry, dear. He'll be here any moment."

Katie walked into the house. There was no one in sight. Her grandmother's drawing room was made ready for guests and presented an impact as visually charming as a stage set. The silk curtains were pulled back to allow guests to view the gardens and the sea beyond. The cushions on the couches had been plumped, magazines straightened, and the fire made up. The room was softly lit by a pair of matching brass lamps, and the flames in the fireplace were reflected in their large round bases. There were flowers everywhere, as Katie expected, since she knew her grandmother loved flowers. Nothing had changed. It was just as Katie had remembered it all these many years. She loved the cottage, the rooms, the furniture, and most of all the people in it—her family. She was so happy to be back in her grandparents' home that she pirouetted in circles around the large familiar room.

Hearing a car in the driveway, Katie raced upstairs to her bedroom. She looked out the window and could not believe her eyes. It's the bellman from the hotel, she thought. What in the world is he doing here? Oh, this can't be! He's arrived in our driveway in an impressive little sports car, and he's wearing a white dinner jacket! She simply could not take her eyes from the scene in the driveway. Her mother was giving the "bellman" a kiss, and her father was shaking hands with him! Through the open window, she could overhear their conversation.

"So nice to see you again," her mother said as the man handed her a bouquet of red flowers.

"Welcome to Penzance. We're honored you could join us," her father said.

Honored? This man can't be a bellman. Oh, no! That must be Adrian Ashley. Katie stared and stuck her head farther into the window enclosure. The man was standing at the end of the garden now, resting one foot on a stone bench while talking to her father. Luckily, he faced away from the house and could not see her at the window. Despite herself, she continued to stare in secret from the curtained alcove.

The sunlight shone on his sand-colored hair, and his wide shoulders strained the back of his white jacket, which outlined his long narrowing torso. He was as still as a statue. A Greek God, she thought absently. Suddenly the man turned and looked up. She jumped backward, as though he might come through the window.

Katie crossed the room and sat hard on her high canopied bed, dazed with the realization that she had given a tip to this man who sponsored the ballet. "Okay, how are you going to handle this?" she asked herself aloud.

Proceeding to dress, Katie paired a skirt with a blue angora sweater. She applied her light makeup in the nearby bathroom, noting her wide eyes held a wary look of confusion and dismay.

The incident with this man, the mistaken bellman, would be ignored. What else could she do? He had taken advantage of her situation, pretending to be a bellman, and he deserved nothing less than a good tongue lashing. At this, she twisted her long straight hair into a tight chignon with unusual ruthlessness and was pleased at the resulting look—sophisticated, almost mature, really. It gave her the courage to face Adrian Ashley.

Finally, taking a deep breath, she headed for the stairs. This had to be gotten over with sooner or later.

As she took the last step of the stairs, her mother came toward her with the "bellman" in tow. "Adrian, this is our daughter, Kaitlyn Rose. Katie, this is Adrian Ashley. He's the mystery benefactor who's helping your ballet out of financial debt."

Katie swallowed with some difficulty and nodded her head. "Hello, Mr. Ashley. Welcome to Penzance."

His eyebrows lifted as he reached for her right hand and placed his lips softly on the back of it. "Miss Johnson, how delightful to be formally introduced to you. I enjoyed your performance immensely," he said with a cultured English accent.

Katie's mind was awhirl. Performance? What performance? Of course. He must have attended the ballet on Saturday night. He is, after all, a sponsor, and I gave the sponsor of the ballet a tip. She could tell by the smirk on his face that he was enjoying this. "Thank you," she said politely, lifting her chin and lowering her eyes quickly.

Just then Olivia invited them to come into the music room. "Grab an hors d'oeuvre and come on, everyone. Gather around." For Adrian's benefit, Olivia added, "Rilla will play the music she wrote for the movie, *Things Remembered*. It will be released next year. She says this will be her last project, but that remains to be seen."

The family and their guest moved one by one into the music room, taking a seat on the plush couches and chairs that were placed around the piano. Rilla's musical score was beautiful.

When she finished and stood and bowed, everyone clapped in appreciation. "Now, I would like to request Mr. Ashley to play us a tune," she said. "Sorry to put you on the spot, Adrian, but rumor has it you are also an accomplished pianist."

Adrian looked embarrassed. "Well, you're a tough act to follow, Rilla. But there's one song I would like to play for you. It's a song that came to me in a dream. It has no name, and I'll probably fumble many times. I'll be playing it from memory for only the second time."

Everyone applauded as Adrian seated himself at the piano, closed his eyes briefly, and began to play.

Katie sat bewildered as she listened to Adrian's music. Suddenly she stood to her feet. "I know that song. I do. I heard it at the theatre the other morning as I practiced."

All eyes were on Adrian. "Yes, one of the musicians played the song for me at the theatre the other morning. He's writing the notation for me. It's a song that comes to me in a dream, repeated identically almost every night."

Rilla walked up to the piano again. "How delightful and mysterious, Adrian. It's a beautiful piece of music." She hesitated. "It's almost Native American in tempo, like some of the Cherokee songs I remember hearing as a child. I'd like to know more about it."

His head turned to her, his eyes looking up. "That's all I know about the song. Like I said, it has only come to me in a dream."

This seemed to arouse Rilla's curiosity even more. "Adrian, it's a known fact that once you've heard a song which meant a lot to you as a child, it often comes back in a dream. Do you think your mother could have played it for you?"

"Perhaps. She often played the piano for me when I was very young," he replied.

"Interesting. Was your mother a student of Native American culture?"

"No. Not that I know of." He hesitated. "But a distant relative of my mother told me she was related to Sequoyah, whoever that was."

"Sequoyah was the Indian who invented the Cherokee writing system. He was a very famous Native American. You might want to study his history if you think you're related. Well, as I said, I would love to read the notation," Rilla said. "Could you send me a copy when you get it?"

Even though she could see little more than his profile, Katie noticed a puzzled look on Adrian's face, then the beginning of a smile.

"I'd be honored." Adrian turned around on the piano bench.

Katie stared at him in disbelief. So this man who posed as a bellman is a philanthropist, a dreamer, and now a pianist? She decided she had never in her life seen a man who looked less like a bellman. How could she possibly have mistaken him for an employee of the hotel? She was feeling much too uncomfortable in Adrian Ashley's presence.

Olivia had slipped out of the room for a minute and now came to the rescue. "Dinner's served. Let's all move into the dining room."

Katie went to the other side of the table to get as far away as possible from the formidable Mr. Ashley. If her family found out, they would never let her live down the story of how she had tipped the ballet's financier. A horrible urge came over her as she looked at the Waterford goblet filled with ice water sitting on the table. She considered flinging the glass of water in his face. She suppressed a chuckle, envisioning the surge of water and the shock on Mr. Ashley's face. Oh, well, she thought, I surely can come up with some other way of getting back at Mr. Ashley for his rudeness, should we ever on some occasion be alone.

The conversation at dinner was rather strained and far too bright and superficial, on her part anyway. Katie had a healthy appetite but ate very little in order to keep her figure slim for the ballet. When she was upset, her need for food, any kind of food, greatly increased in its appeal. She was upset now, and the object of that mood was the handsome man sitting across the table.

She did not want to be gracious or nice or any of the things her mother and grandmother expected of her. She had a difficult time concentrating on any of the conversation or even the food she craved. Every time she looked up from her dinner plate, this man was staring at her. How rude!

She was relieved after the last course of dinner was served and eaten. She could now make her excuse and exit from the table. Just then Olivia looked at her. "Katie, would you like to show Mr. Ashley the gardens?"

Adrian spoke before Katie could respond to her grandmother's request. "I'd love to see the gardens if you can spare the time, Miss Johnson."

"Certainly, Mr. Ashley," Katie said curtly. "I'll meet you in the garden after I freshen up." She left the table and walked out of the room.

Four

Katie sat down on a white wooden bench overlooking the garden and the sea beyond. She did not hear Adrian's footsteps, but she sensed his presence. Lifting her head, she looked up into his eyes. A timeless moment hung between them.

"Your grandmother asked me to bring you fresh ice tea," Adrian said as he sat down beside her. He handed her the glass of tea and smiled at her, a slow, appealing curving of lips that softened his mouth.

His smile made a difference, Katie realized, and she could not let it. She could play the game, too, she decided. She would simply ignore the source of her embarrassment, the knowledge that this man who was a guest in her grandparents' home had misrepresented himself at their first meeting. "Thank you, Mr. Ashley."

"Could we drop the formalities? Just call me Adrian. May I call you Katie?"

"If you wish." Katie took a long drink of the cool beverage and set the glass down beside her on the stone patio. The taste of the soothing beverage brought back a flood of childhood memories. Her family always had ice tea after a meal, even in winter. She looked wistfully at the cottage. "The cottage has changed little since I was here last."

Adrian crossed his arms and stretched his legs out ahead of him. "I suppose that's a good thing," he said.

"Since my first visit here, there have been many times I could even smell Penzance."

"You remembered the smell of Penzance?"

"Yes, the smell of the flowers drifting into my bedroom window in the early morning hours, the smell of Grammy's fresh yeast bread, and the salty smell of sea mist." She looked at Adrian. There's something about gray eyes, really gray eyes that can cut right through you, she thought. For a moment or two she could not speak.

She cleared her throat and went on. "Although it was remodeled some years ago, it's still the same to me. The color is the same, and from the back there are no changes at all. Grammy wanted to keep it pretty much as it was."

"It's a lovely property. I especially like the way the autumn flowers meander down to the water. It seems the sea could touch the petals at high tide."

Katie warmed to his poetic expression and continued eagerly. "You probably know this, but Penzance is famed for its flowers. It's favored by a very mild climate, except for a few dreary cold winter days and lots of rain. Everyone in this town plants a profusion of flowers in their yards and gardens." Her thoughts flitted from the town and back to the house again. "From the front, the house doesn't look the same. The addition of the four bedrooms and formal dining room are evident there." She leaned ever so slightly forward. "I think the spirit of this house has remained the same, while only the people in it have changed."

He sat up straight, and his face took on a puzzled expression. "How so?"

"Well, the older generations have passed, and new family members have been born. When a distant relative first came here in 1912, it had been owned by her fiancé's family for one hundred and twenty-five years. The spirit of this house is one of peace and welcoming. People have always come here to enjoy the comfort of this home."

"You must have some wonderful memories from here."

"Some, yes. My father and mother and I stayed at home most of the time. My father wouldn't take time to leave the ranch in the care of someone else, and I couldn't leave my ballet lessons. I was only here four times as a young girl for very brief vacations, but I remember every hole and corner of this house."

"It's unfortunate you didn't get to spend more time here. This looks like a wonderful property for a young girl, especially with the beach close by."

"But you haven't seen our ranch. It's a great place to raise children." She turned her face to him. "The air is fresh as dew, the beautiful Virginia mountains compare to no others, and my father's horses are a thrill to ride. Do you ride, Adrian?"

When he did not speak, she lifted a brow. Katie could tell he was distracted by her, and it amused her. Through her amusement, she also felt a trickle of first attraction for him.

Finally he answered, "Yes." He nodded his head in affirmation. "Yes, I have horses of my own at Red Oaks."

"Then you know how important they can be to children. They can even help in the care of the horses."

"Well, as a child I never cared for the horses. We employed plenty of help to clean the stables."

"I was taught that hands-on never hurt anyone. Caring for horses teaches discipline and responsibility and concern for all animals."

"I'm certain that's true."

"Tell me where you lived as a child, Adrian."

His voice took on a solemn tone as he began to speak. "My family, as far back as I know, has always lived at Red Oaks in Farnham, southeast of London. Unlike your family's home here in Penzance, it has never been remodeled. I always considered it a cold and unfriendly house."

"Unfriendly? What an odd way to describe a home."

"Red Oaks was never a home. It always was, and still is, a twenty-five room mausoleum, a stone cold, dark, unfriendly house that I dislike."

"Then why do you live there?" Katie asked.

"It's become a habit, I suppose. I never really thought about living anywhere else. My mother left it to my two siblings and me. My brother, Peter, never wanted to live there. My sister, Roxie, loves Red Oaks, but her social life gives her little time to visit. Her daughter, Cara, lives at Red Oaks. It's her home, and she attends boarding school outside London. Anyway, you don't just up and sell an estate like Red Oaks that's been in your family for over two hundred years. So good old Adrian is there to hold the fort."

Katie looked deep into his eyes. Did she see sadness there or was she imagining it? "It's a foolish waste of energy to hate the inanimate," she announced strongly. Immediately she felt a layer of guilt creeping into her consciousness. Hoping to soften the effect of her ill-chosen words, she lowered her voice and said, "Come now, Adrian, I understand your family is royalty. You must have a large, close-knit family."

"Well, royalty in an odd way. We were all morganatic under British Church Laws and not really considered royalty or referred to as Prince or Princess. After the death of my maternal grandfather, my mother inherited Red Oaks, which was always our family residence."

When speaking of his own family, Katie felt him lose the warmth he had when he was listening to her talk about her family.

"Do you mean the Ashley family?" she asked.

"No. My father's name is Wasserman." Adrian dropped his head and put his elbows on his knees, then interlaced his hands in front of him. "I saw very little of him when I was young and see even less of him now. After my mother died and before I started college, I took steps to dispel any connection to my famous father. I took the name of Ashley, which was my mother's maiden name."

"Why on earth would you do that?" Katie watched his gaze roam the darkening afternoon sky for a moment or two. He sighed deeply, and then spoke with an honesty that surprised her.

"Royalty doesn't suit me, Katie. I avoid even the mention of it. I feel that London has its royalty, and they don't need any part of me. I detest being associated with royalty and their stiff, regimented customs and traditions. Ashley's no longer a well known name, and being an Ashley keeps me out of the limelight. Peter, on the other hand, adores being adored, so he kept the Wasserman name, and Roxie, who has been married and divorced several times, goes by Landry, because that's Cara's last name."

"But you still live with your father at Red Oaks?"

"My father lives in South America. He's remarried and has a new family there. Several step-children, so I hear. My business dealings require that I lease a suite at the Strand Palace Hotel in London. I live alone at Red Oaks on weekends or when I take a few days off. I rarely have guests except for holidays when Roxie, Cara, and Peter and his children come to visit. Strangely, the estate's a vision of loveliness during the holidays. In fact, the Christmas holiday's the only time of year when Red Oaks takes on a somewhat warm and friendly atmosphere."

His voice sounded to Katie as precise as if he were doing a business presentation. "Do you visit your father?"

"No. I haven't seen him in many years. He was born George Wasserman of London, cousin to Queen Elizabeth II, and he loves to flaunt his heritage."

"Then your grandfather was also grandfather to the Queen?"

"Yes."

"That's all terribly impressive, Adrian, but you've given me your family history without favorite reminisces from your childhood."

Adrian's face took on a humorless expression. "It wasn't exciting, believe me, and there are few favorite memories. Daily life was a grinding routine with only one goal: growing up to be a man who would never embarrass my father. At least I'm certain I succeeded in that."

He looked toward the sea, then back to Katie. "But what about you? Let's talk about you."

"I'm an only child, although I always wished for a brother or sister. But I have Gretchen, my eight-year-old Scottish terrier. I guess Gretchen and the other dogs we have always took the place of siblings in my life."

"And you live at a ranch?"

"Yes, it's a horse ranch west of Richmond, Virginia. Our home is a simple, large farm house, not opulent like your house must be."

"You're incredibly easy to talk with, Katie. No one has ever gotten so much about my family from me before."

Katie felt sincerity in his voice. "Well, maybe it's because I'm interested in families and family life. I want lots of children who will respect and love me just as I love and adore my parents and grandparents."

There were a few moments of silence between them. Katie wondered what kind of life he led here in England. Was he the type who frequented elegant restaurants with equally elegant women on his arm? Did he watch foreign films and play bridge? Or did he prefer pop or jazz? She had not been able to find his slot as easily as she did with most people she met, so she wondered. Her thoughts also went to her home in Virginia and how wonderful it would be right now to play tag with Gretchen or take a long ride on Nokomis, her favorite horse. Yes, that was what she needed, complete solitude that would clear her mind of these unnerving thoughts this man suddenly aroused in her. But Virginia was thousands of miles and another continent away.

Adrian interrupted her reverie. "Do you have a father in mind for these children you speak of so fondly?" he asked with a tease in his voice.

Katie was astonished at his question. "Of course not!" She felt her cheeks turn red. "I'm not getting married. At least not until I retire from the ballet. Only then will I have time to be a wife and have children." She felt the setting sun fall across her face as she spoke with determination. "Having a family would mean giving up the ballet. No, I wouldn't do that."

"I admire you," Adrian said.

Dismayed, she stared at him. "For what?"

"For being exactly who you are and knowing exactly what you want."

No smooth phrases, no romantic words could have affected her more deeply. She was used to flattery, and flattery, Katie knew, could be brushed easily aside by a woman who understood herself. His words did not sound contrived. Perhaps it was the approaching moonlight, but she felt close to Adrian, comfortable with him. She cautioned herself not to drop her guard. She would not get sucked into another risky relationship.

"Some men find ambition in a woman unflattering, or at least uncomfortable."

"Some men are idiots," Adrian replied.

"I couldn't agree more," Katie said sharply enough that he lifted his brow as he gazed at her.

He quickly changed the subject. "I first met your mother and father at a movie premier of *The Way We Were* in New York City last year."

"Really? Do you visit the states often?" she asked in surprise.

"Only when business takes me there. Your mother is a very talented pianist. I have recordings of every musical score she's written. When I learned she was in the audience that night, nothing could stop me from meeting her."

"You like American films?"

"Certainly."

"I can easily understand why people love Mother's music. The Howell women were talented, and although I seem to have a lot of their spunk, so my grandfather says, I didn't inherit their natural talent. I'm one of them, but I can't write or paint or manage a business. My mother isn't one of them, but you know how musically talented she is. I can't carry a tune in a bucket. So I learned to dance, but it took years of hard practice."

"You'll have to explain to me. Who are the Howell women?"

Without warning, reality dawned on Katie, and the memory of mistaking him for a bellman flashed in front of her again. She could feel her blood pressure rising and bit her lip in an attempt to keep her temper under control. "Only if you'll tell me why you pretended to be a bellman." She knew she sounded cool, but she was fuming again because of his pretense, and she had to get this settled.

Adrian tried to explain. "You've distorted what happened, Katie. I never told you I was a bellman. You just assumed." His voice softened. "Besides, I would never refuse a request to help a lady."

The anger she kept suppressed all through dinner was ignited as she poked his chest with her finger. "Well, you could have said something at least. Do you know how humiliated I felt in front of my family, knowing I gave you a tip for putting my luggage in my car?"

"What should I have said across the dining table, Katie? Perhaps a thank you for the three dollar tip?"

"No, of course not." She could feel her cheeks turn pink with the beginning of a blush.

"Although it would have been amusing to see you squirm," Adrian said with the merest hint of a bemused smile on his face.

Now Katie's anger turned to frustration. "You had no right ... you took advantage of a perfectly innocent mistake."

She knew she was being rude, but felt no immediate regret. He had aroused a powerful irritation in her that she had never before experienced, but it was an irritation that would be short lived.

Adrian rose to his feet and stood looking down at her. "That's a mistake I'll remember the rest of my life, because it gave me the opportunity to learn more about you. I can't apologize for that." He reached out and cupped her chin in his hand and smiled.

His gesture changed her attitude in an instant.

"Oh." Katie let the word trail off, unable to say more, because his eyes prevented her. It had been a long time since a man's words touched her that way. It was a warning sign to her—take it slow, take it slow. She sent him a smile, half bewildered, half shy.

Adrian took her hands and pulled her to her feet. She made a feeble attempt to withdraw her slender hands, but they were engulfed in his larger ones. She had thought during dinner that holding this man's hand would feel something like a cold frog, that she would get warts or something. No, it was warmth she felt, not warts, traveling from her hands and into her arms and face. Her knees melted.

She was certain that even if she knew what to say or if she could give him a logical response to his astonishing statement, her momentary loss of voice would prevent it. She nearly fell against him as he put his hands on her shoulders and continued to look at her. Her eyes fluttered closed, and she gave herself up to sensations that had nothing to do with sight.

She assumed he would kiss her, but he did not. Katie opened her eyes again.

"I've never known anyone like you," he whispered, his voice husky.

She was suddenly aware and entirely conscious of his height, his luminous eyes, and sensuous mouth. He was standing quite close to her, and she found herself breathing with considerable difficulty.

Just then Katie's father walked out of the house. "Adrian, your car is here. Seven o'clock sharp, just as you requested," he called out.

Adrian looked at Katie. "That means I must take my leave." He reached for her hand and raised it, kissing her palm lightly.

Katie stiffened.

"I hope that wasn't too bold of me. I didn't do it to frighten you."

"You didn't frighten me." He did not frighten the woman he could see, but Katie admitted to herself the woman within was terrified.

Over their joined fingers, his eyes locked with hers. "Goodbye for the moment, Kaitlyn Rose." He continued to smile as his gaze lowered to her mouth and lingered there, the look as physical as a kiss.

Katie was speechless again. Within a minute, with a long wave of her hand, she watched his car go down the driveway, and then he was out of sight. He had changed her whole life in a single afternoon, and she was quite sure they both knew it.

Emotions rolled over her, then ebbed like a breaking wave. I'm an idiot! she thought. I'm totally infatuated with this man. It has to be the mystery of him. He comes from a different world than I've known. He's the first man who ever kissed my hand, and it was a very sweet, intimate thing to do. I can still feel the faint pressure on my palm where his lips touched. I really have to be careful now. This is infatuation, the big let down. It has to be, or I'm in for a world of trouble.

This man had opened a new door for her, but she had no idea what to do now. Did that mean she was no longer in charge of her emotions? No. Did it mean she would act irrationally, impulsively, just because the handsome Mr. Ashley had given her some attention? No. Did it mean she was desperate for attention? A most definite no.

So, what was holding her back? Katie had a secret, known only to her family and very close friends in the ballet troupe. Adrian Ashley had aroused unpleasant memories she had kept successfully hidden for the past three years.

Later that evening, the family gathered in the drawing room. Everyone had something to say. It was obvious to Katie that her family was thrilled with the ballet and with her performance. Rilla remarked how delighted she was to get to know Adrian better, and Katie's father agreed. Olivia kept saying over and over how handsome their dinner guest was. Only Katie was unusually quiet. She might have the biggest news of all, but she could not share it. Katie might be falling in love.

"I'm going to take a walk down by the beach," she told them.

"Not too late, dear. The evening air will turn chilly and quite humid. Not good for a dancer's muscles, you know," she heard her mother say.

"Right. Be back soon."

Katie grabbed her coat from the hall tree, loosened her hair from the tight chignon, removed her shoes, and headed toward the sea. She could feel the sand and cool water rushing beneath her feet and the force of the tide pulling the water back toward the full moon. Nightfall made no difference to her. She wanted only to be alone, as she always walked or went horseback riding alone when a difficult dilemma was presented to her. How long or how far she walked, trying to shake the numbing reaction to this handsome man who had walked into her world, she did not know. For the first time since dinner, her mind began to clear, her heart stopped pounding. She knew she wanted to spend more time with Adrian Ashley as surely as she felt the wind lifting her hair above her head.

Back at the house, Katie said her goodnights with brief kisses to the family and went up to her bedroom. She was relieved when the room's peace and quiet seeped into her and some of her churning feelings subsided. She was about to crawl into bed when she noticed she had left the window open. She knew she would not sleep right away, so she walked over to the window and opened the casement wider. She inhaled the damp sweet smell of the gardens and the tang of the sea in the breeze. The padded cushion beneath invited her to curl up, and she did, staring out toward the lush evergreens still illuminated by the moonlight filtering down through ragged clouds. This cottage was really a magical place, like a storybook ancestor in England.

Adrian was still on her mind. What was he doing at the moment? Thinking of business about shares, British stock exchange averages, and bear markets? Or better still, thinking of her, missing her, wishing he were still here with her rather than taking the long drive home.

She wished she could believe in magic, fairy tales, and the simplicity of love ever after. However, Katie did not believe in magic and fairy tales, not really.

Love to Katie was no simple matter. She knew her present way of thinking could only lead to disaster. She must not fall in love with Adrian Ashley. She could not let her affection for him ruin everything she had worked so hard for. The ballet was her life, her love.

This evening her emotions had been spiraling out of control. She had been too weak to resist the romantic feelings that swept over her. Just like when she was in high school and Russell Wiley had almost convinced her to give up the ballet and marry him after graduation. She had fought back those feelings then and later realized she had not really loved Russell, that it was just a school girl crush, her first infatuation.

Then came her three month, life-altering marriage to Jeffery

Bingham, which was the biggest mistake of her life. She was so shocked and humiliated, and made to feel so illogically guilty by his deceptions, that she restored her family name and swore the family to secrecy. Yes, Jeffery was her big secret, and until tonight she had successfully repressed the dreadful memories of their time together, the first great failure of her life.

Why was she so vulnerable tonight? She would fight this attraction to Adrian, and this was one battle she must win. In desperation, she bowed her head and prayed, "Dear God, help me to make the right decision with my life. My family has always taught me that any choice should be made by consulting You and that You would direct my path for the future. I ask You for that tonight. Please. Amen."

Five

As his car sped through the night, Adrian's thoughts were only of Kaitlyn Rose Johnson. She remained a mystery to him, as did the dream woman who visited him every night. Being near Katie all through dinner had made him nervous. When had a young woman ever made him nervous? After all, he was rumored to be England's most eligible bachelor, used to women happy to make his acquaintance. He had an idea Katie Johnson was different than the women who pursued him.

He recalled Katie's slender figure coming out of the French doors of her grandparents' home while he had stood entranced, watching her from across the garden. She then disappeared into the shadows under the trees. The sound of her soft steps on the cobblestone walkway as he sought her out was like a siren's song, drawing him nearer to her.

It had been fun talking to her. She was bright, young, and alive with enthusiasm about her family and their history. He was awed by her innocent remembrances. Katie is not delicate, he thought. Though she was tall and thin, he got the impression of power. Perhaps it was her face, with its large eyes and full mouth. He had become distracted from listening to her, so mesmerized was he by her eyes, her voice. Confidence surrounded her as other women surround themselves with exotic fragrances.

Was she the woman in his dream who invaded his nights over and over, the young ballet dancer who had dazzled him at the theater, or someone altogether different whom he did not quite know yet? His dream woman and the ballet dancer were open, friendly beauties with eyes that touched his soul. Katie's eyes, those dark brown mysterious eyes, seemed to light up when she smiled. Her mouth was wide and generous, always ready to curve joyfully upward. He was having a real problem trying to figure out this young woman to whom he was so drawn. Barely a week ago he had found her to be a beautiful but spoiled brat. Now he found her more like the gentle, lovely woman in his dream. Why did she have to be such a frustrating mix?

He had come to admire Katie without ever wanting to or expecting anything like that to happen. Am I in love with this creature, Adrian wondered.

He arrived at Farnham after the five-hour drive from Penzance, expecting as usual to find his house empty. He liked it that way. He loved the seclusion, the time to unwind and think.

He had excused all the help except the housekeeper, Maude, and her husband, Gus, who lived in a small cottage behind the main house. Gus cared for the horse stables and gardens and did personal chores for Adrian. Adrian knew that Maude would leave him ample food in the warming oven for a late night snack. He hoped she had made bread. Then he smiled, remembering what Katie had said about her grandmother's yeast bread. Had he ever stopped to savor the smell of fresh bread? He would from now on.

Adrian returned home with the knowledge deep inside that his life was changed, that he was changed. Meeting Katie had affected him in a way that caught him off guard. He was excited, elated, and filled with things to look forward to, the first in a long time. He could not erase the memory of her standing in her grandparents' driveway waving him off. It was a new experience for him, and he thought it was ridiculous, but he knew he was falling in love with Katie.

He turned off the road, pushed his car remote to open the large wrought iron gates, and drove up the circular flagstone driveway to the front of Red Oaks. He was surprised to see lights shining from all the downstairs windows. He glanced at the clock on the car's dashboard; it was almost midnight. Roxie's small red sports car was parked nearby. His sister often wandered in unannounced, but since she had visited him three weeks ago, he was puzzled as to why she had returned again so soon, and at this ungodly hour. She normally only showed up for an occasional short visit and for holidays. It was Adrian who kept the family together, at least for Roxie and her daughter, Cara. His brother, Peter, was now in Paris living in grand style with the jet set, which bored Adrian. Just the same, no matter how difficult Roxie and Peter were, they were still his family. He loved them and made allowances for their eccentricities.

Parking the car, he sat staring at the lighted house. How many rooms of Red Oaks have light streaming onto the driveway, he wondered. Strange, I've never counted them. He counted to twelve and stopped. Adrian recalled how Katie lit up when she talked about her grandparents' home in Penzance and said she knew every detail of it by memory from childhood visits. The shining windows stared back at him. The small things she said and did had left a deep impression on him.

He was tired. It had been a long drive from Penzance, and he did not want to see Roxie or deal with her many problems tonight. He closed his eyes, covered them with his hand, as though to wipe fatigue away. He got out of the car, retrieved his briefcase, and walked to the front door. Just as he put his key in the lock, the door opened. Roxie had left the door unlocked.

He saw her coat draped across the hall chair and could smell her perfume. Not that her perfume was cheap, but it was always overpowering. He closed the door and put down his briefcase.

"Roxie?"

He went into the library where she was sitting in a chair facing him, having already raided the seldom used liquor cabinet left by his father. One of her legs was slung over the arm of the chair, her black high heeled pumps thrown haphazardly on the floor. Her naturally blond hair was in place, sleekly falling to just above her shoulders. She appeared pedigreed, but that was not what Roxanne Landry was. Superbly educated, from royal ancestors, and well groomed certainly, but she had a will of her own that often balked at being well mannered and well behaved.

It usually cost him plenty when she came for a visit. Although she received a generous trust fund, it had never gotten her through a month in her life without additional funds borrowed (he used the term loosely) from the family.

"Hello, Adrian," she said in the syrupy sweet voice he hated.

Adrian cleared his throat and looked toward his sister. "Roxie, for heaven's sake, can't you sit like a lady?"

"I'm no lady. Why should I sit like one?"

"Well, at least act the part while you're at Red Oaks."

"Excuse me," she said hotly as she put both stocking feet on the soft Oriental rug covering the library floor.

"This is a surprise. I didn't know you were coming." He sat down hard on the gold tapestry couch.

"I thought once about leaving you a message, but there didn't seem to be much of a point. After all, this is my house, too."

"That I'm aware of, Roxie. Now, get on with it. What do you want?"

"I've come to tell you I'm leaving for the United States tomorrow."

"So?"

Roxie took a mouthful of the brandy and delicately set down the glass on the marble-topped table beside her chair.

"Well, brother dear, don't you want to have a farewell drink with me?"

He did not say anything to this. Across the space that divided them, her gaze met his, her eyes unblinking, somber, and cold.

Adrian bent his head low and silently counted to ten. "Did you find some unsuspecting guy in the United States?"

"Yes, and I'm going to him. He's in California waiting for me."

"So you're getting married again? What is this, the sixth try in sixteen years? Your last marriage to the polo player was pasted all over the London Times. I can imagine what will be said about you living with some poor soul in the United States." Adrian sighed and chose to put that thought out of his mind. He knew the English tell-all papers would pick up the story any day now.

"Adrian, really. You make it sound so terribly cold. It's for love, my dear brother, for love. And I don't intend to get married. That's being foolish in this modern age."

Adrian just shook his head. His sister was unbelievably callus.

Roxie raised her eyes toward the ceiling. "I'm long past the age of minding what people say. Conventions really don't matter anymore, and I definitely don't care what the tabloids say. He has a lovely estate in California."

"Well, I care. Do you think I want my sister's photo pasted alongside all that trash? Who is it this time? Or shall I wait and read it in the gossip page?"

She simply ignored Adrian's inquiry and walked across the room, sat down beside him, and patted his hand. "Oh, Adrian, don't be such a stick in the mud." She kissed his cheek and stood up once more. "I want you to buy my part of Red Oaks. I'm going to need some money."

That astonished him almost more than the fact that she was leaving England. "I always thought Red Oaks meant more to you than anything."

"Not now, it doesn't. It can belong to just you and Peter. However, I'm taking my horses with me, since they were a gift from Father. Ronald has arranged for them to be flown to California."

"Have you talked to Peter? Red Oaks belongs to him, too."

"You know our brother. Since he got his divorce, he spends all of his time with his friends. Maybe he's in Paris, maybe he's sailing the Mediterranean. Who knows? I'll call him later from the United States, and he won't mind. He hates this monstrosity of a house as much as you do."

Adrian's loyalty to his sister was too strong to let her give up the family estate. "Roxie, just let me loan you the money. Don't throw away your part of Red Oaks for another affair that probably will turn sour."

"Well, that depends on how much you can loan me and for how long."

"I'll loan you one-third of the price Red Oaks would sell for on today's market. You can pay me back monthly from your trust fund."

"That sounds reasonable. Have your lawyer draw up the papers and mail them to me to sign." She handed her brother a piece of paper. "Here's my mailing address and telephone number in the United States."

Adrian reached out and took the paper from her hand. "Roxie, this loan will be between us only. No need to get legal about it. I'll deposit the money into your account next week."

"You never change, Adrian. You're your normal sweet, generous self."

He knew she had, as usual, presented him with a totally preconceived plan, her method when she was utterly determined and desperate to have her own way.

"Adrian, I'll never be able to fit into the family mold. You know that."

She was right, and Adrian knew it. "So the man of the hour is named Ronald. Does he have a last name?"

"Well, my dear, I'm sure you've heard of him—Ronald Jackson, the movie star."

"Good Lord, not a movie star!"

"Yes. Aren't you pleased for me?" Roxie walked over to the liquor cabinet and poured herself another glass of brandy.

"Sure. I'm as pleased as punch, but what about Cara? She's still in boarding school. Are you planning to take her out of school and move her to the United States?"

"Cara's sixteen now, and she loves Royal Masonic Girls' School. It's a prestigious school in an exclusive community. She's happy there. I can't just take her out of school. Not now anyway."

"Then when?"

"Ronald and I haven't discussed Cara. I … well … I haven't really told him about my daughter yet."

"If you're going to live with this movie star, I think you'd better tell him about your daughter soon, unless you're ashamed of her."

"You certainly have a way of putting things, Adrian. Of course I'm not ashamed of my daughter. I love her, and you love her, too. She'll come here to Red Oaks during her Christmas and summer holidays as usual. I see no reason to upset her routine."

"Here? Roxie, you know better than that. Her summer holiday is more than three months. I travel a great deal of that time. I'm not prepared to take care of a teenager, no matter how fond I am of Cara. She's just at the age where she needs her mother more than ever."

"How archaic, Adrian. She loves it here, and she adores her Uncle Adrian. Don't you see? I have no other recourse until I have a chance to discuss her with Ronald. Besides, her summers here at Red Oaks are filled with tennis, riding lessons, and visits with her friends."

"Cara went through the sadness of being raised without a father. Being without her mother now could devastate her. You're just like our father, Roxie. I resented growing up like an orphan. Our parents were often traveling all over the globe, leaving me alone like you leave Cara. Don't tell me it doesn't bother her." When Adrian stood to his feet, he could feel his blood pressure rising. He was outraged by what Roxie was telling him.

"Well, I have no other choice. I'll come for Cara later. I've made up my mind. That's why I came to see you this evening. She has to know what's going to happen to her. I want you to go to Royal Masonic this week and explain it to her. You can make her understand it all, Adrian. She adores you."

"What are you saying? You want me to tell her that her mother has left her? Do you realize Cara's looking forward to her Christmas holiday here at Red Oaks with you? That's only two and a half months away."

"Oh, darling, she'll adjust. You'll be here, and Peter's children, and I'll send lots of pretty gifts."

"Don't you see the difference? Peter will be here with his children. You can't just discard her, Roxie, like some material possession you no longer have any use for. She's a smart kid, and she'll see right through your pretty gifts."

Roxie's face hardened, and he knew she was serious. "All right, so it may hurt her for a while, and it's a terrible thing to do to a child, but I had to decide on a course of action that will least hurt her. I think my solution is the right one."

"So you came here tonight wanting me to buy you out of Red Oaks and to give me your daughter?"

"Of course not. Cara will eventually move to California and live with us. This will just be a temporary solution. Don't let's fight over her." Roxie smiled. For the first time that evening Adrian saw a glimpse of the old Roxie at her most charming and persuasive self.

Roxie was difficult, but she had always charmed Adrian into doing whatever she wanted. Yes, he loved her; he simply didn't understand her. "I'm not fighting over her, Roxie. She needs to be with her mother.

I'm not prepared to raise your child for you while you gallivant off halfway around the world with some movie star."

"Then you don't want, Cara?"

"That's not it, Roxie. I love her like my own daughter, but she is, after all, your child."

"She was raised here at Red Oaks, Adrian. This is her home, and …"

Adrian cut her off. "Yes, with you here at least some of the time."

"With you, Adrian, she'll have the best of everything. A good life. I'll come home and visit her whenever I can. Maybe I can even return during her Christmas holiday. For all our sakes, let her live with you. It's the best you can do for her. I know it is. Make the sacrifice, for Cara's sake."

He was so near to her he could smell the stale odor of liquor mixed with her expensive perfume. She would have stepped back from him, but he grasped her shoulders and gently held them. He reached up a finger to her cheek and brushed it affectionately.

To appeal to her senses, Adrian lowered his voice. "Roxie, you need help. You drink too much. Let me get some help for you."

Roxie responded firmly. "Nonsense, darling. I only drink to be sociable. That's what you want me to be, right? Sociable?"

"I only want you to be happy, Roxie. How can you possibly be happy without Cara?"

"I am happy. Really, I am. I wish I could be the way you want me to be, Adrian. I truly do."

He searched her face for some indication of tenderness, something that would make him certain she wanted her daughter more than she wanted the movie star. Her eyes were cold, no hint of what he hoped for. He quickly gave her an ultimatum.

"I'll give you until March of next year when Cara comes to Red Oaks for her Easter holiday. You have to either take her with you then or come back here to live with her."

Roxie put her arms around her brother and hugged him. "Oh, I do love you, Adrian. I really do."

$\mathcal{S}$*ix*

$\mathcal{T}$uesday morning Katie walked downstairs to the smell of hot maple syrup. She knew from the memorable aroma that pancakes were soon to be cooked in the kitchen. Brad was sitting alone at the table enjoying a cup of coffee. She loved her grandfather, loved him very much. He was a handsome man, happy, sometimes silly and childlike, sometimes profane, and sometimes totally outrageous. Once at the ranch house when she was five and peeked out from the railing of the stairs on Christmas Eve, she saw him put presents under the Christmas tree. With his thick shock of silver hair and twinkling blue eyes, she was certain he was Santa Claus and told her mother and father she knew who Santa was. It was a cherished family story she could not live down, but who wanted to? Her grandfather's smile and devilish sense of humor made him quite a dapper Santa.

"Gramps?" She knew she was being impulsive, but she needed his viewpoint.

"Ummm? Yes, my pet?"

She almost lost her courage, then blurted out her question. "Have you ever wondered what your life would have been like without Grammy?"

"Nope. Never gave it a second thought. She's the best thing that ever happened to me."

"The ranch? The horses? You would have done that anyway, without her, right?"

"Hardly, Katie. Without your grandmother to keep me in Virginia, I would have probably wound up in Colorado helping my aunt keep her small ranch."

"But you never gave up your ambition to be a horse breeder because of your marriage to her?"

"No. I'd have been a horse breeder no matter where I wound up. But loving Olivia drove me to be the best I could be." Brad held his coffee cup with two hands and looked at Katie with a questioning look in his eyes. "Why such serious questions this morning, Katie? Does this have something to do with your career in the ballet?"

"Oh, no. I want to be a prima ballerina more than anything in the world. And I'm happy, I really am."

"Of course you are, dear. It's what you've always wanted for yourself."

Katie was very close to confessing the way she felt after meeting Adrian Ashley. Perhaps life with him might be just as fulfilling as the ballet. These thoughts had plagued her all through the night. "Yes. Of course, I still want to be a ballerina." She stopped when she heard the sound of footsteps coming down the stairs.

Rilla walked into the kitchen, stepped to the counter, and poured herself a cup of coffee. "Morning, darlings. You're up early."

"Not really early for me, Mother. I'm usually in the practice room by six every morning." Katie was determined to show her loyalty to the ballet.

"I never thought I'd see the day you'd get up so early and apparently enjoy it."

"Yes, I do love the ballet, Mother. You know that. It's my life. What I've always wanted for myself."

She said the words too quickly. Rilla and Brad glanced at one another.

Katie saw the exchange. She was not good at being subtle and was afraid she may have revealed more than she intended. "So, is this a pancake morning?" she chirped.

Her grandfather studied her through narrowed eyes as he continued to sip his coffee.

The rest of the day was as perfect as Katie could have wished for. She spent time in warm, intimate girl talk with Olivia and Rilla, then walked to one of the local markets for her grandmother. Watching some of the customers greet each other and chat, she wondered what it would be like for children growing up in this friendly, quaint little town. On her way back to her grandparents' home, she wandered along the promenade beside the seafront. Everything about Penzance seemed exotic to Katie, and she was fully aware of the ships in the harbor, the smells of fish and salt air, the cries of the sea birds overhead. She walked slowly, relaxing more with each step she took.

By the time she reached the cottage, she had relaxed completely and was ready for a good game of cribbage with her grandfather. The time flew by as Katie enjoyed the love and attention of her family.

The next morning mother and daughter walked arm-in-arm to Katie's car. "Katie, there's something I must tell you before you leave. I'll do anything to keep you from making the same mistake I made when I was young."

"You made a mistake?"

"Yes, dear. I made a tragic mistake when I didn't marry your father once we fell in love. Even though my Cherokee father didn't give his approval because Will wasn't full blood Native American, I should have married him anyway. Your father joined the Navy thinking I would never be with him. That was a cruel thing for me to let happen. Those were long wasted years. We didn't marry until after my father died and Will returned from the Navy."

"Mother, why are you telling me this?"

"Mothers are probably fated to pass warnings along from one generation to the next forever, even though there will always be a few daughters who will ignore it, to their loss."

Katie was shocked at her mother's transparent excuse. "No, I think I know the reason you're telling me this now. You think I care for Adrian Ashley, don't you?"

"The thought did come to mind. Your grandfather and I knew you were having some doubts about your future when you spoke at breakfast yesterday."

"I guess I blew it. I'm just not quite sure what's real with Adrian and what I imagined."

"Making choices for your life is most difficult, especially when it comes to choices of the heart. I know you'll have some time to read on the flight to New York. Here's a little book you might find of interest."

"What is it?" Katie took the small book from her mother's hand.

"It's your great-grandmother Victoria's diary. Olivia loaned it to me to read just after your father and I got married. Victoria had strength and wisdom and made good choices."

"Thank you. I didn't realize she had written a diary. I'll love reading it." Katie reached over and kissed her mother.

"Olivia wants you to read it, but take good care of it. It's a very private journal."

"I will, Mother."

As Katie drove through the remote towns toward London's traffic and pedestrian congestion, she thought of Adrian. Whatever her feelings for him—and they were deeper, much deeper than she dared to admit— life had to continue as it was. No promises, no vows, no more broken hearts.

She knew full well how lucky she was in so many ways, but thinking about Adrian and how empty her personal life was depressed her profoundly. Her career as a ballerina would end someday. The career of a dancer could only last as long as the stamina was there. And then what? She raised her hand and brushed a tear away.

She arrived at the hotel where the troupe was lodged sometime after 3:00 p.m. The two days in Penzance had been memorable—the time with her family in her grandparents' nostalgic home, the dinner on Monday night, and meeting Adrian. The six-hour drive from Penzance was tiring, but she could still get plenty of rest before tomorrow morning. If the other dancers did not barge in on her, that was.

Sure enough, she had no more than closed the outside door when she encountered two female cast members. They chattered and giggled at her for a whole minute without stopping, telling her something or other about the handsome man they had met backstage after Saturday night's performance.

Katie managed to get upstairs into her room, shut the door behind her, unfasten her ponytail, and throw her coat on the bed before the door burst open. After the merest tap of a knock, two more of her friends came hurrying in to catch her up on more gossip about Adrian Ashley. She listened to them impatiently, and did not tell them about meeting the famous Mr. Ashley. She really did not want to hear about him or reveal that she knew him personally.

There was only one more performance in London, and then she would be off to New York before traveling home to Virginia. She was genuinely glad that the Atlantic Ocean would be between her and Adrian. She would probably never see him again. That would be best for her, she thought, and would easily end all of the turmoil meeting this man had brought her.

Katie had set aside Thursday to practice her part in the third act. She made a conscious effort to forget everything that had happened in the last few days. Everything. She refused to think any more of the stranger who had entered her life, her very being, until she was filled only with thoughts of him. She must bring it to an end.

She got up at 5:00 a.m. as usual and was in the studio warming up by 5:30. There was no rehearsal until noon that day, but she could never bear the idea of missing an entire morning without dancing. She was always afraid she would lose some of her skill.

As she had promised herself, she refused to think of Adrian. She would surely bungle the routine, since thinking of him made her feel clumsy somehow. That could not happen today. If she thought of the dance, and only that, perhaps she could convince herself that everything that had happened Monday evening had been a page from someone else's life.

The choreography demanded perfection, and she completed it as perfectly as it demanded. The one form of discipline she understood was that a routine had to be done no matter what went on around you. Katie felt she had already failed in her personal life, but she would not fail in her professional life. She had known her mother to finish a score of music for a movie while running a fever or while her prized race horse gave birth to a foal. Katie's life with the ballet was a world of intensely hard work. Just as the hard work and dedication of her parents and grandparents made their ranch a success, she knew that same devotion and responsibility to the dance were vital to her art.

Her skill was reaching its peak, and the development of her talent was all that Madame Bettencourt, her beloved teacher, had said it would be. There was never the slightest element of disappointment in her performance.

After the travesty of her marriage had left her mentally in shambles, she finally became focused again and now had the single-minded dedication and purpose that were essential for success. She allowed for no distractions such as those during her first year in New York with the ballet. She lived and breathed and worked and existed only for dancing. She was unlike some of the other dancers whom her teacher viewed with disdain. Despite their impeccable training and whatever talent they had, too often they allowed themselves to be distracted or lured away by romance. The ballet was Katie's lifeblood, the force that drove and fed her very soul. It was everything she cared about and lived for. As a result, her dancing was exquisite. Now her only ambition, her only dream, was of being a prima ballerina with an impressive repertory. She must forget Adrian Ashley.

Seven

*A*drian met the pianist who had made the dream song notation and listened to him play his full version of the song. It was a beautiful rendition. Adrian thanked the man again and went to his office to make a copy of it for Rilla. Because of other business appointments, he could not make the trip to Hertfordshire until Friday morning. He dreaded this day, the day he would tell his young, beautiful niece that her mother had moved to the United States.

Adrian Ashley was born into a world of glamour, wealth, and prestige. He had lived all of his life in one place, a place where only the best was acceptable. In truth, he relished it. Adrian admitted that summering in the calm blue waters of the Mediterranean, soaking up the sun on islands in the Pacific, and winter skiing in the Alps were luxuries he enjoyed.

He would not wish those experiences away, but now he knew his ultimate responsibility was to his niece, Cara, and he would fulfill it for her gladly. He thought of her as she was when a young child, always running to him, her favorite doll tucked under her arm. He had cherished her then and cherished her still.

Love for his niece overtook him with a tightened fist, solid and painful. In all his life he had never known anything as consuming or as fundamentally pleasing as the emotions Cara brought to him simply by being. He set his goals high. He would be more than an uncle and god-father to Cara. He would fill that empty void within her of a father and now a mother, and at the same time fill a need within himself as he looked forward to someday having children of his own.

They walked slowly together but apart around a deserted games field at Cara's school. It was a horrible day, English October weather at its worst—cold, raw, misty. No breeze stirred the almost leafless trees and only the sound of occasional traffic broke the foggy silence. The school buildings stood in the distance. Once they had been elegant country homes with formal gardens and stables, but they had been converted into sleeping quarters and classrooms.

Cara, her head drooping and her hands deep in the pockets of her red coat, kicked at a rock. Wisps of her blonde hair clung to her face as the mist settled on her. As Adrian had suspected, the news about her mother came as a shock to her. Adrian believed this was the way it must be, no flowery speeches about things being fine. He quietly and simply told her the truth and encouraged her as always by declaring his love for her.

"She was never a mother to me, anyway." Cara lifted her head and stared at him. "Uncle Adrian, it's more like you're my father, rather than my uncle. You were the one I could go to when I had a problem, and Mother always encouraged me to do so."

Adrian put his arm around her. "I'm sure your mother has done the best she could. She's different somehow, not attentive to important things like family." He sought for some means of making her feel better and failed.

Cara looked away from her uncle. "Was she sorry she had me?"

The question startled Adrian. He stopped walking and put his hand out to Cara. "Oh, no, Cara!" he said emphatically. "She was pleased, and you were such a beautiful baby. She brought you to Red Oaks when you were only three days old. I fell in love with you the moment I saw you, even though I was only twelve at the time. Then you became all chubby and smiling and trying to walk and talk long before you should have."

Cara stared straight ahead. "I don't remember her being around much. It was always you, Maude, and Gus that I remember. And I faintly remember someone rocking me and singing a lullaby when I was young. She had long black hair." Cara turned to face Adrian. "Was that your mother?"

"Yes, that would have been my mother. She died when you were just four years old. I'm surprised you can remember her."

"Her arms were warm, and she had a light sweet smell of talcum." Cara hesitated awkwardly. "My mother never sang to me, and she never wanted me to call her Mommy. She insisted I call her Roxie. Why has she been gone so much?"

Adrian knew he must be absolutely truthful in his reply, but he did not want to hurt her. "Sweetheart, Roxie and Mother had many disagreements which drove your mother away from Red Oaks. Roxie traveled extensively and lived with friends all over the world. It's the same thing Uncle Peter has done since his divorce."

Cara shook her head. "But it's different with Uncle Peter. He still brings his boys to Red Oaks for holidays, and Robert and Edwin told me he doesn't ever miss their birthday parties. I don't even remember Mother being at Red Oaks for any of my birthday parties."

"But she was always there for the holidays."

Cara nodded her head in agreement and said, "Yeah, she came some of the time."

Adrian and Cara walked for some time before they sat on a bench close to the administration building. Adrian noticed splotches of pink on her cheeks as the air grew colder.

Her brows furrowed as she spoke. "Uncle Adrian, I have my heart set on going to college. Will I still be able to go?"

"Have no fear. You will go, and my little niece will be a doctor someday."

"I'm not so little anymore."

"This is true, Cara. Very true. Listen, I've decided to return here on Sunday to get your grades so I can finalize the paperwork for your enrollment at University College London Medical School. You can go home with me for a few days' holiday at Red Oaks. How would that be?"

She smiled up at him, and his love for her swelled within him. It would all work out. Cara would adjust. He would see that she wanted for nothing. He would give her his love, and all the rest would eventually fall into place.

The two of them were so intently engrossed in conversation that neither of them noticed someone was watching them from an office nearby. Someone was keeping a very close and suspicious eye on Cara and her uncle.

Later that morning after Adrian had gone back to London, Cara walked toward her dorm and noticed an unfamiliar young man strolling in that direction. As she passed him, his arm bumped hers, and their eyes met.

His hat came off instantly. "Oh, I beg your pardon," he began. "Hey! It's you! I know you," he said in a surprised but pleasant tone.

Cara looked at him in bewilderment. Who in the world was he?

"You've forgotten me, Cara," he accused. "Don't you remember at all? You sang in the Christmas pageant with me last year."

Comprehension dawned on Cara's face. "Oh, I remember now." She had met so many people during chorus last year, but now she did remember him, though somewhat hazily. "You're …"

"Don't try," he said. "I forgot your name, too. I remember someone said you were going to be here again this year, and I meant to call you, but for the life of me all I could remember was that they called you Cara. My name's Harry Wilhelm. I'm from Emery. Remember now? Probably you don't, but that's okay."

He was tanned and had crisp dark hair and an amazing profile. His blue shirt, red tie, and dark blue jacket with a school crest on the pocket were traditional for Emery. He flashed a quick smile at her. She thought he must spend all his waking hours on some sort of activity in the sun.

"Of course, I do," Cara said. She was glad to see him, but a little shy at the decided pleasure in his tone. She remembered him now. "My name's Cara Landry."

He took possession of her books. "Mind if I walk along and make sure I don't lose you again?"

"Certainly. What are you doing here at Royal Masonic? Emery's down the road."

"I'm picking up my younger sister. She lives in Rathburn Hall. We're going home for an overnight to see my grandparents, who are visiting from France."

"Who's your sister?"

"Nancy Wilhelm."

"I live in Rathburn Hall also, and I know Nancy. She's a very nice girl."

"She's okay for a sister, I suppose."

"Do you have a car?" Cara asked out of curiosity.

"Sure."

As they walked along, Cara thought he was even more handsome than her rather dim memory of him. He was very friendly in a casual sort of way, and by the time they neared her dormitory they were well acquainted.

He went up to the door with her and then handed over her books. His confident smile flashed down at her again. "Would you go to the cinema with me one of these nights? Busy Sunday?"

Cara shook her head regretfully. She did want to go. "I'm sorry," she said. "Really I am, but Sunday my Uncle Adrian's coming to take me to Red Oaks."

"Where's Red Oaks?"

"It's our family estate just outside Farnham."

"Really? I live in Westchester, barely a hop, skip, and jump from you. In fact, I was at Farnham with my family over the summer. We stayed at a bed and breakfast there."

Cara watched the thin laugh lines around his eyes as he spoke.

"Well, maybe we can get together next week some time."

In the lobby of the dorm, Cara said, "I'd love it." She was already looking forward to seeing him again.

"I'll give you a ring at your dorm before then."

She and Harry exchanged telephone numbers.

"All right. Goodbye for now."

"See you later." He stood with hat in hand before he walked to a reception desk to request that his sister join him.

Cara went through the hall to the stairs with a comfortable feeling of warmth. She had entirely forgotten this young man, but she had a feeling they might easily become friends. He seemed slightly conceited and a little spoiled, but he was nice, and he was handsome. It might be fun going to the cinema with someone other than the girls for a change.

At noon, and much sooner than she wished, Cara was ushered into Miss Monique Ryan's imposing office. Miss Ryan was music teacher and student counselor for Royal Masonic Girls' School.

"Miss Ryan said for you to go right in," the office girl said.

Cara walked cautiously into Miss Ryan's private office.

A tall woman with a pleasant face rose from behind a large mahogany desk. As usual, she was dressed tastefully in a gray suit and crisp white blouse. As Cara walked toward her, her hand outstretched, she detected a genuine gladness in Miss Ryan's tone, even though most of the students did not like her. Cara knew she could be harsh and unkind to the girls if she was in a bad mood.

"Well, well, Cara," she said. "It's good to see you, my dear."

For a moment Cara could scarcely speak. This room and this woman with whom she always had been so shy almost overwhelmed her. One wall of the long office was made entirely of great panes of glass which showed the walkway on the east side of the campus where Cara had walked that morning with her uncle Adrian. Girls were scurrying to and fro, going to classes or to their rooms.

On the floor was a thick tan carpet, and the desk was flanked by comfortable leather chairs. Books in cases rose from floor to ceiling, and on the wall behind her desk were several framed certificates of her degrees and accomplishments. It was, indeed, a beautiful room, one that seemed to fit Miss Ryan.

"Good afternoon, Miss Ryan." Cara smiled shyly as they shook hands.

Miss Ryan smiled back at Cara, and a special kind of charm lit her whole face. "How are you getting on, Cara? Are you well taken care of? Tell me a how your classes are coming."

"I'm enjoying school very much, Miss Ryan."

"And your voice is as good as ever. Are you going to lend us that special gift of yours for the Christmas pageant again this year?"

"Yes, Miss Ryan," Cara replied, feeling her face get very red. "I look forward to the pageant every year."

"The wonderful voices of the boys from Emery will join us again this year."

"Yes, I know."

"So, I suppose you're still aiming on a career in medicine?" Miss Ryan asked quickly.

The abrupt change in subject startled Cara. "If ... if you don't mind, Miss Ryan."

"Mind? Why should I? No, no, Cara. Music or no music, you go ahead and do whatever you want to do. You can use your musical talents wherever you are." By now there was more than a touch of sarcasm in her voice.

Cara gripped her leather school bag tightly between her fingers. "It's really on account of my career choice in medicine that I've come to see you. My uncle will be here Sunday to get my grades and pick up forms for college enrollment at UCL Medical School in January of 1976."

Miss Ryan looked surprised. "UCL Medical School? It is a good school. Of course, you can go wherever you want, and that day will be here sooner than you realize."

"It's not for another year. I'll still have my senior year here." Cara told Miss Ryan all about her decisions, about the realization of the difficult medical studies ahead, and the unexpected offer of a full scholarship to UCL after completing high school.

Miss Ryan listened attentively, and Cara felt that she understood even more than she said.

When Cara finished, Miss Ryan sat looking out a window at the campus in the distance. "You've a lot of work cut out for you, Cara. This medical business is hard at best. Did you tell your family that this college has quite a structured program geared only to the medical field?"

"Of course. Uncle Adrian is my guardian now, and he wants me to attend college at UCL, because it would be the best school for my career. I'll miss the friends I've made here at Royal Masonic. Many of them will attend a college specializing in music."

"So, your uncle is your guardian. Why am I not surprised?" Miss Ryan's voice was barely above a whisper. She turned quickly from the window to Cara and continued, her voice taking on a strong emphasis.

"Cara, music means a great deal to me, more than for most people, I think. When I was young I used to dream of being a singer or a composer, anything to have music very close to me. I had to work hard, desperately hard, as hard as I would have for law or medicine, though few believe it until they try. And getting myself established at Royal Masonic, there was never any time for family, but I always thought that one day ...." Her voice trailed off into silence.

Cara felt embarrassed that Miss Ryan would divulge so much about her personal life to her.

Just then the telephone rang. Miss Ryan picked it up. "I told you I did not want to be disturbed." She put the telephone back in the cradle with a hard fling and pushed back her hair. She seemed nervous as her carefully manicured fingers tapped the top of her desk.

Cara felt uncomfortable.

"I'm sorry, Cara. I dislike being interrupted with frivolous matters when I'm with a student. By the way, you should know I usually don't come to the office on Sunday, but I'll make a note that your uncle will be here on my day off. I do want to talk to him. He must understand how difficult the medical field will be on you. He'll only want the best for you, as I do. I'll wait for him and speak with him here in my office on Sunday."

Cara stood, relieved that her appointment was finally over. She was confused and dismayed at Miss Ryan's demeanor and lack of self discipline.

With the darkening evening sky, the light from the lamps gave warmth to her room, but Cara shuddered and felt she might be coming down with an illness. Her palms sweated, and the memory of the discussion with Miss Ryan that afternoon left her feeling drained. Suddenly, she wished her roommate were there, or better yet, she wished for her mother to confide in. Why aren't you here, Mother? Don't you know how many times and how many ways I need you?

That thought brought Cara a sinking feeling. She probably would not dare to share the details of her meeting with Miss Ryan with her mother, even if her mother were available. Whom could she talk to? Sharing the displeasure of a teacher with another student was unheard of. It would probably get back to Miss Ryan, no matter how much secrecy the friend would vow. She wondered if Harry Wilhelm was in his room at Emery. She reached into her pocket and drew out the small piece of paper with his telephone number. She dialed the number, but then panicked, thinking that Harry would make fun of her disliking a teacher. What if he told his sister, and it got back to Miss Ryan? She hung up the receiver quickly when someone answered.

Eight

On Friday evening, at London's Royal Opera House, the dancers of *Moonglow Fascination* once again held the audience spellbound. The serene beauty of the set was a stark contrast to the energy of the young dancers. When Katie appeared in her solo, she knew every hour of her training was apparent to everyone present. Her leaps and turns were perfect, her Pas de Chat magnificent.

During the final bows, Katie looked across the nearest rows of seats. If Adrian had been there, she could have spotted him. She assumed he had not taken the time to watch her final London performance. Well, she thought, who needs him? She had probably read too much into his words, his gentle advances toward her.

Katie loved a party, and Saturday there was a farewell party for the cast of *Moonglow Fascination*. One of her favorite ways to reward herself for a hard day of dancing was to primp, dress up, and spend an evening with a crowd. It did not matter tonight if anyone escorted her to the party. Most of the troupe members were coming alone. Her strapless forest green gown was new, purchased after a frantic two hours of shopping that morning to find a new party dress. This one did her proud. The slight sweetheart neckline and the softly flared skirt gave her the appearance of a perfect hourglass figure. The jade necklace and tiny jade earrings were plain but elegant. She spent longer than usual on her makeup, experimenting with a new shade of eye shadow she found in a local department store. The other girls had complimented her on the color, saying it was becoming.

After much debate, she hesitated over the perfume her mother had given her at Christmas last year. With a shrug, she touched it to her pulse points. She did not care if Adrian liked the scent. She was, after all, wearing it only for herself. Besides, he probably would not even show up.

She knew a great many people attending the party. Some were members of the troupe, stagehands, choreographers, and musicians. Some English dignitaries and members of the press were also present. She was able to entertain herself by mingling, exchanging pecks on the cheek and fresh gossip.

The fall season had swept down on London in a rush of very cool weather. It was often cold and drafty in large areas where parties and dances were held. Though she had taken a chance wearing this particular dress, the press of bodies heated the room and would keep her comfortable. In spite of her earlier resolutions, she secretly hoped that Adrian would come.

Across the crowded room, Katie spotted him standing alone. He does look fabulous, she mused as she circled the room to come up behind him. His blue raw-silk blazer whispered of understated elegance, the stylish white shirt with tiny pleats spoke of Paris fashion, and the draping of his linen slacks shouted expensive tailoring.

She waited until he picked up a glass of punch. "Hello," she said at his shoulder. "I didn't know if you'd come."

"I have an invitation, but honestly, I usually avoid parties," Adrian said, looking at her soberly.

"But you certainly dressed for the party."

"So did you." His eyes boldly gazed over her. "You look as though you just walked out of my dream."

"Oh, that dream thing again?" Katie smiled. "I suppose you're hearing the music you heard in your dream?"

"No," he said, shaking his head. "Not now."

"When will you tell me about your dream?"

"You'd probably think it was childish."

"Try me, Adrian. I like dreams. My family always thought they had some deep spiritual meaning."

"It was about a young woman."

"Oh, now it's getting interesting. Go on. The woman in your dreams, what did she say?"

"Nothing. She was moving to the music."

"A ballerina?"

"No, I don't think it was ballet, but it was beautiful."

"And she was dancing to this mystical music?"

"It appeared so. She was just there, and then the music began, and she started swaying and moving her feet in the water. Yes, I suppose she was dancing."

"Maybe she was a mermaid." Katie quickly regretted her words when Adrian did not smile at her remark. "I'm sorry, Adrian. It just sounds so magical."

"It was magical. Very mysterious. And she was very beautiful."

Katie could see in his eyes a far-away look. This dream was a very serious thing to him, and she cautioned herself not to make any more jokes about it. "I'm jealous," she said.

He turned his eyes to her. "No need for you to be jealous, Katie. When I saw you dancing in the practice studio the day the musician was playing the music from my dream, it was a déjà vu experience."

"You saw me dancing in the practice studio?"

"Yes, I was walking down the hall of the theatre, and there you were. It was beautiful the way you danced to the music from my dream. I've never seen anything so lovely. When I attended your performance last week, you were lovely then, also."

It was a special moment for Katie, one of those moments she wanted to remember to tell her children some day. Then the warm glow gave way to panic. She looked away, and she knew by her pounding heart how much he meant to her. She also knew loving this man was wrong for her, so very wrong. She could not do this again.

He took her hand, his eyes never leaving her face. Ever so gently he brought their joined hands to his lips.

Katie was not sure she liked the way he was smiling at her, as if he knew the deep dark secret she was keeping from him. Suddenly she felt a strong urge to tell him everything. She did not, of course. Adrian was a stranger. A friendly, uncommonly appealing stranger, yes, but she was not about to bare her soul to him. Only her family and a few close friends knew her secret, and she had vowed to keep it that way. She broke the uneasy silence. "I didn't see you at the performance last night."

"No. I had to see my niece yesterday. After the drive to her school and back, I had a contract to negotiate and then turned in early last night so I'd be refreshed for this party."

The orchestra was playing a silky version of "Moonlight Serenade."

"Everyone's watching you, Adrian. Well, the girls in the troupe anyway." Katie tugged on his sleeve. "Five bucks say they'll swoon if you escort me onto the dance floor and exude some charm."

A broad smile crossed his face. "A three dollar tip and now five bucks. You may become famous for giving out bucks, as you Americans say."

His unexpected humor brought out her best little girl giggles. "Oh, Adrian, really."

Adrian looked around the room. "Don't you have a boyfriend here?"

"I don't date," Katie said.

Adrian lightly encircled her waist and led her to the dance floor. "Why not?" he asked as he held her close.

"I don't have the time for it, or the interest in men. My dedication to the ballet keeps me busy and happy. By the way, you're a nice dancer, Adrian."

"Thank you. I reluctantly attended dance classes when I was twelve."

Katie laughed easily at his gloomy expression. "Part of your royal upbringing?"

He did not smile or respond and when his gaze lowered, she tilted her head up and looked at him.

"Aren't you having a good time, Adrian? You seem very sober tonight."

"I told you, I hate these things. You probably love dances and parties."

"Oh, I do. You'd like this party if you accepted it for what it is."

"Which is?"

"Friends getting together and celebrating a pristine performance before going back to New York and the beginning of another tour."

"I'd already figured that out," he said softly.

The song ended and another began, as they continued to move across the floor.

Giddy with happiness, she did not want to worry about anything while she surrendered to this moment of perfection. Adrian made her feel very feminine. His hands were confident as he guided her across the crowded dance floor, his fingers doing a subtle dance of their own at her waist. Katie squealed like a teenager when he swung her, and she twirled beneath his raised arm as if they had been doing this since childhood.

She began to see her smile reflected on his face. His sharp jaw relaxed, and his eyes glittered with delight in response to her gaiety.

When at last the music faded into silence, they walked away from the dance floor, Adrian's larger and warmer hand swallowing hers. Butterflies fluttered in Katie's stomach, and she was floating on air by the time he led her outside.

As any gentleman would do, Adrian took off his jacket and pulled it across her shoulders. She could smell his scent on the jacket, woodsy and manly. The pounding of Katie's heart was thunderous in her ears. Then he touched his mouth to hers. Although she tried not to give too much credence to the kiss they exchanged, it was a sweet kiss that Katie would not soon forget.

Adrian drew his head back and gazed down into her face. "You're an angel."

Katie heard herself disagreeing. "No, believe me, I'm no angel."

"Yes, you are," he insisted.

She stated more emphatically, "I'm just a woman, Adrian."

Adrian smiled and said in a thoroughly masculine voice, "Yes, you're a woman, but you could never be just a woman. When I kiss you, I feel as though I'm dreaming again."

Adrian Ashley was winning a battle, Katie worried, that he did not even know he was fighting.

Nine

"Katie. Katie Johnson, are you awake?"

Katie groaned at the sound of her name being whispered with repeated pokes in her side. She opened her eyes wide enough to see her room, still shrouded in darkness, and her roommate standing over her, urging her to awaken. What could Alice possibly want at this hour of the morning?

"Go away, please. It's Sunday," Katie muttered while hugging her pillow more tightly. Her arms and legs felt like lead weights after Friday evening's performance and the party for the ballet cast last night. Her brain was foggy and disoriented. Every joint in her body ached.

Alice persevered. "There's a gentleman here to see you. He's waiting in the lobby downstairs."

Katie opened her eyes just enough to see the clock sitting on her bedside table. "It can't be nine o'clock already. Why is it so dark? We just went to sleep."

"Correction." Alice poked her again. "You fell asleep the minute you hit the bed. It's raining outside, and your blinds are pulled."

"Who?" Katie asked, turning over and still hugging her pillow. "What gentleman?"

"Come on, Katie. It's really true. He's waiting downstairs this very minute."

"What's his name?"

"I don't know. The word from the doorman was that some handsome gentleman is waiting downstairs for you."

"No man who is gentle, handsome or otherwise, would come calling so early. Give me a minute."

Then it came back to her. All of it. The dinner in Penzance on Monday, the bafflement Adrian Ashley had left her with, the cast party last night when they danced until dawn, and the wonderful moment when he had kissed her.

Katie pushed herself reluctantly out of bed and pulled her hair back in a pony tail. She slipped on her jeans and an old sweatshirt.

"Here," Alice said. "Take a mint. You don't have time to brush your teeth."

"Thanks." Katie scrambled for her shoes and the door.

At first glance she wasn't sure who he was. He was wearing a dark overcoat, and his back was turned to her as he looked out the lobby window at the rain-drenched London street. Recognition came quickly. Katie stood at the bottom of the steps and cleared her throat. "Hello, Adrian."

He turned around with a smile. "So you're up."

"I am now."

"I have a gift for you." He reached on the chair beside him and presented her with a large bouquet of twelve white lilies.

All at once Katie was aware of how she was dressed and how she looked. "Oh," was about all she could say as she reached out for the flowers. "Thank you. Lilies are my favorite." She lowered her head and inhaled the sweet delicate fragrance. "How did you know, and why the flowers, Adrian?"

"Lilies were my mother's favorite flower. Well, I told you I wasn't going to apologize for the mix up in our first meeting, but I thought the flowers might smooth things over somewhat."

With the flowers in her arms, Katie dropped into a maroon overstuffed chair, one of two flanking the warm, cozy fireplace in the lobby. Adrian sat down in the matching chair.

He reached into his jacket pocket and pulled out a sealed envelope. "This is for your mother, if you don't mind mailing it to her. It's the musician's notation for the 'Dream Song.' I wasn't sure if she'd be in Penzance long enough for me to mail it there. Also, I'm going to

Rickmansworth in Hertfordshire today. Since it's Sunday, I thought you might like to ride along with me and catch a bite to eat on the way."

Katie accepted the envelope, then asked, "What's in Rick ... mans ... worth?"

A smile twinkled in Adrian's eyes when she floundered with the pronunciation. "My niece, Cara. Her school is there. I have to see her counselor for a brief meeting, and then I'm bringing her home with me for a few days' holiday."

"And you want me to tag along?"

"Sure. Why not? I can have you back at your hotel early this afternoon."

She could not resist or refuse or pretend she did not want to be with him. Knowing she might regret it later, she said, "I'll need to bathe and dress. Do you mind waiting?"

"No. I'll walk across the street and grab a newspaper while you're getting ready. I'll be back in, say, twenty minutes."

"Fine."

Twenty minutes meant a brisk shower, not enough time for a shampoo and blow dry, so she slicked her hair back with hairspray into a chignon that somehow did not work. On the third attempt, she thought, what the heck. She left her hair in a pony tail and tied a black chiffon scarf around the rubber band holding her hair in place. The dressing part was easy. She slipped on a fuscia sweater set and a long, slim, black skirt that hugged her thighs.

The shoes, she thought. Where are they? Scrambling on hands and knees on the floor of the closet she shared with Alice, she came up with black leather boots and quickly rubbed off the dust with a washcloth.

She gave herself as objective an appraisal as possible. Hemline okay. No bulges that were not supposed to be bulges, at least. She was blessed with good genes and knew exactly where they came from. Her mother had always been tall and willowy. Katie grabbed her raincoat on the way out and proceeded downstairs where Adrian was waiting.

Right away she saw his expression of approval as she walked down the stairway. Her words caught in her throat mid-sentence. "I'm ready ...."

He walked over to her as she stood with her hand on the stair railing. His hand touched hers.

The look in his eyes was almost an awakening, an awareness of her as a woman. It was a heady feeling for Katie.

Adrian opened the passenger door of a sleek black Mercedes sedan.

"Oh," she exclaimed. "I was expecting your sports car."

"It has room only for the driver and one passenger. I thought the Mercedes would be the best choice for the drive to Rickmansworth." His smile was genuine, but it let Katie know he had counted on her presence.

The thought of Adrian owning a long garage filled with many cars startled Katie. Of course, she finally realized, this man, after all, is royalty!

The drive through London with Adrian was more delightful than she expected. The sun begged to shine and the clouds moved rapidly toward the east. Adrian was playing tour guide. He drove past Hyde Park on the Baywater side. The park's greenness, in spite of the weather, spread for some miles before them. He also pointed out and gave the history—not surprising for someone who was born and raised in England—of various churches and government buildings. Katie found herself enjoying the ride and admitted to herself she also enjoyed his company.

She suppressed a chuckle when she realized she was being driven by the same man she once mistook for a bellman, and she leaned back more comfortably against the black leather seat. Every few moments she sat upright and craned toward the window at the unfamiliar landscape. She had felt the same thrill when the taxi had driven her from Heathrow to her hotel, but now Adrian's comments gave life to what had been a mere view of a very old city.

"Tell me about your niece," she requested, turning her face to him.

"Sixteen, my god-daughter, and given to my care recently by her mother."

"You mean you must take care of her?"

"Yes and no. Most of the time, she's in boarding school, but she always comes to Red Oaks for holidays or when there are school breaks.

It's her home, but it was always hoped her mother would settle down at Red Oaks to be with her. I'm afraid that might not happen for awhile. Roxie has gone to the United States to live with a movie star."

Katie looked at him, shocked by his declaration. "Is Cara upset about that?"

"Yes, but I'm devoted to Cara. I love her very much. She never met her father, and since my father is never around, she depends on me as the father figure in her life."

Katie felt this was a very good time to ask Adrian about his marital status. Better to get the issue out in the open, since many of her friends dated and were later devastated to find out the men were married. "Do you think that's a lot of responsibility for you, being single and all?"

"No." Adrian smiled at her. "My fulltime housekeeper, Maude, and her husband, Gus, have been with the family since long before Cara arrived. They are devoted to Cara and love her like their own grandchild."

"Lucky girl."

"Perhaps, but not having a father has been difficult for her. At least I can give her my love and a consistent, stable environment."

Katie found herself openly admiring his dedication. "She's lucky to have you as a role model."

She did not know him well enough to make that kind of observation, but he blushed at the compliment anyway.

When he grew silent, Katie thought he was probably impatient to be out of the traffic and the uninspiring suburbs. He turned onto a main road and eventually they were in pleasantly wooded countryside. They passed the occasional town or village and small neat fields separated by green hedges which reminded her of the spreading pastures of Virginia. Yet, the charming houses and cottages were so different from Virginia she longed to stop and explore. She sensed that Adrian was anxious to get to his destination and graciously decided not to mention exploration.

Adrian reached across the front seat of the car and squeezed her hand. Finally, he broke the silence. "This part of England compares favorably with any spot in the world," he said. "At times I take it for granted, but you have a way of making me appreciate things, Katie."

"It's lovely."

"Tell me more about yourself." Giving Katie's hand a final squeeze, Adrian pulled his hand away and turned his full attention to the serpentine curve ahead.

She turned toward him. "My home is near Richmond, Virginia. The racehorses Father breeds are truly famous. Perhaps you've heard of Grill's Ranch? It's in a small town called Orlanger."

"Really? As a matter of fact, I have heard of Grill's Ranch. A partner of mine went there a few years ago and found himself two prize young stallions and shipped them off to his home in Australia. Virginia sounds enchanting."

He said this in such a precise Oxford tone that she smiled to herself, realizing her Southern drawl, so normal to her ears, must sound as marked to him as his accent did to her. He was setting about the task of being charming. She might as well follow suit.

"I grew up there, went to public school in Orlanger, and then went to New York to study ballet under Madame Bettencourt."

"You've come a long way," he said, adding, "I can't imagine the time and dedication you've given to the ballet."

"It's not like work for me. I love the ballet."

"In Penzance, you mentioned that your grandmother's an artist. You have a long line of talented ancestors."

"Yes. Some of Grammy's paintings hang in the drawing room at the house in Penzance. Sorry I didn't think to show them to you."

"Perhaps another time."

"Perhaps."

"What about your mother's side of the family?" Adrian asked.

"Well, Mother grew up in a Cherokee village in North Carolina. When she married my father, her parents, who were both Cherokee, were dead, so we never visited their village. But Mother encouraged me to learn many things about her people." She chatted on and on as she had in the garden, not seeming to notice that she was sharing her American heritage with a member of British royalty.

Adrian listened but did not interrupt, so she stopped talking after telling him about her mother.

Once or twice she mentioned the lovely countryside merely to break the spell of silence, because he seemed totally focused on the road. When her comments became repetitive, Katie remained silent and gave her attention to the beautiful view. From time to time she felt him look at her, once long and penetratingly, as if weighing something in his mind.

They stopped for brunch in a small quaint town. The hills rose steeply to either side of it, giving a breadth of view she did not expect. The leaves were turning red, orange, and yellow and would soon be in full color.

"When did you decide to be a ballerina, Katie?"

"Almost from the day I could walk. I always loved to dance. Also, Grammy's step-brother had a daughter, Chloe Cowling, who was a prima ballerina with the London ballet. When I was twelve, she invited me to come and visit her in London during the summer. It was a dream trip for me. She took me to the ballet, out for marvelous dinners, and to her grand house in London."

"So you were inspired by her?"

"Probably, but I knew from the time I was in grade school I wanted to dance ballet. Chloe never married, and I admired her steadfast determination to give herself totally to the ballet. She did inspire that part in me. I knew someday I would dedicate myself to the ballet the way she did."

"Is she still in the ballet?" Adrian questioned.

"No. She lives in New York, but she no longer dances. An ankle injury forced her into early retirement. I get a long letter from her every Christmas season."

"When did you last see her?"

"Last year."

"Do you correspond with her?"

"We talk on the telephone now and then. She attended one of my performances in New York last year, and we had dinner afterward. We weren't that close when I was younger because of our age difference. But, now that I think about it, I will try to call her when I get back to New York. She bought an apartment near Central Park and moved there permanently two years ago."

"Good. I've found that very often acquaintances made years ago are the best."

It was a perfect meal, eaten under perfect circumstances. They ate heartily the steak and thick, crusty bread and finished the meal with cheese, biscuits, and a bowl of fresh fruit.

She would be realistic about Adrian. There was no reason to suppose they could not be good friends. She would go back to Virginia and resume her life as though she had never met him, as though she had never had those silly notions and fantasies of being with him forever. Soothed by this thought, the comfort of good food, and Adrian's enjoyable company, she felt her spirits rise. She told herself that this was another moment she would always remember, in spite of her fears.

Adrian handed Katie a picture from his wallet. "Here's a photo of Cara taken last Christmas when she was on holiday at Red Oaks."

Katie saw a slim girl smiling up at her uncle, her blonde hair pulled back from her face and tiny gold rings in her ears. She wore a dark blue velvet trouser suit banded with some sort of embroidery, and she stood in the curve of Adrian's arm. She looked assured, vital, and happy. Was she really as happy as she appeared in the picture? This was taken before Cara was told her mother was moving to the United States. All of a sudden Katie felt a great sorrow for Adrian's niece. She herself had experienced such a warm relationship with her mother, and she knew it had not been that way for Cara.

"She's lovely. So I'm going to meet her today?"

"Yes. She'll be waiting for us. She's been given a scholarship to University College London Medical School. It's a college geared to students who need studies centered on biology and chemistry, basically a prep school for medical college."

"She wants to be a doctor?"

"Yes. Her grades are at the top of her class, and I think she'll make a fine doctor."

"What field?"

"She wants pediatrics."

"I'm impressed."

"Katie, I have to go see Cara's counselor today. I'll be just long enough to sign the papers that will begin the long, tedious application process required for her scholarship to UCL."

Ten

At noon they arrived on the school grounds, and Katie spotted a young girl who looked like the photograph Adrian had shown her. When Adrian stopped, the girl rushed to the car. Katie saw the surprised look on her face when she realized someone was with her uncle. Adrian went around and opened the car's back door, and she settled inside.

"Cara, this is Kaitlyn Rose Johnson. She's a friend of mine who dances with a ballet troupe from the United States. They just performed in London. She agreed to come along for the ride."

"Awesome! The real ballet?"

"Yes," Katie smiled at Cara. "We just finished our last performance in London Friday night. I wish you could have been there."

"Me too, but I doubt that the school would have allowed it. They're very strict about taking evenings off."

Adrian touched his niece's hand. "Maybe I'll take you to New York when the troupe performs there. Would you like that, Cara?"

"Oh, yes, Uncle Adrian. That would be great."

"All right. You and Katie get acquainted while I visit Miss Ryan."

As soon as Adrian left, Cara became talkative. "Katie, why don't you come with us to Uncle Adrian's house? It's a great house. Do you ride horses?"

"Well, yes, I do, Cara, but …." Katie feared she might intrude on plans Adrian had made.

Katie sensed that Cara was yearning for female company, and she couldn't be stopped. "Wonderful. Then it's settled. You can come with us."

Katie laughed at Cara's spontaneity.

"But, Cara, I didn't bring a change of clothes."

"Uncle Adrian won't mind taking you by your hotel to pick up some clothes. He's great about anything I ask him to do. Come on, Katie, it'll be fun. And you can tell me what it's like being a famous ballet dancer."

"Well, not so famous yet," Katie replied.

Cara abruptly changed the subject. "Katie, do you have any pets at home?"

"Yes, I do, as a matter of fact. I have a dog. Her name's Gretchen."

"Gee, I always wanted a dog, but, Roxie, my mother, never wanted me to have one."

How sad, Katie thought. No siblings, no pets, and attending a boarding school. What a secluded life this young girl lived.

In a short while, Adrian returned to the car. He was frowning slightly, as though the meeting was not all pleasant. He shook his head as if to rid himself of the memory of it.

"Uncle Adrian, will you take us to Katie's hotel so she can get some clothes and come spend my holiday with us?"

Adrian smiled and nodded. "It's up to you, Katie, but we'd love to have you."

Katie had serious doubts about this visit to Red Oaks, but she thought, Why not? I'd like to see firsthand how Adrian's royal family lives. "All right. Thank you. Both of you."

A big smile crossed Adrian's face, and he winked at Katie. "Nothing would please me more." He started the ignition and headed back to the hotel in London.

Katie quickly gathered a few pieces of clothing, hoping her selection would be proper for the weekend's activities at Red Oaks. She scribbled Alice a note to let her know she would not be back until Tuesday morning early. The thought crossed her mind that the females in the troupe probably assumed she and Adrian were an item. She had not heard any gossip, but Katie was sure they had noticed when she spent the whole cast party with Adrian. And, oh dear, what would they think of her now, taking off for a weekend? They would surmise she was with him. I'll explain all about Cara to them later, she decided.

The low, sleek sedan hugged the curves in the road like a racehorse making the final turn toward the finish line. The sun flung visual blockades as subdued peaks of blue and green were thrust against a gray sky. Katie was in awe as wide open landscapes, endless highways, and pleasant grazing fields spread out before them with not a tall building in sight.

Turning her face to the car window, Katie concentrated on the fascinating world opening before her. The closer they came to their destination, the more intrigued she became. The relatively flat land of London turned to softly rolling hills with deep valleys, then a low mountainous region.

Adrian maneuvered the car expertly as he turned off the main road onto a private tarmac. The car began its curving ascent as it wound higher through trees that joined limbs in a conspiracy with the setting sun.

After the turn, both sides of the road were flanked with tall pines and a tall stone fence. At the beginning of a long, sweeping flagstone drive was a white sign with the words "Red Oaks" brilliantly visible from luminaries in the ground. With his remote, Adrian opened the wrought iron gates.

Suddenly, like a mirage, a stone structure appeared beneath a gray slate tiled roof studded with chimneys. Mellow light gleamed from beckoning windows, and floodlights illuminated the landscape. Rather than dominating, the four story structure blended majestically with its surroundings. Behind the grand estate rose a high mountain peak, muted now by the oncoming darkness as if it were some strange sleeping beauty.

Katie could not begin to comprehend what the scenery must look like in bright sunlight. Even her brief glimpse provided a spectacular picture of beauty.

"We're here," said Cara from the back seat, apparently waking from her nap.

It was a place like none Katie had ever seen. The stone mansion with its great expanse of glass windows seemed to draw the onlooker's attention to the wide doors. The stone walls surrounding the estate seemed to sparkle a greeting.

"Tell me the stones don't shine."

"Actually, they do," Adrian said. "There's mica in the stone, and when the light strikes just right, it shines. These stones were brought here from Penzance over two hundred years ago to build these walls."

Katie stood for a moment, marveling at the sounds of nature, almost deafening in the absence of car horns, train whistles, and airplane engines.

As the massive double doors of the house opened, they were met by a pleasant lady, probably in her sixties, with pink cheeks and a bright smile. Beside her stood an older man with a long white beard.

"Master Adrian, Miss Cara. We're so happy you're home." The lady's face was glowing.

"Thank you," they both responded congenially.

Cara rushed up to the couple and gave them a warm hug. Katie could tell that these two were considered more family than servants in this house.

Adrian held out one arm toward Katie as he introduced her. "Maude, Gus, this is Kaitlyn Rose Johnson from the United States. She'll be our guest for a few days."

The couple gave Katie a warm welcome.

The guest room Maude showed Katie was enormous. "You'll be quite comfortable here, miss. Is there anything I can get for you?"

Katie was almost speechless. "Oh, no, everything's fine. Thank you."

"The evening meal will be served at 7:30. Shall I inform Master Ashley that you'll be down?"

"Yes. Thank you." Katie had not yet absorbed her new surroundings, and she was happy it was only 5:00 p.m. She would have time for a bath and a few moments to collect herself after the long ride to Cara's school and back to Red Oaks by way of London.

The room had a pale blue flower-patterned carpet, a fireplace, and two tall windows curtained in blue chintz with gold tasseled ropes to hold them back. The brass bedstead was tall, and the blue coverlet was pulled back to reveal snow-white linen sheets and pillowcases on great, downy pillows. These were elaborately hemstitched and embroidered with what was probably the Ashley family crest. There was a mahogany dressing table and a tall chest of drawers. Beyond an open door was her bathroom.

Even the bathroom was opulent with blue carpeting and a rather comfortable-looking chair. Katie removed her traveling clothes, turned on the faucet, and sprinkled in some bath salts that were in a jar near the large oval tub. The warm water soothed her, and she felt happy, very happy.

After a rejuvenating ten-minute soak, she wrapped a towel around her wet hair, stepped gingerly out of the tub, and dried off. Slipping into a pair of wine-colored silk slacks and a simple matching long-sleeved blouse, she blow-dried and shook her long hair so that it rested alluringly on her shoulders.

Katie found the house comfortingly reassuring. She had been afraid that Red Oaks would be overwhelmingly grand, that here Adrian would be frighteningly sophisticated, and that she would be tongue-tied in such surroundings. But the warmth of the housekeeper and her husband melted her shyness.

It was grand, to be sure, but not stuffy. As Cara took her on a tour of the house, Katie saw that it was tastefully decorated with antiques. There were three reception rooms, a ballroom overlooking a lovely flower garden, a grand drawing room, a huge formal dining room, an intimate family dining room, and an impressive library. Everything seemed to be old, and Katie assumed that all of the antiques had probably been in Adrian's family for years.

The family dining room was paneled and candle-lit. A large Victorian seascape of close detail and charm hung on the opposite wall of the table. Dinner was grilled trout, a salad, and raspberries smothered in Cornish cream.

"Mmm," Katie said after her first bite of the raspberries and cream. "If this is English cuisine, I love it."

Cara giggled and quickly handed Katie the bowl of raspberries. "Help yourself. This is standard fare for us. I've been raised on berries and Cornish cream all my life, and I love it, too. It's yummy."

After finishing their dark, strong coffee, Adrian stood. "I think it's time for some fun. Do you like board games, Katie?"

"Yes. I loved playing board games when I was growing up."

Katie and Cara both rose and followed Adrian into the library.

Cara walked to a large walnut corner cupboard and opened the doors at the bottom. An abundance of boxes containing every board game Katie had ever seen sat on the two shelves.

"Oh, my goodness!" Katie exclaimed. "How do you ever choose?"

This brought giggles from Cara and a big grin from Adrian.

"Sometimes we pull out the box on the bottom, because we figure we haven't played that one in a while. But since you're our guest, you have to choose," he said.

"I have to choose? Okay. How about Scrabble? I'm a pretty vicious Scrabble player."

Laughter rang around the room again, and the vicious Scrabble game began. Katie had a lot of competition from both Adrian and Cara, but her entries were imaginative and unexpected.

"I think this is going to be a very short game," Katie said as she laid her last tile on the board.

This time Cara teased loudly and merrily. "Uncle Adrian, I think we better be careful about playing with Americans the next time."

Katie was shocked when she slept until almost ten the next morning and awoke to find the room filled with bright sunshine. Slipping out of bed, she went to the window. The garden shimmered in the heat of a pleasant, warm autumn day. Gus, in worn overalls, was working in the garden, which was filled with chrysanthemums in shades of rust, yellow and white.

She leisurely dressed in jeans and a white cotton knit shirt and went downstairs. As she neared the kitchen, she heard sounds and voices. There she found Maude in an apron, stirring something on the stove, and Gus, who had returned from the garden with a large pumpkin. They both looked up as she appeared.

"I'm sorry I'm so late."

"It doesn't matter a bit. You needed your rest, dear," Maude reassured her. "Master Adrian headed for the nearby hills on horseback."

"Will he be gone long?"

"Not usually. I'll serve you coffee or tea in the dining room. I've just made some scones and have jam set out for you."

"Would it be alright if I just eat here in the kitchen?" Katie asked.

Maude and Gus looked at one another. "If you wish, dear," Maude said. "I wouldn't want you to be uncomfortable. Miss Cara always prefers to sit in the kitchen for her morning meal."

"We always eat breakfast at our kitchen table at home."

Gus rose from the table and pulled a chair out for her.

"I'll have coffee with cream and sugar, please."

Just as Katie was reaching for a warm scone, Cara walked in. From her cheery attitude, Katie knew, without a doubt, this was her home.

"Good morning, everyone." She hugged Maude's shoulders and gave Gus a cute little wink. In faded jeans and a plaid corduroy shirt, she was the image of a country girl.

"Good morning," Katie and Cara said in unison to each other.

Gus gave Cara a wink and walked out of the room, and Maude stood with her hands on Cara's face, smiling with love and pride. Cara's face mirrored this show of affection.

"And what can Maude make you for breakfast, dear?"

Cara looked at the food on the table. "Homemade scones and jelly! You're the greatest, Maude," she exclaimed. "Maybe a cup of tea with my scone?"

"Tea it is. Your Uncle Adrian is out riding and will be back in a wee bit."

Cara approached the table and eased down into a chair opposite Katie. Maude set a cup of hot tea in front of her and then walked into another room. "Katie, I want to hear all about the ballet now that Uncle Adrian isn't around. I haven't been able to get a word in edgewise since we got here."

Katie smiled. "Adrian is quite a talker. Probably wants to make me feel comfortable."

"I don't know. I've never seen him quite like this. Are you and my uncle dating?" she asked.

"We haven't had an official date yet. For now, we're just friends. I go back to the United States Tuesday evening."

"Well," Cara said with her mouth full of buttered scone, "he's a good catch, you know."

Katie unsuccessfully tried to hold back her laughter. "Really? I'll have to keep that in mind."

"You're the first woman he has brought to Red Oaks."

"I'm surprised at that, Cara, but remember, you were the one who invited me here first. He does date women, right?"

Cara understood Katie's meaning and laughed easily. "Oh sure, but he just hasn't thought enough of anyone to bring her to our home."

"Your uncle has been very nice to me." Katie looked down in her coffee cup. "In fact, I'm not anxious to go back to the United States."

"Then why would you go back when you want to be here?"

"It's complicated, Cara."

"It's because of the ballet, right?"

"Yes. I want to have a successful career in the ballet. I've danced and practiced for many long years to get where I am today."

"Gee, how long does it take to be successful?"

"That depends on a lot of things. How driven you are to practice constantly, how you catch on to the choreography, and if you're willing to live out of a suitcase in dingy hotel rooms for many years."

"But you could dance here with the London Ballet."

"My teacher is in New York. It isn't easy to find someone like her and establish the mentoring relationship I have with her. She's a wonderful teacher and has great faith that one day I'll be a prima ballerina."

"Wow! That sounds wonderful." A thoughtful frown appeared on her forehead. " I wish I knew for sure what was in store for me."

"I thought you wanted to be a doctor?"

"Oh sure, I want to be a doctor, but I mean my life, a life with someone else. I hardly ever meet boys at the girls' school. Some of my friends go into town and hang out. There are lots of boys there."

"That will all change when you enroll in college, Cara. There will be nice boys on campus with the same aspirations as you."

"I can tell Uncle Adrian likes you, Katie. Do you like him?"

Katie felt giddy at the thought of it. "We've only known each other a short time. And yes, Cara, I do like him, but I will never ...." Katie stopped suddenly. She was just about to reveal her secret to Cara. This girl was far too easy to talk with. Katie would have to be more on guard with her.

"Never put anything in front of the ballet?" Cara ventured.

"Yes." Katie sighed with relief that the taboo subject had been avoided. "I love every moment of ballet. It's difficult to explain how it feels to be standing there in the wings before your first solo. The other dancers know. And when you dance, there isn't any pain. You forget it. There's only the wonderful movements for the audience."

"You mean ballet dancing is painful?"

"Yes, very painful when you're practicing every day."

"Why do you push yourself when there's so much pain?" Cara asked.

"Because something drives you. It's so fervent, it's like an inspiration. It's the same for anyone who's involved with athletics. It begins in the morning, the moment your eyes open. The barre, classes, rehearsals, more classes. Seven days a week. It's your life; there's nothing else. Even after you're lucky enough to be accepted to dance with a troupe like the Hudson Ballet Company, you can't relax. There's always someone behind you, wanting your place. If you miss a practice session—even one—your body knows it and tortures you. There's pain in the muscles, the tendons, the feet. It's the price necessary to maintain ultimate flexibility."

Cara continued with her questions. "Uncle Adrian told me you live on a horse ranch. Is that true?"

"Yes. My mother and father live there, and I was born in that very house."

"Do you have lots of horses?"

"Yes. Probably around forty-five right now."

"I've always wanted to see a colt being born. You've probably seen that many times."

Katie could not help smiling at Cara's curiosity. "Yes, I have, Cara."

"Tell me about your dog."

"My little Scottie's name is Gretchen. I just might have a picture of her." Katie pulled out a slim wallet from her pocket, ruffled through a few credit cards, and finally found the picture.

"Oh, Katie, she's adorable."

"Well, I think so. She's always so excited when I get home from my tour."

"Who keeps her while you're gone?"

"My mother and father live at the ranch, and if they go out of town, one of the men who work in the stables cares for her. She loves everyone."

"Gee, that's great."

"Well, having a dog requires a lot of personal attention. I miss my little dog, but it certainly wouldn't do to have her travel with me."

"I suppose not," Cara agreed. Then she announced, "My mother lives in the United States." She said it easily, as though it were perfectly normal for mother and daughter to live apart.

"So your uncle told me. I would imagine you miss her very much."

Cara shrugged her shoulders. "Mother's busy with her friends and travels all the time. I've always been in boarding school and only come to Red Oaks on holidays. When she could, she used to come here when I was out of school. But more often than not, she was out of town. Now I have no idea when I'll see her again. I feel like nobody's child."

Katie saw the beginning of a tear in Cara's eye. She reached over and put her hand over Cara's hand, which was lying on the table. "I'm sorry about that, Cara."

Cara blinked the tear away and answered a little too quickly. "It's okay, Katie. I'm used to it by now."

"Your Uncle Adrian seems to be very good to you."

"Oh, he is. I love him like a father." Cara went on, "And speaking of fathers, I was told my real father died a couple of months before I was born, but I'm not sure that's the truth. Not even Maude or Gus will tell me the truth. I've wondered many times if my mother and father were even married."

Katie was caught completely off guard. "Why would you think that?"

"There's nothing in this house that once belonged to my father. There are no pictures of him. Don't you think there should be pictures of him around here somewhere?"

"I suppose. But you need to find out how long they were together before you were born. Do you know where you were born, Cara?"

"London, I was told. All I know is that my mother brought me to Red Oaks when I was three days old."

"Then this lovely estate is truly your home."

"Yes, I suppose so."

"No supposing to it. This is your home." Katie wasn't about to let their conversation take a downhill turn at this point. "Cara, haven't you met any special young men while at school?"

"There's a boy who attends Emery, down the road from my school. His name is Harry Wilhelm."

"And?"

"He asked me to go to the cinema next week."

"Wonderful. Tell me about him."

Cara's excitement returned. "Okay, he's really cute, which you probably already guessed. He's my age, and he has a car. His sister lives in my dorm, and he and I sang in the Christmas pageant together last year. But we hadn't seen each other since. Then, out of a clear blue sky, I saw him this past week when he was coming to pick up his sister, and he remembered me. We began talking, and it was so comfortable for both of us, he asked me out. I think he'll be a good friend."

At this point, Adrian walked in through the kitchen door, his face ruddy from his brisk ride. "So you two lazy bugs decided to get up today after all."

"Good morning, my very dashing and energetic uncle." Cara gave Adrian a big hug.

Katie was anxious to ride, but did not want to appear too bold about it. "Did you have breakfast before you rode?"

"Yes, Maude never lets a soul out of the house without food in their stomach. What about you? Are you two young ladies ready to get out on the bridle path?"

"We thought you'd never ask," Katie said, as she and Cara scrambled to the foyer for their jackets.

As they walked to the stables, Katie admired the English country gardens, placed strategically around the beautiful property. Adrian had described the estate on the drive to Red Oaks and said it was set on approximately sixty lush acres of beautifully landscaped lawns, gardens, stables, paddocks, a wooded ravine, and a river. Daylight gave her a better look at the house, and Katie thought it reminded her of her old storybooks with drawings of England's castles and magic little people. Hmm, she thought, I'm going to have to keep my eyes open. There's no telling what mysterious things might pop up from beneath the foliage.

Eleven

They rode slowly in pleasant silence for a while, enjoying the crisp October air.

"Cara, do you know who Katie reminds me of?"

"Do I dare ask?" Katie inquired.

"Well, now, let me guess." Cara turned her head to look at Katie. "A princess, a fairy tale princess."

"No." Adrian shook his head.

Cara guessed again. "A celebrity of some sort?"

"No, but you're a little closer." Adrian chuckled. He soon brought the guessing game to an end. "Scarlett. I think Katie reminds me of Scarlett."

"Scarlett?" Katie knew full well who he was referring to.

"Who's Scarlett?" Cara asked, apparently puzzled by her uncle's reference.

"You're teasing me, Adrian. I know who you mean." Katie gave him a mock accusing look.

"Scarlett who?" Cara asked.

"You know. Scarlett. Scarlett O'Hara from *Gone with the Wind*," Adrian prompted her.

Katie let her reins relax. "Cara, your uncle thinks I'm a southern belle. Isn't that right, Adrian?" She bent her head forward and sideways to look at Adrian, who rode beside Cara. Part of it was true; she was southern and proud of it.

"What's a southern belle?" Cara asked.

"Virginia, the ranch," said Adrian. "A perfect setting for *Gone with the Wind*."

Katie came to Cara's rescue. "Cara, during our Civil War, women who were from the southern part of the United States were supposed to be genteel ladies, somewhat weak, and always relying on their men for strength. They were known for their beauty and were referred to as southern belles. Scarlett O'Hara, one such southern belle, was a character in the book, *Gone with the Wind*."

"Oh, Uncle Adrian, you're such a romantic."

"Were the Howell women southern belles?" Adrian asked Katie.

"Yes and no. My family has always lived in the South, but there was nothing weak about my female ancestors," she replied.

"Who were the Howell women?" Cara asked.

"Well, my fourth-great-grandmother, Adrena, second-great-grandmother, Deborah, great-grandmother, Victoria, and Grammy were called the Howell women, simply because that was the family name beginning with Adrena. She lived in a Cherokee village in North Carolina."

"Wow!" Cara exclaimed. "Did they all live in that same village?"

"No. Only Adrena. But they were all strong-willed women who overcame great difficulties for love and family. My mother lived in the same village Adrena once lived in, and although she wasn't related to them, she's a very strong woman, too."

They rode onward, passing a glimpse of a quaint, thatch-roofed, whitewashed cottage far from the trail. Katie pointed to it. "Adrian, what's that old cottage off the trail to the right?"

"Oh, that cottage was once owned by an old man who hunted on this land. He was a distant relative of Mother's and fell on hard times, so he was given the cottage and lived there until he died. I think his name was Humphrey."

Adrian paused for a few moments. "Yes, Old Man Humphrey, that's what we called him. No one has been in there for more than fifteen years, I guess, since the old man died. As a young boy, I rode my horse out here and talked to the old man. Now I can remember things he showed me: arrows, feathered sticks, flint arrowheads, and more. Katie, would you and Cara like to investigate the cottage? We can't get there by horse—it's surrounded by thick, dense ground cover now—but we can walk there."

"I'd love to." Katie pulled at the reins.

"Oh, what fun!" Cara shrieked as she jumped off her horse.

They secured the horses to a tree close to the path and walked. Adrian led the way, with Katie and Cara following up a path that ran deep into the bushes. The sun climbed up into the sky and made the walk quite warm where sunlight filtered through the shadows of the evergreens. They peeled off their jackets and tied them around their waists as the path led upwards. Ahead of Katie and Cara, Adrian whistled under his breath.

The path wound through the mountain behind Red Oaks. Adrian pointed out one of the landmarks from his boyhood, a tree house that Old Man Humphrey had made for him. He then pointed further to the right. "Do you see that little stream there?" he asked.

"Yes," replied Cara.

"In the winter when I used to come here as a boy, I could hear the stream, but I couldn't see it. It was invisible beneath the layers of snow, but the current was strong enough to keep the stream from freezing. When summer would come, Old Man Humphrey helped me fish in that stream. We'd cook the fish and eat it together in his cottage. Whenever I caught a fish, no matter how small it was, he praised me highly. He made me feel very proud."

As they walked farther along the path, they came to a small stone bridge and a waterfall. The waterfall plunged twenty feet or more into a cauldron of white rock. They stood on the bridge and watched an arc of water, bright as a jewel, translucent, and shot with sunlight, curling down to a pool far beneath the bridge.

"It's beautiful," Katie whispered.

"Uncle Adrian, did you know this waterfall was here? It's so pretty. Why didn't you ever bring me here?" Cara's voice was filled with awe.

"I'd completely forgotten about the waterfall. I came here many times as a young boy of maybe twelve or thirteen. You were just a baby then. The cottage is only a little way up the hill now. Better put your jackets back on. As I remember, the overgrowth was denser here and there were thorns."

They all three pulled on their bulky jackets.

"It's like a fairy tale here. Like the story of *Briar Rose*," Cara remarked. "The vines have completely covered the way."

"Yes. It seems so." Adrian smiled at her. "I didn't know you liked fairy tales, Cara."

"I did when I was a little girl. Maude used to read to me every night."

Her mother should have been reading those stories to her, Katie thought sympathetically.

Adrian took Katie's hand. "Let's walk around to the left. As I remember there was a path over there."

Katie thought his hand felt warm and comfortable wrapped around hers. She could not help it, but she felt stupid and sentimental walking hand-in-hand with him through the woods. She was aware of every beam of sunlight, every breeze that held the scent of pine, every sound as their feet crushed the colored leaves below. As she walked beside Adrian, she thought how much her life was like this path, dappled with light and shadows. Three years ago she had vowed to keep her interest in men off bounds. Love had disheartened her once. She did not want that to happen again. After such a negative experience, she had willed her mind beyond the pain and memories of the most dreadful time in her life and had shuddered at the thought of making the same mistake again. That was before Adrian came into her life. Was he different? She thought so. Yet, falling in love with Adrian would be a formidable obstacle in the path of her career with the ballet. Katie had felt this before, and seeing him at his home, with the love he showed his niece, she was sure of it. It would be very easy to love this man.

When they got to one path which led deep into the thick forest, Katie stopped and looked down at Adrian's estate, which the mountain towered over. "I couldn't have imagined all this," she said again in a near whisper. "It's magnificent." She turned her face toward his.

"You should see it in spring when the wild orchids are blooming." Adrian gazed across the scene below.

They walked for some time, and Katie became hot and tired. It seemed they had walked for miles. Only the excitement of getting closer to the little cottage kept her going. They headed left of the overgrown bushes, and there it was, standing silent and still covered with vines.

"Oh, it is a fairy tale. Let's go inside, Uncle Adrian." Cara scrambled through the last of the brush to get ahead of Adrian and Katie.

"Not so fast, Cara. First let me make sure there are no animals or other vermin that have taken up residence here in the last fifteen years."

Katie and Cara stood back while Adrian forced the wooden door open. The Dutch door had a separate top and bottom, and the top of the door released easily against Adrian's strength.

"Can you see inside?" Cara questioned.

"Yes. Come on. Nothing in here but dust and dirt." He opened the bottom of the door.

They glanced around the empty room and walked into another dirty, cluttered adjoining room. The light filtering through the unwashed windows was still bright enough to show a layer of dust on all the surfaces. The floor was aged linoleum, decorated with paint spills. Steel utility shelves overflowed with bottles and jars, tubes and cans, and unfinished paintings were propped carelessly against the cracking plaster wall.

Katie stopped in front of a small watercolor leaning up against the wall at a distance from the others. Red Oaks was beautifully, almost mystically painted. The large mountain behind the estate was dark and mysterious. It must be dawn, she thought. Within the painting she could see the antiquity, the fantasy, and the reality. In the foreground were the iron gates and the sturdy mica stone wall surrounding the property. The wall glistened in the light of dawn.

"It's beautiful. It shows love as well as a touch of wonder. Was Old Man Humphrey the artist, Adrian?"

"I suppose. He often painted as I sat in his rocker reading on rainy days when fishing or swimming was not possible." Adrian touched the frame of the painting almost reverently. "It's like stepping back in time into a fond memory."

Katie could feel her heart moving toward him, and she cautioned herself again. It would only cloud the issue if she found Adrian the most caring, sensitive man she had ever met.

"Are there any others?" She nodded toward the painting.

"There might be. Let's look in there." He walked toward the closet and opened the creaking door.

With Cara peeking over her shoulder, Katie exclaimed, "Oh, look here! There must be over fifty paintings, and they all seem to be finished. The little watercolor must have been drying and was meant to be added to these. Look, there are several of Red Oaks and even one of this small cottage. Adrian, how enchanting. Some of these should be hanging in your house. But look at the initials at the bottom of each painting. BRB. I thought the old man's name was Humphrey."

"Yes, that was his name, Victor Humphrey. Isn't that strange? And they are beautiful. I think you're right, Katie. They should be in the main house. I'll have Gus come back and get some of them later."

"I'm so glad, Uncle Adrian. I think that would be fitting of the man who meant so much to you in your childhood," Cara said.

The next small room proved to be the living area, with an overstuffed couch, a wooden rocker, and a small bed with the linens tautly tucked under at the sides and bottom. Although the room was messy, it looked as though someone had just made up the tidy bed.

Adrian seemed to freeze, and his voice was just above a whisper. "This is odd. I haven't been back here since Old Man Humphrey died, but I'm almost overwhelmed by a sense of his presence." Then he smiled. "See that rocking chair? Old Man Humphrey used to sit in that chair and tell me the most wonderful stories. I would sit right there on the floor," he pointed, "and he told stories you wouldn't believe. He didn't read them. He knew them all by heart." Adrian laughed softly. "I remember one about the 'Raven Mocker Witch.' That story always scared me to death, but I begged the old man to tell it over and over."

Cara giggled.

Lying on the bedside table was the old man's Bible. Adrian trailed his hand gently over the old book. "This was his guidebook for living. He was wise and good."

Another wooden table covered with papers, books, and more dirt and dust sat in the middle of the room. Adrian began rummaging through the items on this table. Katie watched his fingers trace outlines of the items.

"Katie, look. This was his old leather medicine bag, trimmed with beads and fringe. I wasn't allowed to touch it when I visited here. The old man considered it sacred." Looking further, Adrian lifted the lids of several small woven baskets and said, "I don't remember these." In one small basket lay a brightly colored beaded bracelet, tangled as though the old man had dropped it in there without thought. Inside the others were arrowheads, a miniature dream catcher, and a small coin-like object.

Katie reached for the coin. "Oh, look, Adrian. Old Man Humphrey was proud of his heritage. This is one of the metal seals minted in honor of the Cherokees. My mother has one just like it."

Adrian watched her as she looked intently at the artifacts. "Have you seen items like these others before?" he asked.

"Yes, and I'm amazed at how well these are preserved. Fifteen years without care would ruin most things. I mean, look at those books." She pointed to the moldy books that were on the same table. "They're more what I would expect to find, yet the old man's Bible is surprisingly well-preserved, and the medicine bag has barely any dust on it."

Adrian watched her face thoughtfully. "You take all this quite seriously, don't you?"

"Yes, Cherokee people consider all these items sacred. My mother gave me quite an education on Cherokee culture over the years."

"That makes you a student of Cherokee life." Adrian's voice was little more than a whisper, as though he were speaking only to himself.

"Adrian, you're looking at me almost in awe. Isn't it normal for me to be interested in another culture that's also my heritage?"

"It is, but every new thing I learn about you makes me admire you even more." He frowned slightly. "Say, do ballerinas have fan clubs?"

The thought of young fan club members clamoring after ballerinas brought a humorous moment to them, and they both laughed softly.

"Okay, you two, what's so funny over there?" Cara asked from across the room, where she was investigating on her own.

"Your uncle thinks I should have a fan club."

Cara's frown was a close imitation of Adrian's. "Oh, you mean like the Beatles' groupies?"

Their laughter rang throughout the rooms. Old Man Humphrey's spirit, approving of the good natured group foraging the remnants of his home, was felt by all three visitors.

Adrian walked behind Katie and laid his hand on her shoulder. She could feel the warmth of his hand right through the shirt and jacket she had on. Fighting the war inside her, she kept her back to him.

Then both his hands were on her shoulders, turning her to face him. She felt a warm blush along her cheekbones. His fingers caressed her shoulders as she spoke. "I think we'd better get back to the house before it gets too dark."

"Well, I think we should just spend the night here," Cara said, bringing chuckles from Adrian and Katie.

Adrian gave her a quick wink. "Don't worry, Cara. The return is all downhill."

The little cottage had never before felt the liveliness of this afternoon. As the trio turned to leave, Katie noticed that the rooms seemed brighter, not quite so dingy. She saw their footprints on the dirty floors, and knew their spirits had bonded, cemented by the dust they now carried on the soles of their shoes.

Later, lying in bed, watching the stars blink outside the window of Adrian's estate, Katie recalled how delightfully different the day had been. For most of today she had forgotten that her one ambition was to be a prima ballerina, and now she wanted nothing more than to be with Adrian. She refused to consider the possible consequences of caring for him, of maybe even loving him. Turning over and pulling the covers closely around her, she felt that she had never experienced a day more wonderful. In a few minutes, the comfortable bed and luxurious linens lulled her fast asleep.

Twelve

On Tuesday, Adrian's thoughts became despondent. The minutes were drawing near, minutes that would take Katie from him. Once she boarded the plane to New York, he had no idea when he would see her again, or if he ever would. He knew she was strong and had both the intelligence and the will to forget him and give herself only to her career.

He and Cara had driven Katie back to her hotel that morning, and he thought he had said his final goodbye to Katie. There had been no last minute promises or fancy words of regret. He drove Cara back to her school later that afternoon and returned to London without stopping, his mind overwhelmed with thoughts of Katie. She had completely changed his life. She had altered the simple tidy pattern he had been weaving for himself. With her, he needed to soothe, to protect, and to share. There was nothing he could do to change that need even if she walked out of his life forever. By evening, he realized there were words still to be said.

Her flight left at 10:30 p.m., and Adrian ran into evening traffic. Heathrow airport was at least sixteen more kilometers. It was already 10:10. If the traffic did not clear soon, he would miss seeing her off.

He parked curbside at the airport, rushed out of the car, and went through the revolving doors to the terminal. There he glanced at the departing schedule display to find Katie's gate, and hurried in that direction. Ahead of him he saw the ballet troupe huddled together in the gate waiting area. He spotted Katie right away and walked quickly to her side. "Hello! I decided to see you off."

"I'm glad, Adrian. We have about five minutes before boarding."

"Is there somewhere we can talk?"

"Only there. I see two empty seats." She nodded toward two adjacent seats.

They took the available seats. It was difficult to know what to say. There were so many unexpected emotions they both had experienced over the few days since they met.

"Katie, I love you. In my heart, I don't want you to go." He looked deeply into her warm brown eyes, those eyes that would haunt him to his grave, the same eyes he had seen in his dream.

A metallic voice came over the terminal loudspeaker. "Flight 846 for New York City now boarding at gate C10."

He stood, reached for her hand, and drew her up. Though she was tall, her slimness made her appear utterly fragile. That and the innocent way she looked at him, with her head tilted back so their eyes could meet, prevented him from saying another word. He studied her. It was there again, that something, that indefinable something in her eyes that had attracted him even in his dream.

She freed her hand from his and laid it on his chest, as if to keep him at a safe distance.

There was a moment of silence.

This time she was holding back. He sensed it, felt it in the press of her hand against his chest. Not refusing, but resisting. With wisdom that came from somewhere too deep to measure, he backed away from her. He would not pressure her into loving him.

His heart staggered.

She did not move into him. Not this time. Her emotions were simply too raw to risk.

Her heart stumbled.

Her struggle between wanting him and wanting her career had returned during the hours before she left for the airport. There was only one way to stop what never should have started, and she must do it now. She broke the silence. "Adrian, there's something you have to know. To be honest with you, I think I'm in love with you, too, but I don't think I love you enough to stay here with you. It would mean giving up my career, and I'm not ready for that."

She saw by his eyes that her arrow had hit its mark.

"As long as you know how much I care for you, perhaps later there will be time for us," he said. "The test will be when we're separated from one another. Then the answer will come to us. I'm a patient man, Katie."

She kept silent, hoping somewhere down deep inside her soul he would beg her to stay with him. She would not have the strength to say no to him here. She was too emotional and vulnerable, knowing they were parting for a very long time. There was a moment, a heartbeat of time, when it would have been the most natural thing in the world for her to lean into him, lift her face for a kiss. She pictured it so clearly it made her feel foolish. At the same time, she wondered if he felt it too, that momentary connection, an urge that came out of nowhere. She did not have the opportunity to find out.

His voice was soft and full of emotion. "Take care of yourself." He made no move toward her.

Katie nodded in response to him and walked toward the boarding gate. She felt numb, felt she had just turned into a pumpkin and her magical world with Adrian was over. Adrian was a prince. A real one. But Katie knew too well that even a prince could break your heart.

She was who she was and exactly what she wanted to be—a ballerina. Tears fell down her cheeks as she took her seat on the plane. Through her window she could see Adrian still standing inside the terminal, looking out the window toward the plane with his hand over his heart.

Katie fought the sinking feeling within her as the plane lifted. Everyone else on the plane was soon sleeping. But though she tried, she could not find that place inside herself, that quiet, safe, untroubled island where she could usually escape anything that bothered her. It seemed Adrian had followed her there and taken up permanent residence.

The ballet was something she understood, something free of emotional chaos. She told herself she did not want a relationship with Adrian, but a cold terror ate at her heart at the thought of never seeing him again. She covered her face, hating the weakness she felt, but powerless against it.

She had forgotten about the diary. Now she remembered and looked through her carry-on bag for the book her mother had given her when she left Penzance. She reached above her and flipped on the overhead light.

The Journal of Victoria Redman was neatly handwritten on the cover. Katie scanned through the pages, reading phrases here and there, and picking up a sense of the strength in Victoria. Her Cherokee husband, her first true love, had come from the same village where Katie's mother was born. Katie's interest picked up, and she began to follow the text carefully, watching Victoria come to life for her on the pages of the little diary.

Katie's great-grandmother Victoria wrote of her never-ending love for her husband, Hawk, who had become ill and disappeared from home. She searched for him for years, moving to Grill's Ranch when her funds were low, the ranch having been an inheritance from her aunt. She wrote not of him, but to him, sharing the loneliness she felt without him, describing the beauty and growth of their daughter, Olivia, and vowing never to think of a new love until she found proof that he was dead or would never return for some other reason. Victoria's passionate love for him had caused her to live in the past. For nineteen years she had waited, dreading the awful day that proof would come. His parents finally arrived with news of Hawk's grave having been located. A doctor who had treated Hawk had verified that he lost his memory and finally died because of a brain tumor. Only then, after all those years of self-denial, did Victoria agree to marry her old friend, Garrett Cowling, and move to England with him.

That sense of conflict made Katie think of Adrian again. She did not want to think of him. She only wanted to sleep. She rested her head on the back of the seat and closed her eyes. Then she thought she heard a voice. She sat up and looked around, in front and behind her, but everyone on the plane was sleeping. She heard the soft, pleading voice again. This time she distinctly heard her name.

"Kaitlyn. Kaitlyn Rose."

She sat near the window of the plane, and the two seats beside her were empty. Looking out into the night at the flashing strobe lights rotating on the wings of the plane, she saw the face of a man.

She turned off the overhead light and closed her eyes. She was tired and imagining things. Yet the voice called her name again.

"Kaitlyn. Kaitlyn Rose."

Slowly she opened her eyes and stared in disbelief at the handsome face of a man who looked strangely like the portrait of her great-grandfather in her grandmother's sitting room. She willed herself to keep her eyes open and stared intently at the man.

He spoke again. His voice was the kindest and most gentle she had ever heard. "Kaitlyn Rose, if you keep your love locked up, you will become a vessel of your selfishness. Your love will change and become dead, and you will then be incapable of recovering it."

Clutching the armrests of her seat, she closed her eyes again and swallowed the bile that rose, stinging, into the back of her throat. Scrambling down the aisle, she made it to the restroom only to heave up her dinner. She took time to rinse her mouth and splash her face with cold water before going back to her seat. She leaned her head back against the top of the seat and tried to relax, relieved to see that the man was no longer there. Then Katie fell off to sleep.

In London, Adrian returned to his hotel suite from the airport and stood for a long time looking out at the wet night streets. Turning from the window, he was caught unaware by a stab of loneliness and the inner chaos his attraction for Katie had brought. He clearly remembered the soft, gentle touch of her hands, the musical lilt of her voice, the magic of her kiss. He had never felt the need to have a woman in his life until now. There were a few relationships in the years before Katie, but he had never kidded himself, or the women, that any of them would lead to a lifelong commitment.

The dance was Katie's life, and she was committed to it. He was certain of her ability to be a prima ballerina. The natural skill she possessed for dancing and her passion for obtaining her goals were evident. He was sold on a lot of things about Katie. The fact that she was dedicated to the ballet was simply his bad luck. There did not seem to be a hope of her ever being interested in him for a permanent relationship. What if he opened the door to step into her world and she slammed the door in his face? He did not have enough experience with deep relationships to calculate the risk.

He lay down on the bed and reached over to the bedside table to switch on the radio, hoping to distract himself from this litany of conflicting thoughts. Much later, somewhere in the oblivion of another world, he heard the sound of a crooner singing a plaintive love song from a bygone era.

His eyes flew open, and he stared into the night. It was not the girl in his dream who had invaded his senses. It was Katie. A startling realization penetrated his consciousness. Kaitlyn Rose had not disappeared like a dream in the night. She was not, after all, someone he could just put out of his mind at will. She was not a dream, nor was she some kind of magic spell. She was real and warm and alive, and he was madly in love with her.

A little more time, Adrian promised himself, rubbing his temples to clear a headache. Katie needs more time. Can I give her that? At the moment, he needed to consider his personal life. Was not that a part of the problem? He had never had one, had not allowed himself one. Now, a matter of days after he had met Katie, this void in his life was threatening to swallow him.

It was time to reassert some logic. They were dynamically different—in backgrounds, in life-styles, and in goals. Physical attraction was bound to fade, or certainly to stabilize. He had done them both a favor by slowing down, stepping back.

Yet, Adrian faintly heard a mocking voice inside his head calling him a liar and a coward. He stood by the window again, wondering what he was doing by promising himself to back off. The woman he loved—by some twist of fate—might actually love him. Here was a chance for the life he had never allowed himself—real love, a real home, and a real family.

Thirteen

When the phone rang over five times Wednesday morning, Katie was tempted to hang up just as someone on the other end finally spoke.

"Hullo." It was her friend's English accent.

"Chloe, is that you?"

"Yes. Who's speaking, please?"

"Katie. Katie Johnson."

"Oh, Katie, I'm so glad to hear from you. I've been thinking about you. I read glowing reviews of the ballet in London."

Katie was thrilled by Chloe's words. "Yes, the reviews were very good."

"More than that. Did you see how they loved your performance?"

"Yes."

"You were fabulous. Where are you now, Katie?"

"I'm in New York."

"Can you come over?"

It was the question Katie had been hoping for. "Surely."

"Are you available today?" Chloe's anticipation of her visit carried through the telephone line.

"Yes."

"Are you at your hotel?"

"No, I'm at Kennedy. I got here after an eight hour redeye flight

94

and took time to freshen up and have a leisurely breakfast. Then I remembered that you're an early riser."

"How exciting! Grab a taxi and come right here to my apartment. Do you remember the address?"

"Yes. I have it, Chloe."

"Good. I'll be watching for you. It will be so nice to see you again, and you simply must stay over."

At this suggestion, Katie had to beg off. "Thanks, Chloe, but I want to see Madame Bettencourt this afternoon."

"Okay. Although I have no idea why you would go see her. I thought most of the cast members hated her. She certainly has a reputation for being very strict."

Katie avoided that discussion without comment. "See you in about an hour."

"Wonderful."

As she sat down on a large flower patterned couch, Katie noticed immediately that Chloe Cowling's upscale New York apartment was fashionably decorated. The carpet looked like expensive Persian woven art, portraying a graceful pattern of lovely flowers scattered on a butter-toned field. Water lilies floated serenely on a mural painted on the far wall. Lit glass cabinets filled with floral-patterned china lined the other wall.

"I'm a hopeless flower addict," Chloe said over the soft, melodious strains of Chopin coming from somewhere in the room. "Like Monet or Renoir, I must be surrounded by flowers."

"I'd imagine that makes you popular with the local florists." Katie's gaze was drawn to a lush display of full-blown pink roses, casually yet artfully arranged in a sterling vase on top of an antique green marble-topped table.

Chloe nodded in agreement, seemingly delighted at the suggestion. "All the best florists in the city know my name."

"That doesn't surprise me. I doubt there is anyone in this city who isn't familiar with the name Chloe Cowling, London's prima ballerina."

"Aren't you sweet, dear? No, those days are long gone. I'm afraid I'm all but forgotten. Now I'm lucky if the doorman recognizes me."

Tall, with an exquisite stance, Chloe was a magnificent example of womanhood. She wore cream-colored linen slacks and a vivid blue silk blouse. Pale golden hair framed her face like sunlight, and her full, shapely mouth lifted into a smile even as her brows arched.

Katie noticed the cane resting beside Chloe and wondered how much the leg injury still bothered her. Her dedication had been rewarded by sell out performances, but now she would never dance again.

Chloe sat gracefully in a large pink pillow-backed chair. "I'm so happy you've come for a visit, Katie. At last I have someone to talk to. New York is a big city, and I don't get around easily to parties or other social occasions. It's so much nicer to talk to friends in person rather than on the telephone. And you look incredible. Your hair is so shiny. Just magnificent. I know women who would kill for hair so dark, and you seem to have about three feet of it."

Katie was a little uncomfortable at Chloe's praise of her appearance, especially after her disarray from her travel. She did not feel attractive at all and wanted to change the subject quickly. "Do you live here alone, Chloe?"

"Quite alone. Unlike less fortunate ballerinas, I have a substantial income from father's estate. That has allowed me to live somewhat in luxury, with this apartment and the house I still have in London. And, please, don't remind me of the need to have a man around. I gave up on men long ago."

"Why?"

"Katie, decades separate our ages. If I could go back and be your age just for a little while, I would do everything differently."

"Differently?" Katie's sense of curiosity kicked in.

"I let love fall too easily through my fingers; now I'm alone."

"You're alone?" Katie was both fascinated and confused as she repeated Chloe's words.

"Yes." Chloe shrugged her shoulders. "Oh, when I was dancing, I had three very handsome offers, three good possibilities. One tall, aristocratic Englishman who wore tweed brilliantly. One captivating jock from Down Under. And then there was the tall, dark, New York business man aiming for a political career, who almost stole my very soul." Chloe's graceful hand waved in dismissal. "I had no patience for men, but then there were and are times ...." Chloe let her sentence drop and pursed her mouth as if she were considering something carefully.

"There are times you're lonely?"

"Yes. Times when I'm truly lonely." Chloe's words were matter of fact, not filled with self pity. Even loneliness had to be handled with discipline. "I feel, for most of my career, I was just a ballerina doll in a music box, pirouetting endlessly until the music stopped. People were staring at me through the glass dome that surrounded me. I hope you won't feel that way when you retire from the stage, Katie."

"Have you ever thought of teaching, Chloe? So many prima ballerinas do that."

"I thought about it after my therapy was complete, but I realized my great talent was as a dancer, not a teacher. Just recently I was approached by De-Danca, one of the world's leading dancewear manufacturers, to be their Public Relations Officer for North American operations. They're even thinking I could put together seminars and workshops in the highly specialized field of pointe technique and shoe fit for retailers, ballet teachers, and students across the United States and Canada."

"That sounds like a good job for you. You certainly would be an expert in that field."

"I still haven't decided." Chloe waved her hand in the air, dismissing the subject. "Enough about me. I want to hear all about you."

Katie had to smile. Chloe looked like a bright sunbeam in contrast to her own olive skin and dark hair. Katie was about to discover that Chloe's deep summer blue eyes were not only beautiful, but quite discerning.

Chloe stood and crossed the short space between them, the limp in her right leg pronounced even with the aid of her cane. She sat on the couch beside Katie. "Brave little cousin, tell me all about it." She gave Katie a gentle, sympathetic look.

"About what?" Tears stung Katie's eyes, and she knew Adrian Ashley would soon be the topic of conversation.

"About him." Chloe put her hand over Katie's.

At a loss for words, Katie only shook her head. Inner feelings were private. She never had confided in anyone before.

"Katie." The silence was firmly interrupted. "You need to talk. You might not think you look stricken, but you do." Chloe sighed with perfect finesse. "I'm really fond of you, Katie, and I love your family. I know when a certain mister has given this beautiful, talented creature sitting beside me a jolt."

The statement completely robbed Katie of speech. The idea of the exquisite, incomparable Chloe referring to her as beautiful seemed ridiculous. Even more startling was her realization that Chloe had guessed about her conflict.

"Katie, dear. I always pry, but I also know how to keep a confidence."

"He said he loved me," Katie blurted out before she could think better of it and stop herself. This was followed with vivid descriptions of Adrian as she occasionally sighed deeply. Before she knew it, words were tumbling out and tears were shed. She omitted nothing, from the beginning until the very end when she left London yesterday. She even told Chloe about Adrian's dream. Once she began, no effort was needed. She did not have to think, only feel, and Chloe listened.

Chloe was quiet for a few moments before she said, "So what are you going to do about it, Katie?"

"Nothing. I can't give myself to Adrian and the ballet at the same time. I made such a terrible mistake when I married Jeffery."

"Ahh, so it's not just your love of the ballet, is it?"

"No. Three years ago I foolishly married a dancer named Jeffery. I know I let my attentions to him interfere with my practice sessions. After all that, our marriage only lasted three months, when I caught him with another woman."

"I didn't know." Chloe patted Katie's clenched hands.

As fresh tears flowed down her face, Katie asked, "Is love worth the hurt, the terrible hurt, the regrets?"

"Katie, forget about your marriage to Jeffery. You were young and impressionable. Don't let a mistake when you were still a teenager keep you from happiness as an adult. As far as your dedication to the ballet goes, you'll grow older, and the ballet will only be a fond memory, a wonderful dream to cherish. On the other hand, love and sharing your life with the right person is everlasting. Finding and keeping true love is the most important thing you'll ever accomplish in your life." Chloe stopped for a moment before she went on.

"I let Christopher Powell go. He wanted to marry me and take me to places I can now only dream of. He may still be President of the U.S. one day. But I let him go. I let him go because of the ballet, because of my ambition and my dream. I thought the ballet was the most important thing in the world. Just because my father paid a hefty price for ballet lessons, that shouldn't have made it the only thing in the world for me. He never would have wanted me to wind up alone. Now look at me. I'll never dance again."

"Was it a tough decision, giving up love for the ballet?"

"Of course it was. Nothing that's worthwhile can be considered above the other choices without a lot of thought, a lot of weighing alternatives."

"And I must make a choice." Katie knew she must choose the ballet and her career or the love of Adrian Ashley.

"Adrian sounds like a wonderful person. Knowing you love him, could you enjoy the prestige and pride of being a prima ballerina if you gave up love for it? Could it compensate for love, Katie?"

"I don't know. I really don't know, Chloe."

"I fear your dilemma is not with the ballet. Many dancers are married. I think you're still trying to avoid a relationship because of this Jeffery. The choice you make will affect your life forever. I pray you choose wisely."

Then the tears came in a torrent, and Katie shamelessly let them fall before her friend. She ached for love, for the simple companionship of understanding. She wept because she had let a marriage gone wrong keep her from love, causing her to be uncertain she could trust love again. She wept because at this moment she wanted Adrian more than she wanted the dance.

Katie's visit with Chloe Cowling left her feeling sad for this lovely woman who had chosen to abandon love for the dance and then was forced to abandon the dance when her career was at its peak. She was also saddened at the thought of being alone someday if she made the same choice.

Fourteen

The ride uptown took only minutes, and as Katie stepped out of the taxi, Madame Bettencourt was opening the door of her brownstone townhouse to welcome her protégé. It was Madame Bettencourt who had even selected the name of Kaitlyn Rose as Katie's professional name.

She looked at Katie and smiled. "Welcome, my child. I'm so happy to see you."

"It's good to be home again, Madame."

Katie's mentor ushered her into her modest home where hot tea and finger sandwiches were waiting in the sitting room. Katie had been in this apartment many times, and now the sparse but familiar furnishings and décor seemed home to her.

Madame sat on a small chintz covered settee and motioned for Katie to sit in a matching chair near her. "If I remember correctly, you take two cubes of sugar in your tea, dear?"

"Yes, thank you."

"I'm thrilled with your performance in London. Your goal to be a principal dancer is finally on the horizon, Katie."

"Thank you, Madame. Everyone was wonderful to me. I have never felt the way I felt while dancing in *Moonglow Fascination*. I found a strength I never knew I had."

"It's your destiny, my child." The teacher raised her arm into the air dramatically. "Your destiny is finally here." She leaned in close to Katie and asked, "And you are happy, yes, my child?"

"I am very happy."

Madame Bettencourt handed Katie the cup of tea and peered at her suspiciously. "Oh, but your eyes expose you, my child. Something happened while you were in London, something that puts a deep concern on your face."

It was Katie's nature to be honest, and her respect for her mentor would allow for no less now. "I met someone."

"Someone?" Madame Bettencourt frowned.

"Yes. Someone wonderful."

"No!" Madame Bettencourt rose suddenly to her feet. She was clearly agitated, and her voice was harsh. "You must not! You cannot!" Madame was tall and thin and looked suddenly older and more severe than Katie remembered. "Kaitlyn Rose, you must not do this thing! You belong to the ballet! It's your life!"

Katie did not know how to respond to this outcry from her teacher. The use of her professional name contained a clear reprimand. Madame Bettencourt stared ahead in silence and said nothing more as the atmosphere grew thick between them.

"He's wonderful," Katie said in a soft, almost pleading voice. She weighed her words carefully, assessing how much to reveal, since Madame Bettencourt knew of her failed marriage.

"Nonsense, Kaitlyn Rose. Jeffery was also wonderful in the beginning, if you'll remember. Your gift of the dance was not given to waste on some man who will years from now find you unattractive and go to someone else. Just like Jeffery, who was disgusting and rude." She was visibly furious.

Tears began to come, and Katie could not help but let them spill out as she felt a hurt deep in her heart. She was not used to being reprimanded or scolded so harshly by her beloved teacher.

"I want to be with this man with all my heart." The tears flowed down her cheeks as she said it, but Madame Bettencourt showed no emotion other than disdain and anger.

"Do you still love the ballet?" the teacher suddenly asked.

"Yes, Madame, with all my heart."

"That, then, is the answer to your dilemma. You didn't say you love this man. If you choose him over the ballet, you will be making the wrong decision. I guarantee it. He can never give you what your soul needs. You would eventually learn to hate him for taking you away from the dance and the thrill of watching your audience applaud you for your life's work. This is who you are, Kaitlyn Rose, a dancer. This is your love!"

Katie could not believe what she was hearing, although she had heard Madame Bettencourt's point of view before. To her teacher, the dance was a sacred religion and nothing else mattered. She expected all her students, especially Katie, to worship at the altar of this religion. Katie could not imagine how to respond to her teacher. She did love the dance. Her goal always was to be a leading dancer.

Just as suddenly as she had erupted, Madame turned and beckoned her student to come with her, as though no harsh words had come between them. "Come, my dear, you must see the new group of young girls auditioning for our spring program. They have come from Seattle, Pittsburgh, and Atlanta."

Katie followed her mentor as they walked down a long narrow hall to one of the practice studios connected to the apartment.

In the studio, over thirty dancers chatted nervously, carefully wrapping tape around toes and stretching their limbs into improbable positions. Katie realized that some of the them had auditioned for or attended other intensive programs held by Madame Bettencourt. Some were taking their first shot. Their chins raised, concentration evident on their young faces, the students gracefully pirouetted, pliéd, and stretched their legs to an instructor's quick count.

Katie was one of these young, eager girls only a few years ago. Now she almost felt sorry for them, knowing the pain and hours of training they had already gone through and still would have to endure. Ballet is hard on the body. Injuries happen, and pointe shoes can wreck feet with blisters, bunions, and bone problems. Yet, to these eager dancers, there was no question about whether it was all worth it.

"Aren't they beautiful?" Madame Bettencourt asked with a possessive smile.

"Yes. Yes, they're all beautiful." Katie agreed, but she had heard this possessiveness in Madame Bettencourt's voice before.

She noticed Jon Poulevit walking up and down, eying the dancers, and jotting on a notepad. A principal dancer for the New York City Ballet until 1961, he had been an instructor and performer at the Hudson Ballet Company for more than thirteen years now. Katie recalled her own days of instruction under him and knew the dancers would have exhausting days of work ahead.

She had worked so hard, so very hard. Madame was right; it would be wrong to give it up. She would forget Adrian Ashley and dance. That was all that mattered to her—the thrill of the dance!

No, no, she reminded herself. I'm letting Madame influence me too much. I love Adrian, and I want nothing more than to be with him.

Katie would not kid herself. There would be some sadness in giving up the dance, but she was comforted by the knowledge that there also would be sweet, precious memories. She was doing the right thing, she was convinced, in making her own choice. The only difficulty now would be facing Madame Bettencourt with this decision when the time came for her to do so. My love for Adrian will give me strength, she thought with determination.

Fifteen

It was early on a Friday evening in late October, and the older girls at Royal Masonic School were preparing for an evening of fun.

Cara's roommate was struggling with the sweater she was attempting to pull over her head. "Do help me with this, Cara, will you? I've got only ten minutes until I meet the girls in the lobby to go to the cinema."

"Mmm." Cara helped her friend on with her sweater. "Now there. It's a lovely sweater. Is it new, Jayne?"

"No. I just don't wear it often. What about you? Another date? You don't ever go to the cinema with the girls since you met Harry Wilhelm. Goodness, you must have him landed! This is getting serious. Two shows, three dinners, and two lunches. And I saw you two talking in the library until the librarians were giving you disapproving looks. Do you like him, Cara?"

Cara laughed. "Why, of course, I do. I like him all right, silly."

"Good." With that said, Jayne rushed out of the room and down the stairs.

By the time Cara went downstairs, she was unusually serious, and she could not shake off the feeling. She was normally happy when Harry suggested they do something together. He was easy to talk to and was a good friend.

Tonight it was especially good to see him standing there waiting for her in the hall. The passing girls looked him over critically and with definite approval. Cara had taken special pains with her hair and was wearing her best blue silk blouse that brought out the blue in her eyes.

She smiled at him in welcome. "Hi! Hope I didn't keep you waiting too long."

Cara saw his appreciative glance, and she felt repaid for the trouble she had taken in dressing. She and Harry had enjoyed some good times these past few weeks, sandwiched in among all the other things she had to do for school.

"Well, at least fifty females have looked me over, but I've managed to survive. I was early, I guess." He grinned at her.

Harry opened the car door for Cara, and she slipped in. "Would you like something to eat before the movie?" he asked as he started the car.

She thought about it before she answered. "Well, I am a little hungry."

"Good. We have time for fish and chips."

They sat in a small restaurant eating, and Cara finally broke the silence. "Harry, this is for your birthday." She handed him a card.

He put down the malt vinegar and reached for the card. "For me? How did you know it was my birthday?"

"A little bird told me." Cara smiled as Harry opened and read the card.

"Nice card, Cara. Thank you."

"You're welcome. Will you be going home for the weekend to celebrate your birthday with your family?"

"Sure. My mother is a stickler for birthday parties. All my cousins will be there, and my sister will come home for the weekend, also."

"What's a birthday like at your house, Harry?" There was melancholy in her voice.

"We're just ordinary, Cara. Blowing out the candles on the birthday cake and opening gifts are traditions with my family."

"Did they ever miss celebrating your birthday?"

Harry shook his head. "Oh, no. My mother wouldn't do that. And my dad is always there, even if he has to cancel a meeting. How about your birthday, Cara? I know it was last month. Did you go home for the weekend?"

"No. My family isn't able to get together so often." She made a weak attempt at being casual with her answer.

"Even on your birthday?"

"Well, my mother lives in California."

"She does? Oh, Cara, that's sad." He reached his hand across the table toward her.

Cara could not keep the tears back this time. "Yes, it is. I don't think I'll see her very often now." As soon as she told Harry, she regretted it. She did not want to spoil this evening with him, but the tears would not stop.

"Cara, I had no idea." He handed her his handkerchief.

"It hurts. It really hurts. But I love her so much." Cara was able to hold back the sobs that stuck in her throat by swallowing a large gulp of water. She was glad for the privacy of the booth at the back of the restaurant.

"Sure you do. Everyone loves their mother." He looked sympathetic. Then he suggested, "Why don't you come to our house this weekend for my birthday party?"

"Thanks, Harry, but I have a big test on Monday, and I need to study."

"Doesn't sound like fun."

Cara laughed. No, it did not sound like fun, and she wished with everything in her that her family was like Harry's—a mother and a father, both loving and caring. Cara had spent her seventeenth birthday alone. Even Uncle Adrian had a business meeting and was in France for the weekend of her birthday.

The film was one Cara had seen already, but she did not want to admit it to Harry. It was just so nice to be with him. When he reached over during the film and held her hand, she felt awkward, but his hand felt warm and soothing to her.

As Harry drove back to the dorm, Cara's most recent incident with Miss Ryan weighed heavily on her, and she suddenly wanted to share this burden with her friend. "Harry, Miss Ryan has been really friendly with me, and it seems eerie."

"But you said she didn't like you."

"Well, that's what I always thought, but today she invited me to go to her summer home. Apparently, she has rented a house in the country. Somewhere near Coleridge, about three kilometers from there."

"Why in the world would she do that?" He glanced sideways at his friend.

"What?"

"Invite you to visit at her country home next summer."

"I don't know. But it doesn't seem natural, does it? She keeps telling me about her daughter who died and says I was born in the same hospital on the same day as her."

"What? How would she know that, Cara?"

"I have no idea, but it really makes me feel creepy."

"I wouldn't go if I were you. My sister has hinted that no one seems to like Miss Ryan and that possibly she can't be trusted." Harry shook his head as he continued to drive.

Chills ran down Cara's arms when she realized that even Nancy could not openly talk to her brother about Miss Ryan. "I know you're right, Harry, but she's so insistent."

"Just tell her your uncle has plans for your summer, and she would have to talk to him about going with her."

A smile finally lit Cara's face. "That's a good idea! That's exactly what I'll do." Cara hesitated and looked at Harry. Her voice was serious again. "You won't tell anyone what I said about Miss Ryan, will you?"

As Harry stopped the car in front of the dorm, he turned to look at her. "No, Cara. I won't even tell my sister. I understand why you don't want anyone to know. It's just our secret."

Cara felt instant relief after telling Harry about Miss Ryan. "Thanks a million. Now I must run, or I'll be using a late permission, and I didn't even sign up for one."

"Will you be okay, Cara?"

"Certainly. Why?"

"Well, this stuff about Miss Ryan bothers me. Please stay away from her all you can."

Cara sighed. "Oh, she's harmless, I guess, Harry, and talking to you has made me feel better about her. She's just a little wacky."

"I suppose, but be careful anyway. Good night, Cara," he said as she got out of his car.

That was all. Nothing about another night, another cinema, another walk along the winding paths of the campus. It was a trusting friendship that did not beg for reassurances. Cara smiled at him, and walked toward the dorm. Then he was gone.

Sixteen

On that same Friday after his work week ended, when the sky over his garden at Red Oaks turned to a velvet showcase of starry diamonds, Adrian found himself lonelier than he had ever been. Since there was nothing that demanded his attention in the late evening hours and nothing he wanted to do, he tried reading a book. He could not concentrate. Instead, his eyes often became a watery pool which he tried desperately to fight.

He was trying to put his life back together, his simple, peaceful life with no emotional ties and only numbers and profits to worry him. Adrian admitted to himself, however, that he was totally and helplessly in love with Katie. He could not dismiss the reality that her career came first. This was a problem they must resolve—together.

The woman in his dreams did not appear anymore, and he was glad. Katie was now the image forever engraved in his mind. The raven-haired beauty he had watched dance in the ballet in London just a few weeks ago now created turmoil inside him which he could not shake. The matter was not really ended, he knew, and he was eager to know what the outcome would be.

Did she miss him as much as he missed her? Would she call him any day now with words that would put his aching heart at rest? Would she give up the ballet? And why did she think she had to? Adrian knew he would never ask her to quit dancing. It was her passion, and he felt strongly that each of us must have a passion to go forward in life.

He had read that Michelangelo's passion was his statue, "Moses." In fact, the article said, he was so passionate about the statue and it was so real to him, once the statue was finished he took a rod and struck it in the knee, crying, "Speak!" Adrian knew this kind of passion could get anyone where they wanted to be, and this was the passion Katie exhibited toward the ballet.

When the cold, rainy season set in, the last brown leaves gave up and fell to the ground, leaving the limbs bare, except for the evergreens that darkened to yet a deeper green. In mid-November, Indian summer came to the dun-colored property. Adrian took some comfort in this, his favorite season, and he walked the property at Red Oaks, thinking of the adventure he and Cara had taken with Katie and the little house tucked away in the forest. Red Oaks had always been just a place to live, to survive, not a real home until Katie's warm presence had made it one. He wondered at how her short visit here had made him appreciate his home. If she did love Red Oaks as much as she had seemed to, would she be willing to marry him and live here with him? Only time would tell, and so he would wait, but he knew he needed to hear her voice soon.

He saddled a horse and rode up the mountain toward Old Man Humphrey's cottage in the woods. As a child this place had been a coveted and stable place to him. Maybe here he could find the peace he sought.

Entering the little cottage, an old familiar routine ingrained in him by the old man suddenly seized Adrian. He walked slowly into the old man's room and sat in the rocking chair, in the very same spot where it had always been. His eyes fell on the Bible lying on the table beside the old man's bed. He picked it up and opened the front cover. To his surprise, there were these words, obviously written in the old man's handwriting.

Adrian, I would like for you to have this Bible after I pass on to the Land of Souls. Remember to pray. Prayer Changes Things.

Victor Humphrey. Black Running Bear of the Cherokee Nation.

Adrian thought of the small watercolor now hanging in Red Oaks, the one Katie had loved. He remembered the initials printed there. So that was where the initials BRB came from—Black Running Bear. Tears began to sting his eyes, and he held the black Bible close to his heart. He laid the Bible back on the table and folded his hands in prayer as he had done many times at the old man's prodding. It seemed as if Old Man Humphrey did nothing without praying. Adrian had to wait before going to the stream for a day of fishing or swimming until the prayers were completed. Old Man Humphrey was a praying man—a loud praying man—and any words of wisdom he gave, Adrian knew, came from the Bible lying close to his bedside.

As a child, Adrian had often wondered how to pray in those awkward silent moments, and the questioning used to drive one thought after another through his head. Perhaps, he thought, it was because he was too selfish, a deep dark sinner, or did not know what God was all about.

All Adrian knew about a God you could really converse with was what the old man had demonstrated. He once mentioned this to his mother, but got chastised and was not allowed to go back to Old Man Humphrey's cottage for several weeks. When she went out of town with Adrian's father, Adrian had slipped back into the woods and sought out the old man again.

His mother had prayed, certainly, at a local church where she had taken Adrian when he was very young. It had always been a scary ritual to Adrian. His mother tied a black scarf around her head and dipped her fingers into a marble fountain inside the church as she entered. She would walk down the center aisle and make the sign of the cross in front of her chest before slipping onto a bench and kneeling. At times, tears would slip uncharacteristically down her cheeks, but she never talked about God or made any religious references to Adrian, other than to guide him in a childhood prayer at bedtime.

Today there was no Old Man Humphrey, no mother's guidance for his prayers. He must speak the words of his heart. He sat there in the silence, in the brilliant sun-gloried silence of the morning, and a profound peace settled over him, a kind of prophetic serenity. Automatically the words came. "God, I truly love Kaitlyn Rose Johnson, and I want to be the kind of man she needs me to be, the kind of man

I should be. In my mind, I fear I should just let her go, let her live her life as it began without any influence from me. But it's not easy, God, when my mind says one thing and my heart another. Please, give me the strength to wait this out."

After he prayed, he sensed Old Man Humphrey's spirit again. It was only for an instant, but he felt his old friend's love and knew his prayer would somehow be answered.

Seventeen

Three days later, Katie woke early to the friendly kisses of her little dog, sat up, and looked around the room that had been hers since she was born. She hugged Gretchen close to her. Over the bed hung the pale pink toe shoes she had worn when she was only ten. She reached up and lightly fingered the satin ribbons, instantly going back in time to the practices and dances when she had worn them. She remembered when her mother had carefully sewn the ribbons securely to her toe shoes. Her mother was ecstatic after her first recital, and her father's face glowed with gentle awe as he handed Katie her first red rose.

A lifetime ago, she thought, as she let the satin fall from her fingers. Back then I believed in fairy tales and love ever after. Today I'm hoping and praying everlasting love does exist for me. What will I be in a decade when, instead of facing the twilight of my career, I will hopefully be facing a houseful of children? Will memories and clippings be enough of the ballet for me? Can my love and devotion for Adrian keep me from being selfish and one-dimensional?

More memories came to her from those early days of dancing—the music, the movement, the magic, and the time she had first felt her body move without bounds, fluid and free. Reality had come afterward, with unspeakable cramping, bleeding feet, strained muscles. How had it been possible, again and again, to contort her body into the unnatural lines that made up the dance? Yet she had done it. She had pushed her young self to the limits of ability and endurance. She had given herself only to the dance and had continued to give, living for that day when she would become famous as a principal female dancer of the ballet. Those dreams were behind her now. She would give all her energy and commitment to Adrian and a family of her own should he ask her to marry him, and then cherish the ballet as a proud memory.

The misty Virginia air drifted in through the open bedroom window, stirring the curtains. Outside, in the shadowy hulk of the mountains, the early morning light spoke of permanence and endurance. This was her home, a special and peaceful place for Katie. She was happy she could come here for a few days of rest. There was something compelling out there in the early dawn that beckoned to her. She dressed quickly and walked down to the stables.

Katie loved the smell of the feed and the dry scent of hay and even the earthy odor of manure that pervaded the barn. She took off her gloves and stroked the long nose of her bay mare, Nokomis, reveling in the warm velvet texture against her hand and the heat she felt rising from the horse's large body. She again fell into the rhythm her hands and heart remembered—blanket, saddle, cinch, leaving the correct breathing space between horse and leather, and then tacking up, gently pressing downward to get the horse to drop her head. She slipped on the headstall, gently inserting the bit. She was amazed by the way simply being in this atmosphere took her back. Every day after school, she used to ride Nokomis. She loved every aspect of owning her own horse, from feeding and caring for her to riding her in the forest and on the bridle path.

It had been over a month since Katie had heard the stranger's voice outside the airplane. The thought of it still unnerved her. She could not get it off her mind. If she lived a thousand years, she would never forget that voice and the words spoken as the man's face was illuminated by the strobe lights on the wings of the plane.

I'm loosing it, she thought. I've been working too much. Perhaps I will take some time off. Mother and I could go to Florida for a few days of sun and surf.

In reality, all Katie wanted was to be with Adrian again. She urged her mare to a gallop and leaned forward, her face to the animal's mane, encouraging her to a greater speed. The man's voice was still there even with the wind whipping around her. She could not escape the strange things he had said to her. Katie swallowed, feeling the prick of tears behind her eyelids. She could not run away from it, but riding fast and furious was the next best thing.

The speed was thrilling, the danger exciting. The horse's breathing was soon labored, and foam flecked her neck. "Run, Nokomis," she whispered in the mare's ear. "Run."

The wind blew Katie's long hair back from her face, and the scent of fresh earth and pine filled her nostrils. When the sun began to peek over the mountains surrounding the ranch, Katie was reminded anew that God's handiwork could not be imitated by mere man. It also reminded her it was now time to return to the house.

Heaven help me, Katie thought with a sinking heart when she got back to the stable and saw Russell Wiley sitting on the back porch of the ranch house. They had been sweethearts when they were seniors in high school, and at the time she really thought she loved him. Russell wanted to marry her after they graduated, but they were barely more than children at the time. Settling down, getting married, and raising children here in Virginia were things she was not ready for. She knew her future was not with Russell. Once away from him and in New York with the ballet, she knew she was right to break off their relationship the night of the senior prom. The intensity of the activities within the ballet and all the new people she met in New York had made it easy for her to forget him.

As she dismounted and walked toward the house, Russell stood up and jammed his hands into the back pockets of his jeans. The first thing she noticed was that he had put on a lot of muscle since their days together. Back then he was as skinny as a post rail.

Katie stood at the bottom of the steps, a few feet in front of him. "Hello, Russell. It's still early. How long have you been here?"

"Long enough to see you running Nokomis wild and furious. Old Man Jenkins saw you driving into town on your way to the ranch yesterday, so it's all over town that the famous ballerina is home for a visit."

"And would it be proper of me to ask what you're doing here?" Katie waited, fearing what was to come.

"I'm gonna take you to a movie, darlin', and then dancing."

Katie took a really good look at him. He was dressed much as she was, in a Western shirt, jeans, and cowboy boots, the uniform of local farmers and ranchers. She should have been glad to see him, but he just was not part of her world anymore. "That's nice of you, Russell, but I've had a long trip, and I'm tired. We're not an item anymore, remember?" She saw the flush high on his cheekbones and knew she had insulted him. She would never purposely hurt anyone's feelings, and a pang of guilt hit her.

"Oh, shucks, darlin', that's a long time ago. Just two kids not knowing what they wanted. I just thought it would be fun to get together as friends." Russell shrugged his shoulders.

A movie and dancing. The thought no sooner hit her than she saw an image of Adrian. He was handsome, mature, and sophisticated. Compared to him, Russell was still a boy. It would not be right to lead him on. "I'm sorry, Russell. I think too much time has passed, and we'd both end up feeling uncomfortable."

"Sorry you feel that way, Katie. I 'spect you're right, though. I guess it was a bad idea. We've probably both changed so much we wouldn't even know each other."

"You look good," she said, although his eyes, the color of Virginia's sun-ripened tobacco, looked world weary. "So what are you doing now, Russell? Still in college?"

He did not take his eyes from her as he spoke quietly. "No, Katie. My dad died last year, and I quit to take over his tobacco business."

The shock of the news hit her like a slap in the face. "Oh, I'm sorry, Russell. I liked your dad."

"Yes. He was a fine man, a fine man and a wonderful father." The depth of his loss showed clearly in his eyes.

"I can't believe Mother didn't tell me. She must have been preoccupied with her work at the time."

"Well," he said, "I'd best be getting back to the farm. It's been nice to see you again."

"And good to see you. I wish you the best, Russell." Katie sincerely meant her words as she said goodbye to her old friend.

Seeing Russell again made Katie realize that her love for Adrian was stronger than she thought. Or had the man's face outside the window of the plane brought the real feelings deep within her heart to the surface?

Sure, she had made a terrible mistake when she married Jeffery, but she knew now that Adrian was her soul mate. Her love was not enough to shake off the guilt and embarrassment she still felt about her brief marriage, but she knew her love for Adrian would give her the courage to tell him some day.

During the day, Katie went about helping with the chores on the ranch. She loved working in the stables, and she sang a song while she cleaned stalls and filled the water troughs. She was happy, very happy. All her indecision about Adrian was gone. She really loved him more than the dance and would leave it to be with him if he proposed to her.

Katie spent the night peacefully. To her surprise, she slept until mid-morning when she heard her mother's car pull out of the driveway. She pulled her hair into a ponytail, put on her robe and slippers, and walked downstairs to the kitchen where her father sat reading the morning paper. "Morning, Dad."

"Good morning, Katie. Did you sleep well?"

"So-so."

"Anything bothering you, dear?"

"Not really. But I did have a very strange thing happen on the plane ride from London to New York."

"Really?"

She told her father about the man she had seen out the plane window and the strange effect it had on her. She remembered his words exactly and told them to her father.

Will smiled, put down his paper, and took off his glasses. "That was Hawk, Katie."

"Hawk?"

"Yes, your great-grandfather."

"Oh yes, sure." Her tone revealed her skepticism.

"Sit down here, and let me tell you a story."

Katie sat across the table from her father and waited for one of his long stories. What she heard came as a great surprise to her.

"When I was in the Navy, there was an explosion on board ship, and Hawk came to me. I thought it was a dream, but in the dream he told me not to walk toward the light. He even told me that a girl named Kaitlyn Rose was waiting for me. I did what Hawk told me to do and woke up in the ship's hospital with a badly injured leg, but alive. I found out later the doctor had given me up for dead."

Katie felt a jolt of shock, and shivers ran down her arms. "Oh, Dad, you've never told me that before. It sounds like Hawk's spirit brought you back to life."

"He did, honey. That he did. When I got home from the Navy, your mother was waiting for me. We married, and you were born a year later. I knew your name, but I let your mother choose, and she said, 'Kaitlyn Rose,' almost as if Hawk had whispered your name to her also. You've been our special gift from the moment you were born."

She reached out and held her father tenderly. "I'm not the special one. My family is special. Very special."

Will looked directly at her and said, "You may want to consider the words Hawk said to you and come to some meaning about their direction for your life."

Pulling back from him, she said casually, "Oh, by the way, Russell Wiley stopped by yesterday."

Will smiled and winked at her. "I'm glad to hear that. You need to do normal things, aside from being a dancer."

"Well, it was awkward. He wanted to take me to a movie and dancing, but I felt so differently about him. It was like seeing someone familiar, but with no feelings attached."

Her father's words were full of love and concern. "You've grown up, Katie. Your life is filled with hard work and excitement, and it's helped you to mature. But you do need to have more of a social life."

"I guess I'll get it all together some day. You know. When my prince comes."

Will grinned at her. "Well, for now, Cinderella, have some breakfast with me."

If I could only tell you, she thought happily, *my prince has already come.*

Eighteen

That Sunday, Katie once again flew from Richmond into Kennedy airport and resumed her life as Kaitlyn Rose, the ballerina. With the success in London of *Moonglow Fascination*, Hudson Ballet Company had finally made a sizeable profit. This allowed them to hire more dancers and enlarge the variety of their ballet productions, including *The Nutcracker Suite*, *Swan Lake*, and *Romeo and Juliet*. After weeks of practice in New York to learn a new ballet, the tour would include five major cities. The first would be Houston, followed by a brief Christmas break, then Chicago, Los Angeles, Atlanta, and Philadelphia. Hudson Ballet Company had never before scheduled a tour of this length, and Katie looked forward to seeing all of these famous cities.

The old adage, "absence makes the heart grow fonder," proved to be true for Katie. On her first day home from Houston, she called her mother and learned that Adrian had been trying to reach her. Her heart skipped a beat at this good news, and she asked her mother to get a number from him where she could return his calls and to give him her New York number.

He called her in New York the next day and told her he fully intended to get in touch with her on a regular basis. She followed her heart and anticipated his calls. There was no doubt about it; Adrian's love showed through in his voice. Katie found enormous pleasure in talking to him and reminiscing about the lovely hours they had shared in England.

Once again in Orlanger three days before Christmas, Katie found herself fighting her impulse to call Adrian. She realized she needed air. Abruptly, she walked across to the windows and opened one, inhaling deeply of Virginia's cool mountain breeze, filled with the fragrance of pine. The Christmas tree her father had cut and placed in the corner of the living room sat still undecorated. Her gaze wandered to the telephone just as it had so often lately. Taking leave from the ballet for Christmas gave her more time to think of Adrian and made it worse.

All afternoon Katie had toyed with the idea of calling him. But then, he had called just three days earlier. She decided to call him anyway; after all, this was the holiday season. As she reached for the telephone, it rang. Katie jumped back, startled, and then picked up the receiver. "Hello?"

"Hi, Katie, this is Cara."

Katie was delighted to hear Cara's voice. Katie felt like an older sister to Cara, who had become very dear to her over the last few months. They did a lot of talking by telephone, and Cara always filled her in on her friend, Harry Wilhelm.

Sitting down in a small chair beside the telephone, Katie crossed her long, slender legs. She faced the large red and white poinsettias which blossomed from brass pots in front of the fireplace. "Cara, how wonderful to hear from you. How are you?"

"I'm just fine, Katie. Harry will be here any moment."

"Really? You've been seeing a lot of him lately. Is it getting serious?"

"No, but I like him. He's a really good friend, Katie."

"That's wonderful. You sound very happy."

"Oh, I am, and being at Red Oaks for Christmas holiday is the best ever. Uncle Peter is here with my two cousins. We're going for an old-fashioned sleigh ride today with a horse and everything."

"It sounds delightful, Cara. Then you must have snow?"

"You should see it! It snowed about eighteen centimeters last night. Red Oaks looks like a Christmas fairy tale."

"It must be lovely. I wish I could see it."

"Well, that's sort of why I'm calling, Katie."

Katie straightened in her chair, anticipating Cara's request. "Yes?"

"I know it's not much notice, but Uncle Adrian and everyone would be thrilled if you could come here for Christmas. Can you, Katie, please?"

Katie was suddenly sad and felt left out. "Cara, I'd love to be there with you and your family, but I have a performance in Chicago in five days."

"Ah, that's too bad. I was afraid of that." She rushed on in her chatty style. "Oh, Katie, we got your Christmas gifts. Thank you so much. I can't wait to open mine. I'm dying to know what it is. And, it was really nice of you to send a gift for Harry. He'll be happy."

"You're very welcome."

"Uncle Adrian said you probably sent him a lump of coal, since it rattles when he shakes the box." Cara giggled. "We're going to open our gifts early Christmas Eve, and then Harry and his family will be here for our annual Christmas dinner. We'll all go to church on Christmas Eve, because I'm singing with the choir."

"I know you'll have a wonderful Christmas, Cara."

"I know we will. Oh, Katie, one more thing."

"Yes?"

"My mother … Roxie called me today. It was so great hearing her voice. I really do miss her."

"I'm certain you do, Cara. Will she be there for Christmas?"

"No. She's busy, as usual."

"I'm truly sorry."

"It's okay. Really. Hey, hang on, Uncle Adrian wants to talk to you."

"Goodbye, Cara. Merry Christmas."

"Merry Christmas to you, Katie. Bye now."

Katie's heart beat faster when she heard Adrian's voice on the line. "Hello, Adrian. Cara's delighted with the holiday and sounds very happy."

"She's a great girl, Katie. I have to admit I put her up to calling you to see if you wouldn't change your mind and join us for Christmas. It's beautiful here now with the snow. I wish you were here."

"It was always beautiful there, Adrian, but we've been over this before. My performance is in five days. I have to leave for New York the day after Christmas for rehearsal sessions. I have a lead part in the next performance."

"I know, but I miss you, Katie, and wish you were here."

"I miss you too, Adrian. Christmas at Red Oaks sounds wonderful."

"It is."

Katie heard him sigh.

"Okay, I'll say goodbye for now. I'll probably call you again on Christmas day." He sounded resigned to her decision.

"I'll be waiting for your call. Talk to you then, Adrian."

"Goodbye for now, little one. Merry Christmas."

Katie did not put the receiver in the hook immediately. Hanging up the telephone and disconnecting Adrian's voice from her world was very difficult. She wished she were there with him. Her thoughts went to Cara and how tense her voice had sounded when she mentioned her mother. It made Katie want to be with her right now, at this very moment, to hug her and tell her she loved her.

She knew a part of her needed this connection with Adrian and Cara like she needed air and water. He had the ability to see into her heart, and for the first time in a long time, maybe ever, she truly felt part of his world. She finally knew what true romantic love felt like, and its power was overwhelming. Until now, she had made it on her own, but loving Adrian had changed her. She was pleased with the changes.

Nineteen

*I*t was a spring-like day in the middle of March, 1975, one of those freakish breaks in the winter, as though nature was tired of the ice and snow and had banished it to some nether land.

Cara, her head bare and her hair blown about her face, opened the collar of her coat and breathed deeply of the warm, fresh air. How good it would be to have spring come again. She walked slowly across the campus. As she neared the music building, Cara heard a familiar voice.

"Don't you dare use that tone of voice with me, young lady." It was Miss Ryan's voice.

Even though Cara was uncomfortable with her counselor and music teacher, she could not help drawing nearer to hear more of the conversation. She stayed just far enough away so that she did not catch Miss Ryan's attention. Cara was shocked with what came from the woman. With her hands on her hips, she was yelling at one of the younger girls who was standing in front of her.

"Who do you think you are, you little brat? You're only here because your parents can't stand having you around them!"

Cara looked on with alarm as the girl dissolved into tears. Sobbing and wiping her eyes furiously, the girl's voice could barely be heard. "That's not true. It's not true. My father ..."

Miss Ryan cut her off with a swipe of her hand in the air. "Don't tell me about your father. He's an alcoholic, and everyone knows it. Your mother is barely getting your tuition paid. Do you think she would go to the expense if she didn't want to get you out of the house?"

"I want to talk to my mother. She'll tell you it's not true." The girl sounded frantic. She was definitely at Miss Ryan's mercy.

"Call your mother? You are now on detention, and phone calls are off limits until I say so!"

The young girl was crying so hard she slid to her knees on the ground.

Cara focused on Miss Ryan and saw a triumphant smirk creep across her face. The brutality she had exhibited brought Cara a wave of nausea, and she turned and walked as quickly as she could to her next class on a path that would allow her to avoid being seen by Miss Ryan.

Cara tried her best to forget the scene she had witnessed earlier that day. She loved the early evening, when lights from inside the dorms shone through the windows and made them look like jewels. That night was no exception. Shadows long and darkly hued melded into one another so there were no sharp angles or distinct shapes. The sky overhead was a rare and lovely shade of violet, dense and impenetrable. The trees loomed as black etchings against it. Each wild flower growing close to the pond gave off a unique and heady perfume.

Cara had thought a lot about her mother lately. She missed her. Roxie had hardly ever been at Red Oaks, but Cara always knew that at some point she would see her mother. Now, with Roxie living in the United States, she felt a strange loneliness she never felt before.

After long moments of thought and strolling near the pond, Cara walked toward her dorm. Then she saw him.

He was standing motionless beneath the branches of a sprawling oak tree. Her heart rocketed into her throat and her vision blurred. She did not know if he was real or a mirage.

He nudged himself away from the trunk of the tree and moved, silently coming closer until he stood at the brick steps leading into her dorm. Darkness hid his face from her, but she caught the shine of straight white teeth as he smiled slowly.

It was a smile she had grown fond of during the past months, and it matched his tone of voice.

"Hello, Cara." He looked at her, the light from the entrance hall falling on his features.

"Harry, what are you doing here?"

"I just dropped off my sister, and they told me you were out walking. So I waited for you."

"It's nice to see you."

"Thanks. Do you want to take another walk?"

"I suppose. But I have to be in my dorm by eight, or I'll be late."

"We can just walk here on campus."

"Sure, Harry, let's walk"

"You look so serious this evening."

"Harry, I don't talk about people. You do know that, don't you? It's just not in my nature."

"I think I know you well enough to know that, Cara. It's one of the things I like about you."

"I have to tell someone about this." She was desperate. "Harry, this morning on the school grounds, I saw Miss Ryan shouting at one of the younger students. She said horrible things to the girl until the poor little thing was down on her knees crying and pleading with Miss Ryan to let her call her mother. Miss Ryan told her she was on detention and couldn't use the telephone."

"Have you reported this to the principal?" he asked.

Cara shook her head. "Honestly, Harry, I can't. I'm afraid Miss Ryan has lost her mind. No telling what she might do to me out of vengeance. She treats me strangely, anyway. She acts like I'm her pet, even though I haven't encouraged it. If she thinks I've turned against her, she might have me expelled. That could ruin my chances of getting into UCL."

"Ah, she couldn't do that, could she?" Harry asked with lifted eyebrows.

"I don't know what she might do or what she can do, but I'm going to stay as far away from her as I can. The only trouble is, I have my music classes under her."

"Well, you let me know if anything else happens, and we'll try to do something about it together."

Cara was finding out what it meant to have a best friend.

Twenty

Cara's spring schedule at Royal Masonic was a heavy one. Coupled with her work in the school's biology laboratory, it was almost superhuman. It required so much time that she had almost none left for her music or for an evening at the cinema with her friend, Harry. She mentioned this to Miss Ryan one day, and the next day it was all arranged. Miss Ryan saw to it Cara would have her music lessons late in the afternoons, immediately after her laboratory work was over. She felt even more overwhelmed when Miss Ryan often kept her late practicing the scales. Cara's intention was not to have a career in voice, but in medicine. She regretted mentioning her overload to this unpredictable woman.

Cara was happy when the school term was finished in May. She and her Uncle Adrian left for New York City to see a ballet in which Katie would perform. She had never been in the United States, or anywhere outside of England, for that matter. This was her first plane ride, and she loved it. She was amazed by the feeling of sitting still, although she knew the plane was quickly taking them to New York.

It was a pleasant surprise to Cara when her uncle Peter called to say he would meet them at the Plaza Hotel in New York, where Adrian and Cara were staying. Peter's cab arrived just as they were about to leave for the ballet at Lincoln Center. After warm hugs and handshakes, they hailed another cab to go to the theatre where Katie would perform.

"Uncle Peter, I'm so glad you could join us. This is my first trip to New York." Cara chatted on incessantly.

"I hope you're having fun, Cara."

"You bet I am. Uncle Adrian took me shopping today. Have you noticed that everyone here talks funny?"

"Well, Cara, New York is another world, of sorts. I also have business in New York. She's a model for an agency on Fifth Avenue."

"Should have known." Adrian shook his head.

Cara had overheard her uncle Adrian telling Peter all about Katie during the Christmas holiday at Red Oaks. "Wait until you meet Katie. She's really cool, Uncle Peter."

"So I've heard," Peter responded with a smile.

Chloe Cowling walked up to the ticket counter at Lincoln Center. "One of the cast members was to leave me a ticket. Miss Chloe Cowling."

"Yes, Miss Cowling. Here's your ticket. Enjoy the performance."

"Thank you."

With Chloe leaning on her ivory–handled cane, an usher led her to a seat in the center row very close to the stage where two gentlemen and a young lady were already seated.

The young lady looked up at Chloe as if to assess her, but did not say anything.

In response to the clear blue eyes of the attractive stranger, Chloe said hello.

The stranger, who also had an English accent, spoke up. "Hello. Are you from England?"

Chloe smiled at her. "Yes, I was born there, but I now live here in New York most of the time and in London only occasionally."

"Do you know any of the ballet dancers?" the young stranger asked.

"Well, yes, as a matter of fact, I do. Kaitlyn Rose is a friend of mine."

The young lady blossomed as she smiled widely. "Awesome! Katie is my uncle's girlfriend."

"Then you must be Cara Landry."

"Yes. Did Katie tell you about me?"

"She certainly did, including the fact that you'll be a doctor someday."

The gentleman seated beside Cara leaned over to look at Chloe and said, "Sorry, but my niece is quite a talker. She never saw a stranger."

Cara chimed in, "Uncle Peter, she knows Katie."

Chloe returned his smile and the hand which was offered. "No problem," she said. "And good evening to you. I'm Chloe Cowling."

"Hello, Miss Cowling. I'm Peter Wasserman, and this is my brother, Adrian Ashley."

Adrian looked over and nodded approvingly. "I've heard a lot about you, Miss Cowling."

"I'm very pleased to meet you both." She slowly withdrew her hand from Peter's.

After a brief lull, Cara spoke up again. "Are you going to dine with us after the performance?"

"Yes. Katie invited me to join her and her guests for supper. What a surprise that we're all sitting together. I suppose Katie arranged this."

Peter's eyes brightened with pleasure as he looked at her. "Your name sounds familiar to me. Have we met before?"

She shook her head slowly. "I don't believe we have."

He studied her for a moment, stroking his chin and regarding her carefully. "Cowling. Yes. Chloe Cowling. You were a prima ballerina with the London Ballet."

Chloe noticed his well-groomed appearance, which seemed to her inconsistent with his suntanned skin. His dark hair, just graying at the temples, was still full. "I'm impressed that you remember. Yes, but that was years ago."

Peter nodded. "I saw your performance in 1965. *Cyrano de Bergerac*. You danced with Tamara Rossi, whose husband was a friend of mine."

"Yes. She was a lovely woman."

The conversation came to a halt when the orchestra began.

"Miss Cowling?" Peter said, straining to look across Cara. "May I buy you a glass of wine during intermission?"

His voice, deep and sensual, sent a ripple of awareness through her. "Certainly." Chloe was thrilled with his offer, and she leaned back in her chair suppressing a sigh when the curtain rose.

Peter Wasserman hardly watched the ballet. Chloe could feel his eyes on her now and then throughout the performance. During intermission, they talked as though no one else was around. Chloe knew he noticed that she used a cane and had a slight limp, but he said nothing about it. It was obvious to Chloe that her disability did not matter to Peter.

They all joined Katie backstage after the performance and went to a nearby steak house for a celebratory meal.

At the restaurant, Peter and Chloe sat next to each other and continued their own conversation. Peter remarked to Chloe how perfect Katie was for his brother, and Chloe agreed. It was evident to them that Adrian and Katie were very much in love.

After supper the group went out onto the street to hail a cab.

Chloe turned to Peter. "Peter, I live close to Central park, and it's a long way from the hotel where Adrian and Cara are staying. I'll take a separate cab."

Peter took her hand and asked, "May I escort you to your apartment?"

"If you wish," Chloe said, pleasantly surprised by his generous offer.

Once at her apartment they talked over coffee until the wee hours of the morning. Peter was a true gentleman, and Chloe and he found they had a lot in common. They liked the same plays, the opera, and, of course, the ballet.

"Chloe, would you dine with me tomorrow evening?" he asked as he was about to leave her apartment.

"I'd like that very much, Peter."

Adrian, Katie, and Cara went up to Adrian's hotel suite, and Katie tucked Cara into bed.

Cara looked up at Katie. "Katie, I'd like to call my mother."

Katie looked into her wistful eyes. "I see no reason why you shouldn't. And this would probably be a good time, since California is three hours behind New York."

Katie walked into the living room. "Adrian, do you have Roxie's phone number? Cara would like to call her mother."

"Certainly." He handed his phone book over to Katie. "She's listed under Landry."

From the time that passed, Katie guessed that the telephone in California must have rung several times before Roxie answered.

"Hello, Roxie," Cara said. "Uncle Adrian, Uncle Peter, and I came to New York to attend Katie's ballet. Oh, you should have seen her performance. She's just the best ballerina ever!"

Katie listened to Cara's end of the conversation and watched Cara's eyes go from excitement to a heartbreaking sadness.

"Well, school's out for the summer, and I don't start tennis lessons for another week or so .... We're going back to London tomorrow. Uncle Adrian has business things to attend to .... Yes. It was lots of fun." Cara hesitated longer this time. "Good bye, Roxie."

Katie realized from Cara's sadness that the telephone call was not as uplifting as it could have been. Cara simply gave Katie the telephone and rolled over. Katie smoothed Cara's hair back, pulled the blanket up around her, turned off the light, and walked out of the room.

Twenty-One

It was late spring, a time of renewal, strength, and hope, a time that called lovers together. This was Katie's favorite time of year, especially in Virginia. Today, however, she was in New York preparing for a June 7th performance. There was a light knock on her private dressing room door. She drew her dressing gown close around her. As she opened the door, she shook her head, feeling dazed. "Adrian, what are you doing here? Is Cara with you?"

He looked at her awkwardly and spoke with difficulty. "I ... uh ... no, Cara's not with me this time. I came to see your mother's premier. And if you don't believe me, I have an invitation to *Things Remembered* here in New York tomorrow night. Your mother sent it to me." He patted his jacket pocket to indicate the invitation.

Katie felt a rush of doubt. "Adrian, you don't sound too convincing." She stepped aside to allow him into the small room. Out of their awkwardness, they both remained standing.

"Katie, I'm not sure how to say this to you, but ... I ... uh ...." He moved closer to her and reached out, taking her hand in his. "I love you, Katie," he said, now sounding stronger and older than he was. "I love you very much, and I would like for you to be my wife."

A diamond sparkled brightly in the little black box he held open in front of her. Her dreams had come true. Now she must face him with the story of her past.

"Well? What do you think?"

131

All Katie felt was dismay and near panic at the thought of revealing the secret which had plagued her since the day she met Adrian. She wished he was not standing so close to her. She felt her face and neck grow warm.

"You've caught me off guard. I feel vulnerable. My emotions are all near the surface, and I don't know what I want right now, Adrian. I didn't expect this so soon."

"But you did know I would eventually ask you to marry me?" Adrian simply drew her close, nestling her head against his chest.

"Oh, don't," she whispered and shut her eyes as she leaned against him. A warmth flooded through her, and she felt her defenses melt.

"Tears?" He spoke quietly, as if considering. "I thought my proposal would make you happy, not sad."

"Adrian, you don't understand."

"Yes. I think I do understand, Katie, but you seem very fragile right now, and I don't know what to do with you," he murmured. Taking a handful of her hair, he let it run through his fingers. "It was simpler before I found out you had this fragile side. I don't think I deal very well with weakness and tears."

Puzzled, Katie drew back from him. She had not felt fragile until he touched her so gently. Knowing there was no safety in the feeling, she tried to shake it off. "I'm not frail at all," she denied, then stood straight and faced him. No one had ever made her feel fragile before, and she was afraid if he touched her, she would feel weak again.

"Katie, you feel fragile because this is all new to you. Has anyone ever proposed to you before?"

She ignored his question.

"But that doesn't have anything to do with our getting married. Look, Katie, I'm in love with you. I want you to be my wife, but I also want you to be what you've always wanted to be. No matter what it takes. I don't know where you got the idea I'd want you to quit the ballet if we were married. I've never felt that way, but I had to wait until you had more faith in me to talk about it. Just tell me you love me and will marry me." He stepped closer and held her face in his hands, kissing her lightly.

Katie was stunned, not ever having realized he would approve of her staying with the ballet after they married. She spun from a kiss that melted the iceberg of her previous misconceptions and left her sailing in uncharted waters. Her mouth trembled. When she tried to find a response, the only truthful one to give him was what was in her heart. "I love you, Adrian," she whispered, overwhelmed by his tenderness and her maelstrom of emotions. "I do want to marry you, but there's something you have to hear first. I'm afraid there's a dark side to my past."

They sat down on a small settee, facing each other.

"I'm listening," Adrian said, with no emotion showing on his face.

"After I left Virginia on my graduation day from high school, I went directly to New York and the ballet company. Soon I met another ballet dancer by the name of Jeffery. I was dazzled by his performance in the dance and by his attention to me. In a short time, we married, unknown to even my parents, in a small ceremony at the court house. My marriage to Jeffery started out like a fairy tale. It was quite a heady experience for a girl from tiny Orlanger, Virginia. Did I ever really love him?" Her eyes drifted to the ceiling, as if she were carefully considering her answer. "I think I must have in the beginning. I was drawn to his talent as a dancer and his dedication to his profession. But it was less than three months later I found out he was unfaithful. I caught him with another woman. He didn't even care that I knew about his infidelity. I felt helpless and degraded. I divorced him immediately and took my maiden name back." Her face was a deep red from the guilt she still felt.

"I went home after that and threatened to leave the ballet and give up my dreams of being a dancer. But with the gentle love and understanding of my family, I pulled myself together and went back to New York. Jeffery had left the ballet and had gone off to Canada with the other woman. That was the only good thing about this story. I'd never have to see him again. I vowed then I would give myself to the ballet as never before. I wouldn't date or even think of dating anyone ever again. That was until I met you. I knew that weekend at Red Oaks that I was falling in love with you, and still I hesitated to make my feelings known to you. I just assumed you would want me to quit the ballet. And I could never marry you without telling you about my horrible marriage. I would never keep such a story from the man I love."

After making her confession to Adrian, she felt drained but somehow unknotted. Telling him about her failed marriage and the trauma that had upset her world unfurled the tension inside her. He was a good listener, asking nothing but accepting everything she said. He did not pretend to understand. He did not try to offer advice or tell her how to fix her feelings. By simply listening, he helped her. She felt like a new person with all the guilt and the dread of telling him her secret off her chest.

Adrian drew her to him and held her cheek cradled against his chest. "Katie, my little one, I don't know what to say."

Katie felt enormous comfort there, where she could feel the beating of his heart. "Does it make a difference in the way you feel about me?"

"No, Katie. Your life before we met makes no difference to me whatsoever. Your relationship with Jeffery was a mistake. Simple as that. I'm afraid you've let your desire for perfection in the ballet carry over into the rest of your life. Being an adult means being able to let go and carry on. You'll remember that my own family has quite a few divorces."

"Then...that's all you have to say about it? Because I'm sitting here confessing that I love you, Adrian. You changed my heart. I'm no longer bitter toward love."

He kissed her lips, a sweet kiss of love which said more than any words could.

She admitted to herself that she felt safe, protected, with his arms around her. She could only think about tomorrow and the future he sketched so easily with his talk of marriage, including her career. She knew he meant what he said.

"So you will marry me?"

"Oh, yes," she whispered.

"That's all I need to know," he said as he placed the ring on her finger.

"Oh, Adrian, there is something else. You know I love my Gretchen. How do you feel about having her live with us?"

Adrian threw back his head in easy laughter, then drew Katie close to him. "My darling, you may have a million dogs if that's your heart's desire."

They went to dinner that evening and made plans for the future—where they would live when they were married, how they would travel the Caribbean together, how many children they would have when Katie decided to retire from the ballet, and how they would make a real home and a real family for Cara by including her in all their plans. Katie would continue her career with the ballet, which to her meant having the best of both worlds.

When Adrian left to get a taxi and return to his hotel, he kissed her, sealing their agreement. Their second kiss quickly followed on the heels of the first. Then there was immediately a third and a fourth, and very soon Katie lacked the inclination or the presence of mind to keep count.

His kisses said she was beautiful, said he liked kissing her, even loved kissing her. They said he wanted to go on kissing her. How could a man's kiss do so much? She ceased to think; she simply was. Adrian made Katie feel whole, feel like a woman.

The next evening Adrian and Katie attended the premier of *Things Remembered*. It was held in the Reade Theatre at Lincoln Center. Afterward, Will stayed with Rilla as she answered questions from the press and chatted with her many friends in the movie business. Katie and Adrian met her parents later at a small, intimate Italian restaurant.

The music in the restaurant was low and romantic and Katie had never been so happy. Adrian beamed as he gave Katie's mother a hug and shook her father's hand. They were seated quickly.

Katie made an effort to hide her left hand, so her engagement ring would not be discovered before she had a chance to tell her mother and father that she and Adrian were engaged.

"Rilla, the music was fabulous," Adrian said.

"Thank you, Adrian. As you know, Katie's conductor asked me to write a revised score for 'Dream Song,' which they plan on adding to the end of the third act of *Moonglow Fascination*. I've decided once and for all that will be my last orchestral score, although I've had a great time working on it."

Katie looked at her mother with pride, knowing she would someday dance to her revised score. It gave her shivers each time she recalled anew how Adrian had dreamed the song before he and Katie met.

Rilla went on. "Afterward, I think it's time for Will and me to retire and do some traveling and see more of the United States." She sighed deeply. "Oh, by the way, Adrian, here's a tape of 'Dream Song' and a printed copy of the first score."

Adrian reached for the envelope which Rilla offered him. "Thank you, Rilla. That was very thoughtful of you. I look forward to hearing it."

"Mother, the troupe is all a-buzz about the new music, and I don't want to cut short our admiration of it, but I'm shocked to hear of your plans for retirement. What about the ranch if you and Dad retire?"

"Oh, it can be run by our talented employees. We trust all of them," Rilla emphasized.

Will spoke up. "We cut back on buying any new stallions this year. In fact, for the past year, we've talked of turning most of the grazing land into tobacco farming. Then the stables and breeding will be phased out in a few years. We can hire people to raise and harvest the tobacco crops."

Katie was alarmed. "A farm?"

"Sure, honey." Will replied. "Tobacco farms make good money these days."

"It just sounds strange. Are we going to call it a farm?"

"We won't make that change until all the horses are gone, but sure, why not? Grill's Farm has a nice ring to it."

Katie and Adrian looked at one another and smiled at the mention of the word "ring."

Adrian said, "Go ahead, Katie, tell them our good news."

"Mother, Father, Adrian and I are engaged." She proudly extended her left hand, on which the diamond sparkled brightly.

"Congratulations!" Will exclaimed.

Rilla looked intently across the table at her daughter. "Your ring is lovely, and I know you two are meant for each other, but what about the ballet, Katie?"

"We both feel I can continue dancing as long as I want to, even after we're married."

"Adrian, that's very generous of you," Will said. "You certainly have our blessing."

"Thank you, sir," Adrian replied.

Rilla still seemed hesitant. "But where will you live, London or the United States?"

"I'll live at Red Oaks with Adrian, Mother."

"Will you continue to travel with the troupe? That sounds like a lot of traveling for you, dear." Rilla's voice was full of concern.

"I realize that, Mother, but we'll work through it."

"And what about children?"

"We'll have to put off having children for several years, but all of these matters will work out when the right time comes. You have to trust us with these things, Mother. I guess I've never talked about children, but I definitely want to be a mother. I just hope I'll be as good with my children as you have always been with me."

Rilla rose from the table and went to her daughter. "Oh, Katie, Adrian, I'm happy for both of you. I really am." Rilla embraced them, and Will and Adrian shook hands again.

This time when Adrian's plane left for London, Katie felt different. Very different.

The diamond on her hand was his token of love. He really loved her just as she loved him. Katie's world was happier than she ever dreamed it could be.

The next weekend Katie returned home for a week long vacation. The trees proudly displayed their tender leaves on the Virginia hills around the ranch. Willows swayed golden in the sunlight, and dogwood blossoms, fragile as a whisper, looked like white butterflies flitting on the mountainsides.

After the initial shock of realizing Adrian had actually proposed, Katie explored the adventure of being in love. It did not make her light-headed as some songs promised, and she certainly did not lose her appetite, but it did make her desire for the dance seem less important to her. She had successfully ignored Madame Bettencourt's scorn. It had been her choice to accept Adrian's proposal of marriage. She knew it was not falling in love that had dictated her decision, but the special person with whom she had fallen in love. Deep inside her, she had known that if she ever fell in love again it would be with someone who adored her and whom she adored. That, in a nutshell, was Adrian.

Twenty-Two

"Cara, how nice to hear from you again. Is anything wrong?" Katie shifted the telephone closer to her ear.

"Not really, Katie. I just wanted to tell you how pleased I am that you and Uncle Adrian are engaged. He told me when he got back home. While he was telling me, he broke down and cried because he felt so lucky and happy. He said you have changed him so much he doesn't even hate Red Oaks anymore." Cara's soft laughter could be heard coming from her end of the line.

"Thank you, Cara. I'm very happy, too. What's going on with you?"

"Well, Harry and I are going on a picnic today. Several of us are going down to Barnes Lake to swim, and the school made us box lunches with Coca Cola to take along."

"That sounds like fun for a hot July afternoon, Cara."

"I'm looking forward to it. But there is only one thing."

"What, Cara?"

"Miss Ryan, my school counselor and music teacher, gave me a very stern talk about Harry. She said he was no good for me, that I am royalty and shouldn't think of dating a commoner. Isn't that strange, coming from a teacher?"

Katie thought for a moment or two. "Well, yes, Cara, it does sound strange. Does your Uncle Adrian know about this?"

"No. He has met with Miss Ryan several times but never says anything bad about her, so I thought it was just me."

"Maybe as a counselor she is just unduly concerned about your welfare."

"I suppose."

"If you don't feel comfortable with her, just stay away from her as much as possible. When I was in high school, I had a teacher who thought my joining the ballet was a waste of time. She thought I should go to college and get, what she called, a proper education. She was harmless and probably meant well, so I just listened to her, was respectful, and did what I wanted to do. You have to do the same, Cara."

"I will, Katie. It's so nice to have you to talk with."

Cara's silence on the other end of the telephone line was evidence that something else was on her mind.

"Cara, is there something else bothering you?"

"I spoke to Roxie the other day, but she was too busy to talk."

"I'm sorry about that. I'm certain your mother will call you back when she has time."

"I guess."

To get Cara's mind off this unpleasantness, Katie asked, "How is your extra class going?"

"Fine. I'm also taking another chemistry class this summer, so I won't have to take that one when I get to college in January."

"Good idea. Do you have a lot of free time at school during the summer?"

"Yes, but I stay busy. There are quite a few girls still here taking college classes. We hang around on weekends going to the cinema and such. And I've been spending a lot of time with Harry. He's also taking some summer classes."

"Where will he go to college, Cara?"

"University of London. He wants to study economics.

"I suppose you won't see much of him come January?"

"No. I guess not. Although he has a car, so he can come and pick me up on weekends for dates. I went to his house last weekend. His parents are very nice."

"Good, Cara. Harry sounds like a good friend."

"He is."

On August 3rd, Katie returned home from Dallas and an exhausting triple performance. When the telephone rang at Grill's Ranch, she picked it up reluctantly. Her spirits lifted when she heard Adrian's voice. She had not spoken to him for several days. It was always exciting when he called. They chatted a few minutes about the ballet, the weather, and Cara, but Katie knew the subject of setting a wedding date would come up again. It did.

"Yes, Adrian, I have thought about it, but late summer wouldn't be a good time for our wedding. I still have Chicago and a performance in Seattle later this month."

"Are you certain you still want to get married?"

"Of course, Adrian."

"Well, it just seems to me you keep putting off setting a date."

She could hear the tension in his voice. "No, Adrian, that's not the case. It just has to be at a time when I have several weeks between performances."

"Maybe I'll come to the United States for a few days. Could I see you then?"

"If I'm here. Please remember that we discussed this when you were here in May. You wanted me to continue with the troupe, and when there was time we would set a wedding date."

"I didn't think it would take so long. Can't you look at your schedule and tell me when it's a good time for you?" His voice almost had a pleading quality.

"Hold on, Adrian. I have my date book in my purse."

Katie put down the telephone to get her purse. "December. I have over three weeks free. Then I have to return to New York for another tour of the West Coast."

"Well, that's better than nothing. Shall I go ahead with plans for a wedding in December? How about December 6th? That's the first Saturday of the month."

"December 6th? Yes, I think that could work. I don't have to be in New York until January 8th. From there we'll be going to San Francisco, but this leaves us time to go on a honeymoon and get back to Red Oaks for Christmas. Cara and our other family members can join us for both the wedding and then the holidays."

When she hung up the telephone, Katie knew Adrian would have preferred a much shorter engagement. But after all, it was his suggestion that they marry and she continue with the ballet. It was her dream, but she agreed that it really had not been fair of her to put off their marriage for so long. Now a date was set. The date she and Adrian would be married. How could I have doubted that I truly love him, she thought.

Twenty-Three

Four months later in a small English town, a woman sat staring into the frozen woods outside her office window on the campus of Royal Masonic School for Girls. Monique Ryan was fairly attractive at forty-five. From the top of her smoothly coiffed brown hair to the tips of her shining crocodile pumps, every detail indicated that she was a classy lady. Why not? She was a respected music teacher and student counselor. But looks could be deceiving.

Miss Ryan's posture was a characteristic one. She sat with her legs crossed, left elbow resting on the desk, her chin supported by her right hand, and a cigarette between her left fingers. Its smoke billowed before her eyes. Those small beady eyes, as dark as black coffee and deeply shadowed, stared out the window at Cara Landry walking with a group of friends. Cara was being studied by the counselor as though she were a fascinating new specimen caught between the glass plates of a laboratory slide.

Just as she did every afternoon, Miss Ryan picked up a pen to write the progress she had made toward her seventeen year goal. On the desk lay a black journal, opened to her latest entry.

December 1, 1975

Secrecy is the most important factor. I must be accurate and finalize my plan without anyone knowing.

The wealthy could always buy a child; I could not. My only attempt

143

to have a child ended in tragedy when my daughter died eight hours after she was born. I was banished by my family for disgracing them with that pregnancy. There must be atonement for those judgments against me. So I will take the child born the same day as my daughter. The wealthy British Monarchy will never miss her. At last I will have a child born with royal blood, but she will be mine.

Cara Landry. What a joke. Her name will be Elizabeth Ryan, not Cara Landry. Soon, very soon now, my daughter will be with me, and we will never be apart again. She will love me as she never loved her bitch of a mother. I will show her what real motherly love is. I will care for her and love her like a mother should. She will grow to love me, and then, of course, she must die, and I shall die with her. There can be no greater love than that. I will leave each step recorded in my diary, even up to our final breaths of life, and someday someone will find it and publish it as a wonderful story of a mother's love.

Miss Ryan was nearly done with every detail of her plan to kidnap Cara. Adrian had asked Cara's school to provide a round-trip car and driver for his wedding and reception. Miss Ryan had joyously volunteered. She knew exactly what had to be done. She even knew how to go about doing it, but she must be careful. She must be very careful. She had the finances finally, so now all that was left was to dwell on the pleasure of having a daughter. She would be patient and wait for the precise moment, and no better time than when she was driving Cara back to school after her uncle's wedding. She had a house rented in the country and every detail was carefully planned. The drive would take over an hour, which would give her plenty of time to sedate Cara.

As she began to write again in her journal, she smiled, a hideous smile of hate and deception.

Cara will never see her so-called mother or her Uncle Adrian again. I have gone seventeen years without a daughter at Christmas; now I will have her all to myself.

My daughter. My lovely daughter, Elizabeth …

Twenty-Four

Katie was filled with anticipation. It was December 4th, and in two days she would be Mrs. Adrian Ashley. Some of her close friends from the ballet troupe had given her a luncheon and bridal shower before she left for London. Her parents were flying from Virginia to the wedding, while her grandparents were driving from Penzance. She knew this was what she had been destined for, to live in England with Adrian, and she would continue her dancing as long as she wanted. Adrian was adamant about that. The world was not such a big place, and air flights would take her wherever the troupe was performing. Adrian had even set up a practice studio, with mirrors, wood floor, and barre for her at Red Oaks. She knew her decision to marry him had been the right one.

Because the wedding plans were made by telephone, Maude had enthusiastically agreed to take care of the cake and reception food, all the flowers, and Katie's favorite music for both the wedding and reception. She and Katie had talked about the details at length through phone calls and when Katie visited Farnham in October, and Katie felt quite confident in Maude's abilities. Her wedding gown had been consigned from a Boston designer and would be waiting for her at Red Oaks when she arrived.

The newlyweds would have a two-week honeymoon in Australia, return to Red Oaks for the Christmas holiday, and in early January of 1976, Katie would fly back to New York to begin another tour. She had promised herself they would include Cara in all their future vacations. It would be a good life. She was sure of it.

Today Katie was flying to London. She settled back in the luxurious first-class seat of the jet that was taking her to Adrian. In seven hours, she would feel his arms around her again. As she turned her head to look outside the plane window, just as before, she saw an image emerge from the early morning darkness. This time she knew who it was, and she simply smiled at Hawk's image.

She whispered, "Thank you, Hawk. Somehow in this crazy mixed up world, you came from across the Land of Souls and guided me in making the right choice."

The image smiled back at her, and then was gone. She knew she would probably never see him again, but if she did, he would not frighten her as before.

Katie arrived at Red Oaks to find a flurry of caterers and floral specialists busy at work, but Adrian and Maude insisted she go right to bed after she was served tea and a sandwich.

"I won't be able to sleep. I'm too excited," she declared. But that was not true. She slept for ten hours and woke up rested and ready for a day filled with last-minute planning for her wedding.

Friday was hectic for her and Adrian both as they wandered around the house. They were amazed at all the workers still busy with preparations. Maude had done a wonderful job coordinating everything, and each detail Katie had suggested was perfectly put in place, only in a manner she could not imagine. Katie was not used to this lifestyle—the grandness of it all—but she was determined to adjust.

In the formal dining room, three twenty-four foot long tables were set all in white with a lace tablecloth on each. Formal white china on silver chargers, crystal glasses, silver place settings, and lovely flower arrangements were spread the length of the tables.

"Adrian, this is the china pattern I picked out, but there's so much of it."

Katie knew Adrian disliked parties. He preferred quiet, intimate affairs, as opposed to opulent get-togethers. Katie also knew this was her day—her wedding day—and Adrian had pulled out all the stops for her.

"Remember that I told you that anything you wanted would be at your disposal for the wedding and reception afterward? There will be other occasions when it will be needed, so I ordered enough for our reception. Do you like the tablecloths, Katie?"

"Yes, they're exquisite."

"They were used at my parents' wedding. They're Irish lace and were handmade for my great-grandmother's wedding over 130 years ago."

Each chair, upholstered in white brocade, would be adorned on the back with lilies of the valley for the reception. An orchestra was setting up their instruments in the adjoining drawing room. The music they would play had been chosen by Katie three months earlier. This large room would easily feed the one hundred guests who would attend the noon wedding and reception.

"I'm afraid I'm overwhelmed, Adrian."

"Stop worrying, darling. Everything will go just as planned. After the meal is served, the drawing room will be opened for dancing, and the dining room will be set up with coffee, tea, drinks, and the wedding cake."

Adrian was probably right; Katie's nerves were showing. She had never attended anything this grand. This would be the most important performance of her life—her marriage to her prince.

Twenty-Five

*I*t was very early morning in the dormitory of Cara's school. Outside the snow was coming down in fat little flakes, slowly piling drift upon drift until the wind came along like a gigantic broom and swept it up close against the window sills.

Inside it was quiet, the special quiet which precedes the coming of the dawn. All the rooms in Rathburn Hall were given over to the soft, regular breathing of girls relaxed in sleep. Forgotten were all the problems that filled their days with demands for attention. Gone now were the classes, the cinemas with friends in town, the near romances, the competitions and strivings for knowledge, and the dread and preparation for exams once the Christmas holiday was over.

Cara was too anxious to sleep, so she busied herself getting ready to go home for the wedding. Her excitement stemmed from her enrollment in college after the Christmas holiday, as well as her Uncle Adrian's and Katie's wedding. Yet, she wished her mother were going to be there with her. Tears began to fall, but Cara would not let sad thoughts and loneliness for her mother spoil her happiness. She was to be Katie's maid of honor. Her clothes for the ceremony were already at Red Oaks. She dressed warmly now and would change again before returning to school.

Tomorrow Cara, her friend, Jayne Forsythe, and Jayne's parents would leave for France. Cara would stay with them on the French Riviera for two weeks and was eager to experience new adventures with

Jayne. She wished Jayne could go to the wedding with her, but Jayne's mother wanted to take her daughter on a London shopping spree before the foursome flew to France.

Miss Ryan would be driving Cara to Red Oaks and bringing her back to school after the wedding reception. Cara was uncomfortable with the idea, but she felt she would be ungrateful to complain. After all, the school had accommodated her by providing their car and faculty member to transport her to a family social event.

She decided she would pretend to be asleep for most of the trip, making it unnecessary to talk to Miss Ryan.

Very early the morning of the wedding, Adrian and Katie enjoyed a light breakfast together in the intimacy of the Red Oaks kitchen at Katie's request. Maude had prepared a fresh batch of blueberry scones and Cornish cream. This was a big day for them. As the couple ate, Katie realized her speech was dominated with meaningless, nervous chitchat.

"You've every right to be tense, my darling. I've heard brides are always nervous on their wedding day."

"I suppose, Adrian. But it's so grand with so many flowers and so much food."

"Get used to it, Katie. Red Oaks will always serve you in grand style. Now let's quickly get ready. Cara will be here any minute. I think you need to slip on something other than your sweat suit."

As they stood and walked toward the stairs, Katie asked, "How is she getting here?"

"The school is providing transportation for her to the wedding and the reception, and then she'll be whisked right back to school."

"The poor girl ."

"Don't worry about Cara. She's so happy to have you in the family, she'd even be satisfied with a horse and buggy for the trip."

Katie laughed and nodded her head. "Cara and I became close that first weekend we met and have grown closer ever since."

"I know that, Katie, and I know she loves you very much."

"I feel the same way about her." Katie stopped walking and looked up at Adrian. "Is Roxie coming for the wedding?"

"She called last week with her regrets. Her movie star friend in

California is having a house full of guests, and she felt she must be there." He took Katie's hand and continued walking toward the second floor hallway.

"I'm sorry, Adrian. I know Cara would have liked her mother to be here for the wedding."

Adrian could not stop himself from being judgmental toward his sister. "It's not the first time Cara has been disappointed," he said through tense lips.

"True."

At the second floor, Adrian put his hands on Katie's shoulders. "We don't have time to do a proper rehearsal, so when Cara gets here we'll do a quick run though, and then dress for the wedding."

"So much in so little time."

Adrian drew Katie into his arms and kissed her tenderly. "It'll be fine, dear. I promise."

"If you say so." She was not convinced they could pull it off.

"I'm going back downstairs to the library and check on your family and Peter. You get dressed, and I'll meet you there."

Maude approached Katie as she was coming back downstairs. "Katie, another of your guests has just arrived."

"Thank you, Maude, but it's probably the party planner. She wants to go over the final arrangements before the wedding. The lilies on the reception table are suddenly wilting." Katie was hopeful. "If that's the only thing that goes wrong, I can handle it."

When Katie walked toward the front door, she saw Chloe Cowling standing tall, serene, and as lovely as ever. "Chloe, I'm delighted you made it for the wedding!"

They embraced, and Chloe said, "This is a wedding I wouldn't miss for anything. I'm staying at the house in London until after the holiday. Then back to New York. Now I'm going to fade away and let you get on with your wedding preparations. I'll see you at the reception."

"But it's almost three hours until the wedding. Whatever will you do all that time?"

"Peter Wasserman and I have been dining and attending the theatre here in London the last few weeks. I'm certain he can find something for us to do for a while." The blush on her pale cheeks was like the glow of sunset on snow.

"Chloe, why didn't you tell me?"

"It's nothing serious yet. I find that Peter is a great friend, and we enjoy each other's company."

Katie did not believe Chloe's reference to Peter being just a friend was credible. The happiness showed in her smile and her twinkling eyes.

"That's so great, Chloe. See you at the reception."

Katie gave Chloe another hug, then watched her friend walk away leaning on her cane for support. Peter walked up to Chloe and took her hand. He waved at Katie, then he and Chloe walked off together hand-in-hand. Katie saw Chloe lean her head back and gaze into Peter's eyes. What a great pair they make, Katie mused, and what a lovely surprise.

Cara and Miss Ryan arrived shortly. Cara rushed into Katie's arms with hugs and kisses and then ran into the library, where she knew the guests would be waiting.

"Did Cara's mother show up for the wedding?" Miss Ryan asked Katie.

"Roxie?"

"Yes, as I remember, that's her name."

"Have you met Roxie Landry?" Katie questioned.

"Oh, yes. We were friends some years ago."

"Really? No, Roxie isn't able to attend the wedding."

"How unfortunate." Miss Ryan's voice betrayed her disdain for the absent mother.

Gus escorted Miss Ryan to a drawing room in his and Maude's cottage where she could relax during the festivities.

After a brief rehearsal, Cara joined Katie and Rilla in the dressing room. Rilla helped Cara get into her sapphire blue bride's maid gown, her first floor length dress.

Rilla clasped her hands in approval of the new look, a sophisticated, lovely young woman. "Your turn now, Katie."

"Katie, you're beautiful," Cara said in awe as she watched Rilla help Katie slip into her wedding dress. It was made of white silk organza, cut on the bias, with just a slight pouf in the top of the long tapered sleeves. With the gown cut low in the front and back, the silk glowed softly against her olive skin. Her simple, yet elegant, train fell only to the hem of her dress from a circle of white roses on her head. All of the white was stunningly bright against Katie's dark hair.

"Do my nerves show?" Katie asked.

"No. You only look a little frazzled," Cara laughed

"Thanks a lot." Katie shook her finger at Cara, then walked over and hugged Cara. "I'm so glad you're here and that you agreed to be my Maid of Honor."

Cara didn't reply, but her eyes misted, and she returned the hug to Katie. "Katie, where's Gretchen? Didn't you bring her to Red Oaks with you?"

"I didn't think this was the proper time to bring her to Red Oaks. Adrian and I decided not to bring her here until we get settled in. Better she stays at the ranch for now."

Rilla smoothed Katie's hair and the skirt of her dress as they looked in the mirror.

"Is that really me?" Katie felt she was in a dream world.

"Yes, darling. It's really you. And you look so happy you're almost glowing." Rilla hugged her daughter.

At that moment Olivia came into the room. "Katie, it's a beautiful dress. However, something seems to be missing."

"Missing, Grammy?"

"Well, yes, the top of the dress seems too plain," Olivia said seriously.

Eight eyes looked into the mirror in front of Katie.

"Mother, hand me the diamond earrings. Maybe then it will look better." Katie fastened on the earrings which Rilla had loaned her to wear today.

"Now, Grammy, is that better?" Katie asked.

"No. Not yet." Olivia's brown eyes twinkled as she took a dark blue velvet pouch from her purse, walked behind Katie, and pulled out a beautiful blue cameo surrounded by diamonds that glittered in the light from the windows. She placed the chain around Katie's neck.

"What is this?" Katie asked, detecting the antiquity of the cameo.

"It was my great-aunt's engagement brooch. She gave it to her maid before going down on the Titanic in 1912. Her maid was rescued and honorably saw to it that the brooch was brought to my mother, who gave it to me on my wedding day. I had it put on a golden chain for you."

"It's lovely," Katie said as she hugged her grandmother.

"Now you have something old, something new, something borrowed, and something blue," Cara teased.

They all giggled.

"I was afraid the dress would be wrinkled," Katie said, eying herself critically in the mirror.

"For the price you paid for this dress, you could be sure the design house would know how to ship it so it wouldn't be mussed," her mother said.

Then Katie heard the music drifting in from downstairs. Her heart warmed to think of Adrian waiting for her.

"It's time," said Cara. "Gee, what do I have to be nervous about? I'm just going to lead the bride in front of one hundred people, all gawking at me. I hope I don't trip and fall."

They all hugged each other again. Cara handed Katie her bouquet and reached for her own smaller version. Rilla pulled Katie's veil over her face, as motherly tears continued to roll down her cheeks.

"Don't cry, Mother."

"I have a right to cry. I bet your father cries, too."

After the wedding and the preliminary activities at the reception, Katie and Adrian said their goodbyes to Cara and Miss Ryan as they headed back to school. The dancing and festivities went on until late evening.

When the celebration was concluded, all of the Friday overnight guests collected their belongings and left to give the happy couple some privacy. Adrian told Katie she was the most beautiful bride he had ever seen, and Katie's world was perfect and happy.

For once, Katie had performed without her feet hurting. She was suddenly surprised at herself. What a silly thing to think of on her wedding night.

Twenty-Six

A t 8:00 o'clock on Sunday morning, the telephone rang at Red Oaks, where Adrian and Katie were packing to leave on their honeymoon.

"Master Adrian, there's a call for you."

"Thank you. I'll take it in the library, Gus." Adrian walked quickly downstairs into the library and picked up the telephone. "Hello, Adrian Ashley here."

"Mr. Ashley, this is Mrs. Bentley, headmistress at Royal Masonic."

"Yes, Mrs. Bentley?"

"First of all, I wish to congratulate you on your marriage."

"Thank you." Adrian knew the call could not be just about his wedding. "Is something wrong, Mrs. Bentley?"

"Mr. Ashley, we were expecting Cara to return to school last evening."

His concern deepened. "But she did return," he said quickly. "The car was driven by Miss Ryan, and they headed back to the school after our wedding last evening around 5:00 p.m."

"I'm very sorry, sir, but neither Cara nor Miss Ryan has returned to the school."

"Cara is leaving today to go to France with Mr. and Mrs. Forsythe and their daughter, Jayne. Perhaps she's with them."

"Mr. and Mrs. Forsythe and their daughter are here with me. They haven't seen Cara. We all are very concerned."

"Have you checked with other students to see if they know of her whereabouts?"

"We interviewed all the girls who are known to be friends with Cara, and no one has seen her since she left for your wedding." Mrs. Bentley was obviously distraught.

"Thank you, Mrs. Bentley. My wife and I will start checking from here." Adrian felt as though his heart was about to jump out of his chest. With his throat tightened and his body trembling throughout, he went back upstairs to inform Katie of the bad news.

"Adrian, we can't go on a honeymoon knowing Cara is missing."

"Absolutely not. We must make other plans."

"Of course, but don't forget I have to be back in New York by January 8th," she added in a weak voice.

"Well, that's more than three weeks from now." He sounded agitated, and quickly turned the conversation back to Cara. "Miss Ryan probably became sleepy, and they decided to spend the night in a hotel. I'm certain Cara will call us any moment now as to their whereabouts, or they might even be back on the road driving now. We'll just cancel our flight today and reschedule in a day or two."

"I hope you're right, Adrian."

Katie came down the stairs later that afternoon just as Adrian hung up the phone.

He spoke slowly. "I called the Thames Valley Police. They put me in touch with a Sergeant Graves, a Duty Supervisor for Missing Persons. He began a Risk Assessment as we spoke and immediately assigned Cara's case to the High Risk category. He assured me that he would add Cara's name to the Missing Children Database and notify Child Rescue Alert and other groups which will immediately begin the official search."

Katie walked over and faced him. "I'm so sorry, Adrian. So very sorry. I'm frightened for our Cara."

Cara came to slowly, with a rush of nausea and a blinding headache. A nightmare, still black at the edges, circled insistently, like a vulture patiently waiting to drop. She squeezed her eyes tighter, rolled her head on a pillow, and then cautiously opened them.

Where? The thought was dull, foolish. Not my room, she realized, and struggled to fight against the chain that held her wrists to the headboard of the iron bed on which she was lying.

She could smell jasmine or roses or vanilla, a very strong scent which added to her nausea. There was no choice but to accept it.

Snippets of her memory returned—the car being driven by Miss Ryan; the way she had rolled from one side to the other in the back seat as the car swerved and speeded ahead; her screams, seemingly not heard. Cara knew for a certainty that Miss Ryan had gone mad. About half way through the trip, Cara recalled, Miss Ryan had insisted Cara drink a soft drink she had brought along for her. A severe dizziness soon had overcome her. She remembered the car pulling up in front of a small house. Miss Ryan had helped her out of the car and into the house just before everything went black.

The chain now rubbed Cara's wrists as she tried to change positions and realized that Miss Ryan had kidnapped her. Her family would be forced to pay for her safe return.

Then she heard the singing. The mad woman was singing as Cara's breath came in ragged gulps while she pulled on the chain which held her. It was useless.

She relaxed and made herself survey what she understood now was her prison—a room sparsely furnished with only a chair, an old table, and the bed she was lying on. The windows were bare, and Cara could see the wind whipping the snow outside.

While looking around the room, Cara noticed the rough hewn wooden table and saw several candles sitting there flickering where the wind came in around the windows. They were the source of the nauseating flowery smells. Her stomach knotted greasily.

Finally, Cara heard the lock on the door click. The door opened, and Miss Ryan stepped inside.

"Elizabeth, you're finally awake. Good morning, my darling. You've slept a long time. Are you hungry, dear?" Miss Ryan reached over and unlocked the chains around Cara's wrists. "If you will come with me, please."

Cara swallowed a bubble of hysteria. Seeing no immediate

alternative, she knew it would be wise to play along until she could find some way to escape this mad woman's clutches. As her feet touched the floor, she realized a moldy smell was coming from a shabby wool carpet on the floor.

Five days passed, and Adrian was experiencing the most difficult time emotionally he had ever gone through. He was completely absorbed in his efforts to find Cara. He knew that Katie, on the other hand, was feeling alienated from him, but he could not deal with both of them at once.

He came in from a search of Farnham's city streets and, still wearing his hat and coat, dropped into a chair in the drawing room. He was very tired and knew his nerves were shot, and he was near the edge of a breakdown.

Katie quickly followed him into the room and knelt by the side of his chair. "Adrian, I'm as worried about Cara as you are, but do you see what this is doing to you? You've taken on the full responsibility for the search. You're exhausted, and you won't let me help you. I feel like an outsider. Please don't let this terrible thing come between us."

"Don't do this, Katie. Don't criticize me now. I want you to stay at Red Oaks. Stay at the house so I don't have to worry about you being in danger, too" Adrian pleaded.

"But you're not letting me do anything. You never include me in any of the leads you run out to investigate. Last night you were gone most of the night searching for Cara. I didn't even know you had left the house. I would have wanted to go with you."

Adrian was insistent. "That's out of the question. You're safer staying here."

"I think it's time to call Roxie and let her know Cara is missing. It's been almost a full week now."

"I don't know if Roxie will come back to London."

"Of course she will, Adrian. Cara is her daughter," Katie said angrily.

Without saying another word, Adrian walked to the phone and called his sister. After giving her the briefest of details, he insisted she return to England during the wait for news of Cara. He sensed alarm in his sister's voice, but there was no good way to tell her the terrible news about her daughter.

"And you say she disappeared right after your reception? Adrian, that was almost a week ago. Why didn't you call me immediately?"

"We thought there might have been an accident, and we waited until all the hospitals and clinics were checked. And quite honestly, I didn't know if you would be willing to leave your new love for the sake of your daughter." He knew he had said it bitterly and felt it was wrong, but he couldn't restrain his true feelings in this moment.

"Well, I really deserve that one, don't I? I'll make it up to her somehow. I want to come home, Adrian. The only thing stopping me is money. Or, rather, the lack of it." Roxie's voice was filled with sincerity, and she seemed to be on the verge of tears.

"I guess it's time for both of us to forget the past." Adrian sighed heavily into the telephone. "Your daughter needs you, and I need you here with me. I'll arrange for a flight for you by this evening. Will you be able to get to Los Angeles International by then?"

"Yes, I'll pack immediately and wait for you to call me with the flight information."

"No, don't even wait," Adrian urged her. "Just get a cab to the airport and check in with the TWA desk. Your ticket will be waiting there."

"Oh, thank you, Adrian. I do love you. I don't know what I'd do without you and your kind heart."

Just knowing Roxie would soon be with him, Adrian calmed somewhat in spite of the crisis around him. "We'll both have a good long talk when you get here. We have a lot of things to discuss. Goodbye for now, Roxie. I'll see you tomorrow."

When he hung up the telephone, Katie, her anger forgotten, spoke from across the room. "Adrian, we're not even close to a solid lead. What if this goes on for weeks? What am I supposed to do?"

"If it's the ballet you're worried about, just call and tell them to use a stand-in."

Katie felt a cold shock run through her body. This was not the Adrian she knew. "How can you think I'm concerned about the ballet?

My commitment to the ballet is second to my loyalty to you. And you're completely overlooking how much I love Cara."

His voice rose. "Then what do you suggest, Katie? I need one thing from you, just one thing—to stay in this house where you'll be safe!"

"What about us, Adrian? You barely even speak to me."

"I can't believe how you're putting your own needs before this crisis. If you feel so put down, then go back to New York, Katie. I don't care what you do! I'm going to the police station again today. I want to personally follow-up on every lead they have so far."

Adrian was out of control. He jumped to his feet and was shouting. "Gus will take you to Heathrow!"

"Take me to …?" Katie's heart was shattered. "All right, Adrian. If that's what you want, I'll leave for New York today."

"Do whatever you want to do, Katie. I don't care anymore."

He walked out of the drawing room and called loudly to Gus as he opened the front door. "Gus, Katie will need a lift to Heathrow today!" The door slammed loudly behind him.

Twenty-Seven

Roxie's mind was in turmoil during the flight. So many questions. How could she face her family now? Would they accept her? Would Cara ever forgive her for leaving England and moving to California with Ronald? Could she go back to Red Oaks, the only place she ever felt loved and safe?

At the airport, Adrian embraced her, and they both shed tears, tears of joy for their happiness to see one another again and tears of sorrow for the terrible thing that had happened to Cara.

"Katie sends her apologies. She had to return to New York earlier than she expected," Adrian said solemnly.

Not knowing of Katie's deep love for Cara, she accepted his excuse for her. "I understand, but, Adrian, have you had any news of Cara?"

"No, nothing yet."

"Does Peter know Cara has disappeared?"

"Yes, he and I have talked several times this week."

Snow fell on Roxie's hair and melted into her white cashmere coat while she waited for Adrian to unlock the car door. She grimaced as her lovely Prada leather luggage sat in the pile of snow at Heathrow's curbside. Oh well, so what, she thought as Adrian reached out his hand to help her climb into the passenger seat of the car. I've got a lot to learn, she realized. All of a sudden the cashmere coat and the expensive luggage meant nothing to her. The only thing that mattered was to find her daughter and hold her close.

Roxie fastened her seat belt in preparation of the snow-slick road. Adrian drove quickly from the airport parking lot, navigated several roundabout turns, and finally pulled out onto a large highway. Patches of blowing snow obscured visibility, and huge flakes splattered the windshield as fast as the wipers could remove them. Only a few cars were moving slowly along both sides of the road.

"There isn't much traffic," Roxie said after several minutes. "Is the storm so bad that people aren't driving?"

"Probably." Adrian looked serious.

There was not much for them to say to one another during the drive. Concerned thoughts of Cara enveloped Roxie, and she knew her brother felt the same way.

Roxie looked down at her black leather gloves, folded together on her lap. Yesterday she was in sunny California and had said a final goodbye and good riddance to the worst ordeal of her life. Ronald Jackson had been a movie star all right, but over the last year he had grown into a has-been. Liquor and his drug-laden friends had overtaken him, leaving Roxie penniless and discouraged. He had flown into a drunken rage when she mentioned returning to London to await Cara's return to the family.

She had done a lot of thinking over the last year, and even before the tragic news about Cara, she had decided to go back to England and to her home—if she still had a home. Even though Adrian had bought out her part of Red Oaks, she had spent each and every penny on Ronald's starlet friends, their partying and booze. Roxie had not gotten into the drug scene, and thanks to Ronald, she had given up drinking several months ago. It made her sick to see him a slave to his addictions. Weeks before Adrian's telephone call, she was just waiting for a chance to leave California and go back to her family.

A wide road stretched out before them like a white carpet. Evergreens, mingled with blackened branches of deciduous trees, lifted their arms as if to catch the crystalline falling snow. Christmas would soon be here, and signs of it were on every house and street post in the small towns. Houses, each with their own individual designs, sat charmingly against and below the rolling snow covered gardens. Curling white smoke rose from chimneys, and Roxie could imagine the families inside sitting around a warm fireplace, playing games or sharing stories and all talking happily at the same time. That's what family is all about, Roxie now realized. In a quaint little park in the center of a town, snow fell upon angels guarding the baby Jesus in the manger, safe and warm inside the stable. Her eyes stung with tears that finally tumbled down her cheeks.

"Now," Adrian said as they drove toward Farnham, "all we have to do is drive up this mountain, slide down the next hill and around the bend to our driveway, and we've got it made."

Roxie gave Adrian a small nod, but truthfully the drive was unnerving her.

He glanced over at her. "They don't get snow in California, do they?"

"Not in the southern coastal area, and I don't recall this much in England." She unclenched her hands and smoothed her coat.

They approached the driveway of Red Oaks. It was once a welcome sight to Roxie, but not today, knowing her daughter was not here.

Adrian gestured toward the house. "We're home."

"It's so good to be here." Tears rolled down her cheeks, and she brushed them away.

He reached over and took her hand. "I know, Roxie. I know it's good to be back home. I'm glad you're here again. This will always be your home."

He parked the car near the front door, and an outside light glowed on the walkway where someone had shoveled a pathway to the house. She knew the someone was none other than Gus. He had cared for Red Oaks for as long as she could remember. She wondered if she had been kind to Gus and Maude in the past. She had so much making up do. She prayed silently it was not too late.

The next day, Roxie received a phone call while Adrian was out. "Hello?" she asked with fear in her heart, not knowing if more bad news was on the other end of the line.

"Roxie? It's me, Katie. Are you alone?"

"Yes," she replied. "Adrian is with Sergeant Graves again."

"I thought he would be. Roxie, I want you to know I didn't turn my back on all of you and selfishly run to New York for the ballet. I'm worried sick about Cara, and I'm worried about Adrian. He's under so much tension, he's not his usual self."

"Katie, I believe what you're saying. Adrian is different. I'm worried, too, but I haven't lost my sense of time and place. I think maybe Adrian has. We all love Cara, but Adrian seems to feel responsible for her disappearance."

"What can I do from here?" Katie's voice sounded desperate.

"I don't know, Katie. I'll call you every couple of days to let you know what's happening. Give me a phone number where I can reach you."

Roxie wrote down the number, and the two said a sad goodbye.

For the next two weeks, Adrian continued his frantic search. Whenever a new lead arrived, Sergeant Graves called him, and he hurried to the police station to look at photos or to travel with the sergeant to interview people who claimed they had seen the missing girl. Adrian kept to this routine, although it seemed endless. None of the leads helped. Out of panic, he always asked Roxie to remain at home for her own safety, as he had done with Katie.

Roxie pleaded, "But Adrian, I need to go with you."

He was adamant in his denial. "No! You must stay here."

Adrian had not called Katie since she left London. He excused himself by blaming it on his search for Cara, but he knew deep in his heart he should have called her. He knew Roxie was keeping in touch with her, updating her on the events that were taking place. In his present state of mind, he felt this was all Katie needed.

Finally, the worst message of all arrived.

"Dead?" Head still foggy from nightmarish sleep, Adrian pushed up on one elbow as he answered the phone. He tried to shake himself awake enough to think straight. It was the sergeant in charge of Cara's disappearance. "Dead?" Adrian asked again. "You found a dead girl?" Heart jump-started by the horror of such a thing, Adrian squinted one eye at the alarm clock sitting on the table beside his bed. It was five in the morning.

"Yes, Adrian. Sorry to have to tell you this, but it could be Cara.

She has blonde hair and a deep tan. Has Cara been anywhere lately to get a tan?"

"No. Not that I know of."

"And Adrian, was her hair blonde and shoulder length?"

"Yes, that all describes Cara, except the tan."

"I have no idea who this young girl is, but it's normal procedure for me to call you when something like this comes up."

"I understand." Through a throat filled with gravel he said, "I'll be right down."

"Yes, sir. I'd feel the same way if it were a relative of mine who was missing."

"Thank you."

From the night he had picked Roxie up at the airport, Adrian had combed the streets of Farnham and the surrounding towns. On that particular night, he had spent most of the preceding twenty-four hours in his old four-wheeled jeep. He had been in bed less than three hours. In five minutes flat, he showered and dressed in jeans, a T-shirt, a wool jacket, and winter boots.

Before he could get out the door, Roxie came running down the stairs fully dressed and grabbed her coat from the foyer hall tree. "I heard your end of the conversation, Adrian. I don't care where you're going or why, but I'm going with you."

Adrian silently nodded his head and put his arm around Roxie's shoulder as they left Red Oaks to check out the latest information in the search for Cara.

"Darn snow!" Adrian downshifted to second gear, drew himself closer to the wheel, and strained his eyes. Through the frantic swing of the wipers on the windshield, all he could see was a wall of white. No winter wonderland, Adrian thought, as the snow pelted down in large icy flakes.

The wipers worked furiously to clear the windshield. There were seconds of white vision followed by seconds of white blindness. Adrian shuddered at the thought of Cara somewhere out there, afraid, cold, or worse—in the morgue.

Neither Adrian nor Roxie spoke. Each of them was concentrating on the weather and getting to Sergeant Graves as quickly as possible.

The tension in Adrian's shoulders began to ease somewhat when he pulled up in front of Farnham Police Station and helped Roxie out of the vehicle. They forged their way through the blizzard to get inside the building.

When Adrian opened the door, the sergeant was waiting. Adrian introduced Roxie, standing timidly behind him, as Cara's mother. "What happened?" he asked.

"The autopsy will be performed later today, but it looks like the poor thing simply froze to death." Even in the early morning with the temperature barely above freezing and the sun only peeking above the ice-crusted horizon, sweat beaded the officer's forehead. Death and kidnapping were hard work for anyone. "Are you sure you want to see this, Mrs. Landry?"

"Yes, if it's my baby, I have to be there for her."

Sergeant Graves nodded, but his expression was grim. "Come on. Follow me downstairs."

Adrian's heart pumped anxiously. He prayed it was not his niece.

The sheet over the body was pulled back for them, and Adrian stepped toward the slab. It was a beautiful young girl, but it was not Cara. Adrian and Roxie stood there holding onto one another in the morgue. Adrian breathed deeply for the first time since the telephone rang that morning. He rubbed the back of his neck and blew out a weary sigh.

Roxie was pale and shivering. "I never thought I'd be glad to have another false alarm, but this time I'm relieved. I'm so relieved, Adrian."

"Let's go back upstairs to my office." Sergeant Graves was still very serious as they climbed the stairs.

Once back again in his office, Adrian and Roxie sat opposite him at his desk. "I don't suppose you've received any mail concerning Cara?" the sergeant asked.

Adrian spoke without hesitation. "Mail? What kind of mail?"

The sergeant looked them in the eyes, first one, then the other. "I'm afraid we have to include the possibility of kidnapping in our search efforts."

"Kidnap?"

Adrian interrupted her. "Sergeant Graves, I can assure you if we had received any mail pertaining to a ransom, I would have called you immediately."

"Well, I thought so, but in these cases, some people try to take care of matters without the aid of the police. I'm glad you're not in that group. I know I can trust you to cooperate, and I'll continue to call you about every lead I get, no matter how small."

By now Roxie was sobbing. Adrian once again put his arm around her shoulder as they walked to the car.

Back at Red Oaks, Maude and Gus stood in the doorway still dressed in robes and pajamas.

Adrian could see the fear in their eyes. "It's alright," he said. "A heartbreaking trip to the morgue, but it wasn't our girl, thank God."

Roxie took him by both arms so that he stood facing her. "But it so easily could have been, Adrian. You must promise me that from now on, any time there is a call about a young girl being found, you will tell me and take me with you. No matter what time of the day or night, I can't be left out of anything."

"I understand, Roxie. Of course, I'll do that for you. In trying to save you pain, I'm afraid I've just increased your anxiety. It won't happen again, I promise. I did the same thing to Katie. That's why she left early. We had our first serious argument, and I turned away from her. I doubt she'll ever forgive me."

"Of course she will, Adrian. She's your wife, and she loves you."

"I hope you're right, Roxie."

They held each other for solace while walking into the house where Maude and Gus had a fire roaring in the library fireplace.

Adrian walked Roxie upstairs to her bedroom and pulled a blanket over her as she lay across the bed. "Try to rest, Roxie. This has been a trying time for you. I'll bring you up some hot brandy."

"No! No, thank you, Adrian. No brandy. Hot tea would be nice." She looked up at her brother. "I love Cara. I really love her."

"I know you love her, and Cara knows it, also." Dark thoughts overtook him. "I wish I could tell you everything will be fine, but we don't know. We just don't know."

"Tomorrow is Christmas day, Adrian." Roxie's eyes filled with tears.

Adrian tried to keep his tears at bay, but now they fell shamelessly. "There will be no holiday festivities at Red Oaks this year."

Twenty-Eight

Before dawn, Cara tried her best to sleep, but her mind refused to stop. She had no idea what day or time it was. The days and weeks had melted together in one long horrible terror. She turned over and over from her back to her left side and back again. Last night Miss Ryan had chained only one leg to the bottom of the bed, which was a much more comfortable position than having both her wrists tied above her head as they were most days.

Cara could feel the bone-deep icy cold of the winter storm reaching invisible fingers through the cracks in the windowsill. She pulled the thin wool blanket up around her chin. The snow and sleet pounding against the windows made her shiver.

Random bits of thought tore her to pieces—analyzing, questioning, despising until she had no peace. Often she could not sleep, even during the few hours Miss Ryan left her alone. Worst of it all was the hate that had taken possession of Cara.

She hated Miss Ryan.

Hate was something new to Cara. Before her kidnapping, she had never known the meaning of the word. Pride, an oversensitivity, a little smugness, occasionally anger—all these, yes, but not hate.

She finally drifted off. An hour later she awakened from a restless sleep with startled suddenness.

What in the world was that? she wondered with alarm.

There had been a noise, a strange, bumping noise in the hall. There it was again!

The bedroom door opened, and the light from the hall glared in Cara's eyes. She put her hand up to shield the light, only to see Miss Ryan coming toward her with an arm full of wrapped packages. Cara remained motionless as she wondered what this evil woman was up to now.

"Good morning, my darling, Elizabeth. I have presents for you. In case you forgot, it's Christmas day, and I thought you would enjoy opening your gifts first thing."

Cara thought better of even speaking to this despicable person, but she remembered that Miss Ryan was the kindest when she at least acknowledged some of her supposedly generous acts. "Thank you," Cara said, "but I have nothing for you."

Cara looked at Miss Ryan sitting there with a smile on her face, and all at once the only thing she could feel for her captor was pity. This was a very sick woman. The hot hate that had taken over Cara disappeared. She knew her Uncle Adrian, Katie, and probably her mother were looking for her, worried to death, not knowing where she was. They would come for her soon, and this nightmare would be just a bad memory. A tiny voice in Cara's head asked, they will come, won't they?

"You're welcome, dear, and don't worry about gifts for me. Just having you with me for this Christmas day is the greatest gift I could ask for. I'll hand your gifts to you to open, and then we'll have a wonderful Christmas breakfast together."

"Could you untie my leg? It feels numb."

Miss Ryan's voice became soft and seemed somehow distant. "Oh, no, dear. I couldn't do that just now."

Miss Ryan handed Cara a small box. When Cara held it and opened the lid, a little dancing ballerina doll turned and turned to the tinkling music.

"Don't you just love this music box, dear? The music is so soothing, it will help you relax."

"It reminds me of Uncle Adrian's wife, Katie. She's a ballerina." Tears fell from Cara's eyes, and she wiped them away with the back of her hand.

"Elizabeth, remember, they never really loved you, your royal family. Especially the little phony who called herself your mother. She traveled all over the world and neglected you horribly."

"But she ...."

Miss Ryan spoke matter-of-factly. "Dear, you have no idea what a mother's love is. I'm going to show you that love in the next few days. I've waited for this opportunity for seventeen years."

"But you're not my mother, and my name is not Elizabeth!"

"Oh, but I am your mother, my dear. I'm the only mother who really ever loved you. I named you Elizabeth when my own baby girl died. I was there when you were born. I was very comforting to your mother at that time. I planned for seventeen years how I could have you with me, and now it has finally come to pass. I even took a position at your school just to be near you, Elizabeth."

"Please, Miss Ryan, please let me go home. Please." Cara couldn't conceal the raw pain in her soul.

"Elizabeth, you will never go to the Ashley home again. But you won't miss those nasty, hateful people. Think about that wedding. I didn't expect to be a guest, but they insulted me by isolating me in that horrible cottage. I felt degraded by them. Now you and I will be together forever, and we'll never again feel their insults. Do you understand what that means?"

"No, Miss Ryan, I don't understand."

"Well, darling, I could never let you go home after taking you and keeping you here in this ugly little house. I will burn the house, and we will burn with it."

This brought a shock of horror deep within Cara, as she suddenly grasped the meaning behind Miss Ryan's plan. Tears sprang from her eyes. "But why? Why must you kill both of us, Miss Ryan?" She swallowed and bit her bottom lip to keep from crying out. Surely there would be some way she could escape and run for safety. The room was cold, but Cara felt little drops of sweat run down her forehead.

Miss Ryan went on. "If we ever left here and went to a nicer place to live, we would eventually be recognized. Police would come and separate us. This way, we will be together for all eternity. No one can take you away from me again. And we will be famous. You see, my dear, there will be a book published one day, a book about us, and it will tell the world what true motherly love is."

Cara felt her pity for Miss Ryan slip away. She knew the deepest meaning of insanity and now felt only a paralyzing fear. Wanting to distract her captor from words of death, Cara asked in a trembling voice, "Could I see the rest of my presents, please?"

"Oh, Elizabeth, you do understand, don't you? Of course. Here is a new purse I simply fell in love with."

Cara looked at the cheap pink cloth purse and said, "It's lovely. Maybe you and I could go shopping?"

"I'm sorry, dear. No shopping trips for us. Only the wealthy can afford to go shopping. I wish I were wealthy, Elizabeth. I would buy you anything you wanted. But wait. The next gift will please you even more, I'm certain."

"My Uncle Adrian has money. He'll give you all the money you want. Then we could go shopping."

"Now, now, dear, don't get yourself worked up. Everything will be fine. Here, look at this lovely bracelet I bought for you."

"Why would you buy me gifts and then burn them?"

"Just to show my love for you. And I know you love me, don't you, Elizabeth?"

"Yes, ma'am, I do," Cara said meekly as she held the flimsy rhinestone bracelet in her hand.

"I'm going to make our breakfast now. You just rest."

"Could I have a shower? And I need to go to the bathroom, too."

"A shower isn't necessary, dear. I'll come and get you later and take you to the bathroom. You really shouldn't drink so much water. It's a lot of trouble chaining you up again and again."

"I'm sorry," Cara muttered as she drew a long breath. She watched Miss Ryan leave the room and close the door. Tears rolled down the side of her face.

Twenty-Nine

I t had been four weeks since Cara disappeared. An overworked Sergeant Graves looked up from his desk as an aide brought a young man into the room and pointed toward the sergeant. The teenager walked over to Sergeant Graves and stood in front of his desk. "Sir, I believe I have information that may be important in the search for Cara Landry."

"Is that so? And what is your relationship with Miss Landry?" Sergeant Graves inquired, after noting the young man's nervousness.

"We're friends, sir. My name is Harry Wilhelm. I attend Emery Boys School near Royal Masonic. Cara and I spend time together in the library and at the cinema. Not exactly a boyfriend, but I care a lot for her."

"Have a seat, son." The sergeant motioned for Harry to sit across from his desk. "What is this information you have?" Sergeant Graves asked skeptically. He had never had a reliable teenage witness before, and he wondered what the boy could know of any importance. But Harry looked intelligent and was well dressed, so he would at least listen to what he had to say.

"Well, sir," Harry began, "the music teacher at Cara's school is known to be hateful at times, yet Cara confided in me that this teacher, Miss Monique Ryan, has been unusually chummy with her. Cara said it made her feel uncomfortable. Once, Cara saw Miss Ryan give a tongue-lashing to one of the younger girls. The student fell to the ground crying. Then later, Miss Ryan told Cara she had rented a summer home, near Coleridge, it was, and she wanted Cara to spend time with her there. She also told Cara she had a daughter who was born the same day as Cara, but the baby died soon after she was born. Cara had no idea how she knew when she was born. Cara didn't know if she looked up her birthday on her school records or even if this really happened. "

"Calm down, Master Wilhelm. Go slowly," the sergeant urged.

"Well, this teacher was the last person we know was with Cara. She drove her to her uncle's wedding and was supposed to bring her back to school. According to my sister, Miss Ryan is missing also."

Sergeant Graves decided Harry was a good informant after all. "I think you're on to something, Master Wilhelm. My deputies will contact Cara's school and also begin interviewing estate agencies right away. Thank you for coming in, son. Be sure to leave your name, address, and phone number with our receptionist. I've a feeling I may need to talk to you later."

All telephone calls at Red Oaks were welcomed as the household hoped there would be good news about Cara.

Adrian was quick to pick up the telephone on the second ring. "Yes, Sergeant, do you have news?"

"Do you know a teenage boy by the name of Harry Wilhelm?"

Adrian was surprised to hear Harry's name coming from Sergeant Graves. "Why, yes, I do. He's a friend of Cara's and has been to our home several times. In fact, his parents were here with him for dinner about a month ago."

"Did Cara ever mention her music teacher, Miss Ryan?"

"Miss Ryan was the girls' counselor as well as their music teacher, and, actually, I once had a rather disturbing meeting with her. She asked far too many personal questions about Cara for my liking. Cara never said anything derogatory about this teacher, so I didn't discuss it with her."

"That closely matches what the Wilhelm boy told me. I'm curious about something. Tell me, if you were uncomfortable with Miss Ryan, why did you allow her to be your niece's driver to and from the wedding?"

"That's one error in judgment I'll never forgive myself for. Do you think Monique Ryan may have kidnapped Cara?" Adrian's heart felt like lead. He had not trusted Miss Ryan from the first time he met her and now feared even more for Cara's safety. He had relied too heavily on the sound judgment of the administrators at Cara's school.

"It's too soon to tell, but we're running down the information Harry Wilhelm gave me and checking rental agencies. It's going to be difficult to find the house he described in this storm. Meanwhile, I'll go over to Royal Masonic this afternoon and talk to the headmistress. Surely she'd know if Miss Ryan had shown erratic behavior."

"Thank you, Sergeant Graves. I'll be waiting for more information from you."

"I'll call you if I find out anything."

After Sergeant Graves said goodbye, Adrian stood for some moments with the telephone still in his hand. It would be hard to tell Roxie what the sergeant had just related to him, but he must do it. He had promised not to leave her out of the search.

Adrian and Roxie sat in the living room while he told her the latest from Sergeant Graves.

"I think I know the woman you're talking about," Roxie said with tears immediately streaming down her face and her voice quivering.

"You know Miss Ryan? You weren't at the wedding, and besides she stayed at Gus and Maude's house during the ceremony. How could you have known her? Did you ever go to Cara's school?"

"No, no, no. Not from the wedding. Not from Cara's school. I'm almost certain I met Monique Ryan seventeen years ago."

"Go on," Adrian said, sitting back in the chair.

"When Cara was born, a woman at the hospital had a baby girl who died. As I recall, the babies were born within minutes of one another. We shared stories and tried to encourage one another while we were in the same labor room. She came to my private room soon after her infant died, and I allowed her to talk, since I felt sorry for her."

"Did you tell her of your royal status and that Cara was from royal blood?"

"I think I did." She rubbed her hands together. "I never thought it would go anywhere. She and I bonded to some extent. I was all alone in London having a baby without a husband, and so was she. Then, when her baby died, I tried my best to console her. I even gave her several thousand dollars when we left the hospital, because she had no money. I never saw her or heard from her again."

"I'm surprised the reporters didn't pick that up."

"She probably didn't say anything. But one thing she said sticks in my mind. She asked me if I would be willing to sell my baby to her."

"Sell?"

"Of course, I told her no. I thought she was only kidding, and we both laughed about it. She even encouraged me to go back to my family and assured me they would welcome me and my baby girl with open arms, which you did. Oh, Adrian, what have I done?"

Adrian rose from the table and headed for the telephone. "Roxie, just relax. This information may be a great deal of help. I must call the sergeant back right away. He needs to know this." He walked quickly to the telephone and began dialing.

Sergeant Graves had told Adrian he would meet him at Royal Masonic Girls School. When Adrian arrived, the sergeant was already there and waiting in the foyer. The two men shook hands, then Adrian brushed the fallen snow from his trench coat before the receptionist led them into Mrs. Bentley's office. A strange nervous twitch beside the headmistress's right eye caught Adrian's attention as she walked across her office and shook hands with the two men.

"Sergeant Graves, Mr. Ashley, I've been checking with some of the students during the last two weeks. I must say, I was most surprised by what I learned. I was just going to call you," Mrs. Bentley said nervously to Sergeant Graves. She motioned for the men to sit down and returned to her desk chair.

"You'd better tell Mr. Ashley and me about it," Sergeant Graves said.

"It seems there has been a ritual of secrecy on campus that administration has been totally unaware of until now. I've made a list of names and the quotes I obtained. Here, you may have this for your follow up." She handed the sergeant the list and went on. "The girls who knew Miss Ryan as a teacher or counselor all told me the same story. She has a history of being bitter and vindictive toward the girls.

They've actually been afraid of her, so afraid they did not confide in each other or in their parents for fear of reprisal. Some were threatened with detention and even suspension from the school. They didn't know Miss Ryan alone could not accomplish that. Others were denied privileges, others chastised to the point of trauma. Sergeant, I deeply apologize and assure you that steps are being taken to educate all of our students as to their rights and the names of staff they can safely confide in about anything." She paused. "There's more. Miss Ryan had actually compared the girls' faults to the perfection of Cara, saying, 'If I had a daughter, I would want her to be like Cara Landry.'" Beads of perspiration had appeared on Mrs. Bentley's brow.

"Mrs. Bentley," Sergeant Graves said, "as you say, there was a conspiracy of silence among your students, a silence driven by fear of Miss Ryan. At this point, would you consider her behavior harmful enough to make her a suspect in her and Cara's disappearance?"

Mrs. Bentley bowed her head. "Yes, I'm afraid so, Sergeant."

"Then we must focus our search on her whereabouts during the days preceding the disappearance. Did Miss Ryan have rooms here on campus?"

"No, her apartment is off campus, but my receptionist can get you her personnel file," Mrs. Bentley offered.

"Yes, I'll want to see that and also do a thorough search of her office before we search her apartment."

"Certainly, sir."

"Adrian, I'll call three of my deputies to help me run down this lead. You best go back home and inform Mrs. Landry of this new information. If anything comes up, I'll call you immediately."

"Thank you," Adrian said on his way to the door.

Later that day, Sergeant Graves called Adrian again. There had not been any leads from Miss Ryan's office or her apartment. They would be making an all-out search of estate agents' offices that might be governing rental property in the Coleridge area.

For two days, the deputies and police officers conducted futile searches. Just when they believed Miss Ryan might have gone as far away as London to find her summer house, Sergeant Graves interviewed an estate agent who volunteered to show him a contract signed by "M. Ryan."

Sergeant Graves called Adrian and Roxie, who rushed to the sergeant's office where they met the estate agent. The three looked closely at the papers.

"Adrian," the sergeant said, "this contract gives us specific instructions on how to find the house, which is in a secluded area near Coleridge. This matches what the young man from Emery told me."

They compared the signature on the contract with a signed paper Sergeant Graves had found in Miss Ryan's office.

"We're going to search this property immediately," declared the sergeant. "I just hope we're not too late."

Thirty

Cara knew she must escape. There was no choice. She must get the window open. That morning for the first time, Miss Ryan had chained her into the solitary wooden chair in the room. She leaned over in an attempt to reach the window, which she could see was unlocked. Driven by a strong survival instinct, she knew what she must do. If she could only open the window, perhaps she could get out of the house and run to safety. She had been in this dungeon of a room for weeks with no hope of delivery from Miss Ryan's insanity.

In another room she could hear Miss Ryan singing, strange singing that almost drove Cara crazy. There seemed to be two Miss Ryans, the cruel one who had kidnapped her and an unrelated, carefree one who sang happily when alone. Unbelievably, Cara had listened to the voice of her captor, then heard the words again in a more mechanical duplicate, leading Cara to think that the mad woman was tape recording her voice. The recorded voice began talking, but Cara couldn't understand the words. This part of the recording must have been made while Cara slept or even before the kidnapping.

Last night Miss Ryan had said they were going away where no one would ever bother them again, and they would be happy together forever. Cara's whole body shivered from fear. She knew the woman was hinting at their imminent deaths.

Cara would not give up without a fight and a chance to escape. She struggled with the chair, rocking back and forth as hard as she could.

With her fear ever mounting, she tried to lean in the direction toward the window. Her desperation was a source of strength that surprised her. When the chair finally tipped over to the left, Cara fell to the floor. The flimsy chain on her left side snapped under her weight. Her left wrist was scraped, reddening the skin. Her left leg, however, was raked from hip to ankle. The chain had cut through her leotard as though it were so much paper. Blood oozed from the top of the wound, but she ignored it as she worked to unwind the hated chain from her right arm and leg. She lay there for a minute, listening for Miss Ryan to come into the room. She was relieved when she heard the continued sound of Miss Ryan's voice on the tape recorder and realized the old carpet had muffled the sound of her fall.

Cara stood up, opened the window, and leaned out, looking at the ground below. It was not so far down. She could jump. Walking quickly back to the center of the room, she picked up the fallen chair and propped it under the door handle so Miss Ryan could not come in. With all of her adrenalin surging, she did not even notice her red coat hanging on a hook on the back of the door. When she was once again standing close to the window sill, she glanced across the room and saw it. There was no time to get it now. She would have to brave the winter storm the best she could. Like a bad omen, she heard Miss Ryan singing again. Her voice seemed to be closer. This was Cara's only chance to escape.

She climbed out the window, dropping to the ground below. Her arm was hurt again in the fall, and the pain stung almost as much as the bitter cold. She stood, and the wind hurled snow and bits of ice into her face. It stung her skin and brought tears to her eyes as she walked carefully toward the road in the front of the house. Without her coat to stave off the cold, Cara was glad she wore a wool sweater with a turtleneck underneath. The snow was deep. With only her oxfords and no boots, it was difficult for her to keep her footing. The woods around her were deserted and bare of habitation. The trees seemed menacing with the wall of white snow banked up around them.

She could see the road ahead, covered with snow drifts. Occasionally she heard the motor of a truck driving by slowly. She thought if she could get to the main road, someone would help her. She struggled down the shorter end of the circular drive, stepping clumsily, unsure of her footing on the icy snow. As she progressed with greater and greater difficulty, it became merely an uncertain path through the mountainous heaps of snow.

The wind increased. The drifts grew deeper. The sky was dark and lowering, and it was hard to imagine that above the snow clouds the sun must be shining. Occasionally she lost her footing and went tumbling into the soft feathery mass that was so light, so cold, and so implacable.

The five weeks being held captive had been a frightful experience for Cara. She thought about Miss Ryan giving her gifts and calling her "my daughter." She thought about her real mother and her Uncle Adrian and Katie. She missed them dreadfully, especially her mother. Right now, if she saw her mother, she would run joyously into her arms. Cara knew Miss Ryan had lied when she said Roxie did not love her. Tears stung her eyes, and she cried out with all the strength she could muster, "Mommy, Mommy."

Her hands were numb with cold. Her body bent against the wind, her face red from the effort. Once she side-stepped to avoid a ridge of ice, and her foot sank deeply at the side of the road. She stumbled and fell. Her mouth and eyes full of snow, she used every ounce of her strength and courage to stand. Her legs were stinging and cold, and her shoes were packed with snow. Blood from her injured leg stained the snow.

Afterward, Cara would remember only fragments of that awful trip on foot through the snow. As she walked, she had a confused realization of bending eternally against the wind and going on and on. Her legs seemed mere stumps of wood to be raised and set down, raised and set down, until she thought she could not bear it another minute.

The road was just beyond her. She was relieved when she saw a marker ahead with fragments of the words "Coleridge 3 KM" (kilometers). Snow clung to the sign and to trees hanging over the trail on either side. The trees afforded temporary relief from the wind, but they were so black and forbidding that she almost cried aloud with panic and fear. She must not get lost. No one would ever find her here.

Then she was lost. Although the snow had stopped, the road and its marker, which before had pointed the distance to Coleridge, were now covered by drifts of heavy windblown snow and were indiscernible.

She did not know whether she was following the road or if she had wandered from it. There was not a vehicle in sight.

She was so tired, so very tired. It was then Cara, cold and hungry and stiff beyond all endurance, gave up. She sank down into the snow. "I must rest awhile ..." Her weak voice trailed off into the eerie silence as she curled up and closed her eyes.

Adrian and Roxie followed closely behind the rescue entourage, which drove up the first end of the circular drive they came to. Snow plows moved slowly to remove the snow on the road, then cars with red blinking lights and an ambulance stopped in front of the little house where the police thought Cara might be held captive. As Adrian and Roxie got out of the car, they were surprised to hear loud voices in the distance behind them. Swarms of curiosity seekers and media anxious to get the scoop had followed closely behind and now rushed up toward the house.

Sergeant Graves gave instructions for his deputies to cordon off the suspected crime scene so the paparazzi could not get closer. Then he motioned for Adrian, who had cautioned Roxie to stay out of harm's way, to join him. He removed his weapon and held it ready as he walked carefully toward the little shack of a house set deep in the woods.

"Is a gun necessary?" asked Adrian

"Adrian, I think we're dealing with a psycho here. Anything is possible. Be careful and stay close behind me."

He did not see anyone or anything that constituted a threat as he walked into the house, but he could smell something like gas.

Adrian and Sergeant Graves followed the smell through a hallway. Smoke was coming from the bottom of a closed door off to the right. When the sergeant carefully opened the door, they saw Miss Ryan's body lying on the floor, engulfed in flames.

Sergeant Graves replaced his weapon and coughed several times before shouting to Adrian, "Get out!"

There was a loud explosion as they ran out of the house. The flames and the heat of the fire kept the men from going back inside. The wooden house began to burn like dry kindling.

Adrian went immediately to see that Roxie was at a safe distance. "I saw Miss Ryan's body lying on the floor just before the explosion."

"Did you see Cara?" Roxie cried out.

"No, Cara was not in the room."

Adrian ran around back of the house where it was not yet affected by the fire. He saw an open window and hoisted himself up into the room. He saw a chair with a broken chain attached, braced under the door knob to keep anyone from entering the room. His knees buckled as he saw Cara's familiar red coat, and he quickly grabbed it. He realized Cara must have secured the door with the chair before she went out the window. He jumped out the window just before the flames engulfed the door of the room.

"There's no one in there," Adrian said to Sergeant Graves as he was helped to his feet, "but it looks like Cara escaped out the window before the fire started." Relief and hope struggled to beat back fear.

They were walking back to the front of the house as Sergeant Graves said, "I'll call for back up. We'll have to try to search the woods, trail, and road, but we only have a few minutes of dusk left. Finding someone in the deep snow drifts and storm would be all but impossible in the dark."

They watched in amazement and shock as the house, now completely engulfed in flames, stood before them.

Roxie rushed up to Adrian and touched the red coat in his arms. "This is Cara's coat! Oh, Adrian, Cara was here! She was here!"

"Yes, Roxie, she was here." He shook his head wearily. "We just have to find out where she is now. I don't think she could have gotten very far. Are you okay, Roxie? Are you cold?"

"I'm fine, Adrian."

Adrian realized Roxie was not concerned with the cold and wanted only to find her daughter. He motioned for Sergeant Graves to come over where they were standing.

"My sister is joining in the search at this point. We're going to take the other path toward the main road. There was no trace of her as we drove in, and the map indicated that part of the drive is shorter. You can almost see the end from here."

Sergeant Graves gave them a small, quick salute. "Good luck to you. Dear God, good luck to us all."

Adrian and Roxie bent their bodies against the wind and started down the path. The snow had now stopped, but it covered most of

Cara's tracks. Only small blood stains in the deep dents in the snow where she had fallen several times gave them hope they were actually following her. They were careful with their steps, not wanting to walk over even a trace of anything Cara may have left in her path. Because they were dressed more appropriately than she had been, they covered the distance much more quickly.

In less than three minutes, Adrian put his arms around Roxie and turned her face to his. His voice was shaky, his face grim. "We must be getting close to the end of the road. If we find her, let me go alone to see if she's still alive."

"She'll be alive. She has to be alive." Roxie had never sounded so determined about anything, even when she was arguing with her brother about going to America. Adrian was pleased with this new version of the old Roxanna, one who had learned the meaning of family through this awful experience and who was not letting anything hinder her from helping in the search for her daughter.

After a short distance, Adrian shouted, "I see her! It's her!" He quickly turned and tried to restrain Roxie, wanting to spare her a possible heartbreak if they had arrived too late to save Cara.

An ambulance siren wailed, and then the shrill call of a fire engine was heard in the distance. Before Adrian could stop her, Roxie yanked herself out of his arms and ran toward the still form lying in the snow. The frantic mother's entire body trembled, and she gave an anguished cry that Adrian would remember in his nightmares.

"Cara! My darling, Cara!" Roxie's voice was ragged. She began sobbing uncontrollably.

The sister Adrian once considered tough and hardened now shattered before his eyes. She fell to her knees on the crust of snow and gathered Cara in her arms.

"I'm sorry, so sorry," she muttered against her daughter's hair.

"Is it Cara, Mrs. Landry?" an officer following them inquired.

"Yes, officer. It's Cara. It's my daughter."

A moment later, the officer said, "An ambulance is on its way."

Adrian was standing beside Roxie with his hand gripping his sister's shoulder tightly. He reined in his impulsive thoughts of bending to Cara also. Interrupting this critical moment between mother and child was not the kind thing to do. He gently wrapped the red coat around

Cara and patted Roxie's back until her racking sobs subsided. Cara lay in her mother's arms curled up in a fetal position, and her face was as pasty white as the snow that was banked all around her.

Within seconds, the ambulance that had been parked in the yard of the burning house drove up behind them. As they lifted Cara onto a stretcher and into the ambulance, Roxie climbed inside and stayed close enough to keep a hand on Cara, who was beginning to move restlessly. Adrian stood by, and gave Roxie this moment with her daughter.

Cara, covered now in woolen blankets to ward off the cold, turned her head and smiled. Her voice was soft and breathy, but her words were unmistakable.

"Mommy. Mommy, I knew you'd come for me. I called out to you, and I knew you'd come."

"Yes, darling, I'm here. And from now on, I'd love it if you would call me Mommy or Mother. You can't know how good that sounds to me." Roxie was crying again as they closed the doors to the ambulance.

The ambulance drove as fast as possible in the heavy snow to get Cara to the closest Emergency Room. Adrian drove closely behind. Once in the ER, a doctor diagnosed moderate frostbite in her fingers and feet. He determined that her arm was only sprained in the fall, stitched the gash in her leg, and ordered a nurse to attend her for observation for the next three hours. He then told Roxie to have her family doctor see her daughter after they got home. Roxie, Cara, and Adrian left the Emergency Room at 2:00 a.m. the morning after the rescue. They pushed Cara in a wheelchair to Adrian's jeep, which was now parked near the Emergency Room door.

As they expected, the paparazzi had followed them to the hospital. Knowing their thoughtless tactics, Adrian suspected they had camped out at the hospital all night. Notebooks and flashbulbs were pushed into their faces as they fought to get into their vehicle and leave without making a comment.

Adrian pulled into the driveway at Red Oaks, parked as close as he could to the front door, and carried Cara into the house. Maude and Gus were waiting for them.

With tears in his eyes, Gus welcomed Cara home.

Maude, who always was more verbal than Gus, could not keep from talking to Cara. "Oh, my sweet darling, it's so good to have you back with us. We were so frightened for you."

Adrian kept walking with Cara as Maude spoke. "Maude, please help Roxie get Cara whatever she wants or needs. I'll carry her up to her bedroom. Then I have some phone calls to make."

As soon as he laid Cara safely onto her bed, he gave Roxie a quick hug and rushed to the phone in the downstairs library. After calling the family doctor to come and examine Cara's condition more thoroughly, Adrian called his security guards and ordered them to flank the main gate at the entrance to Red Oaks to keep out all paparazzi. This had been necessary at times in the past, and the guards knew exactly how to handle the situation.

In less than thirty minutes, the Ashley family physician arrived with his medical bag in hand. As he took off his hat and coat in the foyer, he complained to Adrian about the trouble he had trying to drive through the crowd of cars on the main road.

"The guards let me in the gate with no problem, but the tabloid journalists and photographers have a nasty snarl of traffic on both sides of the road." His voice held obvious contempt of the paparazzi.

Adrian could only shake his head. "It's one of the pitfalls of being from royal blood. The newsmongers try their best to get every ounce of it."

He took the doctor upstairs to Cara's room. Adrian took comfort in the fact that this man had been the medical caregiver for his family for many years and was close to the entire family.

The doctor soon gave his approval of the stitches on Cara's leg, but spent more time in the examination of her hands and feet. After a lengthy exam of her reflexes and a determination that she was not in shock, he gave Roxie written instructions on how to treat the frostbite and counteract the emotional trauma this young girl had suffered. He recommended that she stay in bed for at least three days with meals served bedside.

He smiled at Cara and gave her a soft pat on her shoulder. "You've been a patient of mine since you were a baby. I'm not about to let anything get past me in my care of you."

Cara smiled back at him and laid her hand gently atop his. "Thank you. I'll try to be as good a doctor as you someday," she said in a weak voice.

"That you will be. Mark my word. That you will be. And I know your mother and Maude will follow my instructions and have you up and around again in no time. I'll come by in three days to see if you're ready to leave your bed."

As the doctor turned to go, he stopped at the doorway, turned around, and blew Cara a kiss.

Thirty-One

Adrian called the ranch in Virginia and asked if Katie was there. She was on the telephone in seconds. He quickly told her that Cara had been found. "It was a horribly frightening experience for all of us. Her crazy counselor kidnapped her, Katie, but she's going to be okay."

"Do you mean Miss Ryan?"

"Yes. She had all of the school administration fooled about what a witch she was. She apparently stalked Cara for years before making this move. She rented an old, run-down house near Coleridge and was keeping Cara chained like a prisoner." Adrian's voice shook with anger and regret as he spoke.

Katie's sobs blurred her words, and she tasted the bitter salt of her tears. "Oh, poor Cara! Adrian, I'm so sorry I left you. I didn't know what else to do when you were in such a state of mind. Cara told me many suspicious things about Miss Ryan. If I had stayed, I might have been able to remember."

"We all make mistakes, my darling. It's all over now. Miss Ryan is dead."

"How is Roxie handling all of this, Adrian?"

"She's doing well, Katie. I think this has opened Roxie's eyes to what family really means."

"That's a blessing, anyway."

"Cara was in the Emergency Room for several hours, but they

187

didn't keep her. I'll tell you the details about finding her later, but right now I want to tell you how sorry I am that I drove you off. Come home to me, Katie."

"I want nothing more than to be with you right now. Is Cara bedfast?" Katie asked.

"Only for three days, as far as things look now."

"Alright, I have an idea. In view of all that Cara and all of you have been through, what do you think about giving Cara, Roxie, and you a retreat here at Grill's Ranch?"

Adrian did not have to think about it before he answered. "Considering the way the paparazzi surrounded us at the hospital, I think Virginia would be a wonderful place for Cara to rest and a way to avoid the press. Yes, Katie, I think it would be good for all of us to be away from England for a little while. And about our honeymoon …"

Katie interrupted him before he could go any further. "Adrian, we can take a honeymoon any time and any place we choose. No matter when or where we go, it will be our special time to give all our attention to each other."

"You're still my angel, Katie."

"Well, we can discuss that later, also," she said softly.

After Katie hung up the telephone, a myriad of emotions overtook her, and she sat in the living room and shook. Tears stung her eyes once more as she ran instinctively out the back door and sat down on the top step of the porch, hugging her knees to her chest.

Rilla grabbed Katie's coat, followed her out back, and sat down beside her. She slipped the coat over Katie's shoulders.

"Darling, tell me the news of Cara."

"They found her, and after a trip to the ER, she's back home at Red Oaks. They'll all be coming here for a visit next week if Cara's ready for the trip." Sobs ripped from a deep place inside Katie.

"Katie, I'm so glad. Oh, the poor dear. What a terrible experience for a young girl. This is a relief for everyone. The fears and tension are over."

"I should have been there! I should never have gone back to New York!" Katie cried and shook even more.

"Katie, you did what you thought Adrian wanted you to do. It was probably the right thing to do at that moment. Don't question yourself now that it's over."

"How dreadful for Adrian and Cara's mother." Katie's chest hurt from the violent sobs, yet once she started, she could not stop. It was as if she had to get out all the sadness and isolation she had been keeping bottled up inside. Her voice gasped and hiccupped like a drowning victim. After a few minutes of this, she fell into her mother's arms, weak and drained. The wind blew her long hair, and Rilla brushed it back from her face. Katie looked up into her mother's eyes, giving her a half-smile. Rilla offered a handkerchief from her coat pocket, and Katie wiped her face.

"Just concentrate on their visit here. You need rest, darling. You've had a grueling schedule, and with the worry put on you by Cara's disappearance, I don't know how you ever performed."

"Those weeks felt like a dream. Nothing was real. I only wish it could have been a dream."

Thirty-Two

Two days after Cara was rescued, the phone rang at Red Oaks.

"The Ashley residence. Good afternoon."

"May I speak with Mr. Ashley, please?"

"Certainly. May I tell him who is calling?"

"Hello, Gus. It's Sergeant Graves here."

"Yes, sir. I'll get Mr. Ashley right away."

Adrian picked up the receiver with no idea of the importance of the call. "Hello, sergeant." His voice carried the admiration he now held for this man.

"Adrian, I just received something in the mail that I'm sure will interest you. Could you come down to the station right away?"

"Certainly. Does it have something to do with Cara's kidnapping?"

"Yes, Adrian, it does."

"I'll be there within the hour."

When Adrian walked into Sergeant Graves' office, the sergeant handed him a large bulky envelope. Adrian opened the envelope to see a black notebook inside. "What is this?" he asked.

"Open it," the sergeant said in a low, confidential voice.

Adrian sat down in the chair opposite the sergeant's desk and leafed through the notebook. He paused at some of the dated writings. In less than a minute, he looked up in astonishment. "Miss Ryan's journal?"

"Yes," the sergeant replied, shaking his head.

190

"She really was crazy. I can't believe what I'm reading here. Did she really think we'd give this journal to the press to have a field day with it?"

"More than that, Adrian. She thought it would make a good book. One entry says it should be published as a description of a mother's true love."

"Ridiculous!" Adrian clenched his hands to control his outrage. "So she mailed this book before we got to her?"

"Apparently so. The envelope was postmarked from Coleridge three days ago. I think she intended to burn the house with her and Cara in it. I called you down here as soon as I received this in the mail. What do you think I should do with it?"

"Burn it, of course." Adrian handed the book quickly across the desk to the sergeant.

"My thoughts, exactly. Come with me."

The sergeant put the book under his arm and led Adrian to the back of the building where an incinerator stood. He handed the book to Adrian. "Be my guest."

Adrian opened the incinerator door and stepped back away from the intense heat, quickly closing the door again. He looked at the sergeant questioningly.

"Go ahead, Adrian. Destroy that evil woman's words. No one has seen the book but you and me, and I'll never reveal it to a soul."

"Nor will I," Adrian said as he opened the incinerator door again and tossed the book into the blazing coals. He closed the door and turned to the sergeant, who was now smiling.

"That's a good ending to a sad story, Adrian. Thank you."

"The pleasure was mine, Sergeant. Can you imagine what a delight that book would have been for the media?"

"Yes, I can certainly imagine the grief it would have added to your family's distress. Now, go home to your family, Adrian. Love Cara, and she'll recover. She's a strong girl."

"Thank you again."

They shook hands, and Adrian got into his car and drove back to Red Oaks. It was a secret he would take to his grave.

Thirty-Three

On January 12th, Grill's Ranch had three welcome guests. Twilight was beginning to fall, and the dullness of the late afternoon was turning a deeper gray that gently folded into itself the rigid outlines of the Johnson's lovely country home. Like a scene from a beautiful painting, the lights from the windows gleamed softly on the bright snow-covered ground. Christmas wreaths adorned with red ribbons still hung on each of the windows upstairs and down.

It was a large three-story house, set upon the crest of a small rise overlooking the massive sweep of pastures. Barns and stables sat within white wooden posts and rails. The large surround porch on the house was illuminated by a ceiling light, and on each side of the door stood two white rockers, looking as though they were waiting for summer breezes to move them back and forth.

As Adrian, Roxie, Cara, Rilla, and Will got out of the car and walked up the steps to the porch, an old brass knocker gleaming on the white door welcomed them. A Christmas tree, with colorful lights and aluminum ice sickles glowed through the front window.

Rilla approached the door just as it was thrown wide open by Katie, who was now home for a month's vacation. Rilla rushed inside and began to take off her coat, gloves, and boots. Katie grabbed Cara first and hugged her warmly. She then hugged and kissed Adrian.

Cara, Roxie, and Adrian stepped into the foyer and found themselves in a central hall with a wide stairway curving up one side. This was a gracious, lovely foyer, welcoming them under the mellow light of a brass chandelier.

Katie looked at the tall slender woman wearing a white coat, still beautiful in her late forties, no matter that she now had streaks of gray in her blond hair. Hers was a beauty largely of bone structure, for her narrow face was delicate, almost exquisite.

"You must be Roxie. Thank you so much for all the phone calls keeping me up to date," Katie said, stretching out both hands as she approached.

Instantly Katie's fears slipped from her, as if they'd never been. One glance from those brown eyes told her she was going to like her new sister-in-law. "How do you do?" Roxie responded warmly to Katie's embrace.

Roxie's eyes were intelligent, and there was something of Adrian about her. She was close enough for Katie to see little laugh lines around her eyes and to sense something about her that was both sophisticated, pleasant, and mixed with serenity.

"Oh, dear! You don't have boots on, Roxie. Your feet must be frozen."

"Not really. The car was well heated." She slipped off her gloves and laid them and her purse on a nearby chair.

Rilla took everyone's coats and hung them in a closet.

After bringing in the luggage, Will stomped the snow from his boots, switched to his barn coat, and said, "I'm heading back to the stable to check out the horses. Rilla, I'll join you for dessert when I get back if you want to wait for me."

"Sounds lovely," Rilla assured her husband. "I'm going to the kitchen now and heat water for tea."

Will nodded to his guests and walked toward the back of the house.

Katie could tell that Roxie was somewhat tense. What did she feel after being away from England for so long and not seeing her daughter in all that time, then going through the fears of Cara's disappearance and rescue? Katie wondered what she herself would be like if it had been her child who had been kidnapped. She pushed the dreadful thought from her mind.

Just then Katie's dog, Gretchen, came bounding down the stairs.

Without hesitation, the little dog pranced over to Roxie and looked up, happily wagging her tail.

"Well, hello," she said as she leaned down to pet Gretchen on the head.

Cara saw her at the same time. "Oh, she's adorable," she said excitedly.

"Everyone, this is Gretchen, my faithful friend and companion." Katie also reached over to tousle Gretchen's hair. "If she gets in your way while you're here, just tell her 'shoo,' and she'll give you space. She's really quite wonderful."

As she talked, Katie ushered her guests into the dining room, where the wonderful smell of hot apple cider greeted them. This was an old room with the gracious spirit of another age. A fire burned in the fireplace, where brass andirons held logs beneath a large wooden mantel strewn with green holly and red candles. Quaint colonial wallpaper in shades of gray repeated a design of old houses.

The Johnson home told guests more about Katie and her family than words ever could. Here were beautiful things, some of them old pieces, and yet there was nothing to suggest they were old, just pieces that were well used and loved.

"You must be hungry after that trip. I know how long it is, and you don't get fed decently on flights. Mother has some hot Virginia ham, fresh biscuits, and homemade plum butter on the buffet. Please help yourselves, and I'll see if I'm needed in the kitchen. I'll be right back with you. Just make yourself comfortable."

When Katie was sure her mother did not need her in the kitchen, she rejoined her new family. Adrian had taken charge of carving the ham and was serving his sister and niece. Katie could not help thinking this was the first time she had met her new sister-in-law in person, and Cara was now her niece. She liked the sound of that. My family is growing by leaps and bounds, she thought.

After they finished eating and were drifting to the living room to relax, Cara asked Katie, "Would you mind terribly if I go to bed now? I'm awfully worn out from the trip."

Katie put her arm around Cara's shoulder and motioned for Roxie to follow them as she led the way up the polished wooden stairway. "That sounds like a good idea. You still need a lot of rest."

"Yes. Mother, Uncle Adrian, and Maude made sure I got rest at home."

"And well they should," Katie replied as she opened the door to a teenage girl's dream of a bedroom. "Cara, this was once my room."

It stood out because of its pink colors. Even the Oriental carpet was white, pink, and gold. The four-poster canopied bed was decorated with pink batiste fabric which matched the window curtains, and next to a white fireplace stood a white writing table with a matching pink upholstered chair.

"This is great. I think I'll sleep really well here."

"Good, and if you need anything, your mother will be right across the hall."

Once Cara was settled in, Katie led Roxie to a white and gold room, large and airy, with four large windows. The windows overlooked the terrace and frozen gardens at the rear of the house. Lights in the back yard revealed spaces between the barren trees through which the white fences and large white buildings could be seen.

"I knew you were on a horse ranch, but this seems to be a large business."

"Yes, it's a stud ranch for racehorses. It was my grandfather's dream and became my father's pride and joy, also." Katie smiled. "I'm sorry I wasn't able to come to the airport to meet you, Roxie. I've been exhausted from my work with the ballet combined with my worry about Cara, Adrian, and you, and I'm trying to rest up. I slept most of the day."

"That's fine, Katie. I do understand. Your father and mother are very nice. It was kind of them to invite us here and pick us up at the airport."

"Yes. They're the best."

Opposite a lovely sleigh bed was another white marble fireplace over which hung an oil portrait of an old Indian woman. Her eyes seemed fixed on anyone who entered the room, and her look was serene and lovely. There was also a white sectional sofa and a Queen Anne writing desk with a matching chair. On the floor lay a thick oriental carpet in white, taupe, and gold.

"It's exquisite, Katie" Roxie exclaimed. "I'm going to love being here."

Roxie sat down on the bed and tears gathered in her eyes as she looked up. "Katie?"

Katie went over and sat beside her. "What is it, Roxie?"

Roxie felt safe with Katie and needed to confide her fears. "Will Cara hate me? Will my daughter always hate me?"

"No, Roxie, she doesn't hate you."

She reached for Katie's arm. "She's been through so much. I should have been there for her all along. I must know she doesn't hate me."

"Look, Roxie, just relax." Katie put her arm around her sister-in-law. "It'll be fine, I promise. Cara is your daughter. She talked to me about you often. She has always loved you, and she loves you now. Don't forget that."

"But mistakes take a long time to be erased." Roxie's voice was barely a whisper.

How well Katie knew the truth of that. "We all make mistakes. We recognize them and rectify them the best we can. We wait with love, no matter how long it takes. Why not go horseback riding while you're here? I think that would be a good time for the two of you to catch up on some of the things you want to say to each other."

Tears rolled down Roxie's cheeks, and Katie could tell she was truly sorry for neglecting her daughter all those years.

"Family is bonded with a thread of love that can be mended." Katie put both her arms around Roxie and held her for a few moments before leaving.

"Katie, although you're young, you're very wise."

"My family has always been there for me, no matter what mistakes I made. Your family is there for you also, Roxie, and don't forget, I'm part of your family, too."

As Katie stepped into the hallway, she heard quiet sobbing coming from Cara's room. She looked at Roxie, and the two of them rushed to Cara.

Roxie threw her arms protectively around Cara, who was sprawled face down on the bed. "What is, my darling? What's wrong? You're safe here, and no one can ever take you from us again."

"Oh, Mother, Katie, I've missed my enrollment at UCL."

Quiet relief settled over Roxie and Katie.

Roxie gently turned Cara over, held her in her arms, and wiped her hair from her tear-filled eyes. "Cara, what's the date for the second term enrollment?"

Cara sat up and rubbed her eyes. "It's sometime in March. Why?"

"Don't you see, my sweet daughter? You can start then with very little, if any, damage done at all. The whole of London has watched for your safe return, and the Director at the Medical School has already called your Uncle Adrian and assured him that you can start when you're ready."

Katie was thrilled to hear the genuine concern in Roxie's voice and to see Cara begin to relax as she listened to her mother's alternative plan.

"If you both could use some hot chocolate and pound cake, I can fill that request in the twinkling of an eye," Katie said.

It was just what they needed to hear to lighten the moment, and Roxie looked at Katie with deep gratitude. "Would it be too much trouble to bring it here for us?"

"That would not be a problem at all." Katie headed toward the door.

She quickly returned with the food and drink, then left mother and daughter to have their dessert together. She nearly skipped down the stairs and into Adrian's waiting arms.

"Oh, darling, I've missed you so much." Katie wanted her husband to know she had completely forgiven him and was happy to see him.

"And I missed you, too. I'm so glad to be with you again. I love you, I love you, I love you." The kiss was deep and passionate. "We must never leave each other in anger again, not even going to bed at night when either of us is angry."

"That, my husband, is a promise."

A short time later, they were interrupted by Katie's parents, who walked into the living room carrying their dessert and smiling mischievously.

They always loved to present secrets to Katie, and Katie suspected they were about to share a secret with both Adrian and her.

"Katie and Adrian, your father and I did more than just leave the Christmas decorations up for you. We hope to give all of you a truly peaceful, leisurely remembrance of Christmas tomorrow that will be filled with reverence and love."

Adrian seemed embarrassed by the Johnson's generosity. "This is too good of you. We really didn't expect anything like this. We came unprepared for it."

Will patted Adrian on the shoulder. "Now, don't worry about gifts. We've all had a lifetime of gifts. Rilla and I want to give you the true sense of Christmas with family, good food, and our traditional Christmas tree, topped by the Star of the East."

"The food is already prepared," Rilla assured them, "so there's nothing to bother with but warming it and bringing all of us together for a feast of celebration." Rilla's voice became softer. "We want to celebrate life, because Cara has been returned to life with her family."

Katie and Adrian looked at each other as tears slipped slowly down their cheeks. Adrian spoke for both of them. "Through Katie and the two of you, I've learned what a loving family truly is. I thank you for that, from the bottom of my heart. With all my own worry, I forgot there were others who were also distraught about Cara's welfare. I was obsessed with finding her and returning her to the safety of our home. I left out everyone, even Katie and Roxie, although Roxie soon insisted that she be actively included."

Adrian told his new family the details of the search for Cara, including the fact that Miss Ryan was undoubtedly insane. There, in the comfortable living room with a fire cozily burning in the brick fireplace, Katie knew Adrian was finally able to release all the tensions that had previously bound him.

Afterward, they sat together, each in their own thoughts, with only the lights from the fireplace and the Christmas tree casting a magical glow upon them. When Adrian looked at Katie questioningly, she rose and gave her parents a warm hug and kiss, then led Adrian up the stairway.

The following day was highlighted by all the merriment of their Christmas holiday. Only four wrapped gifts were beneath the tree. Rilla gave Adrian a copy of her album with the complete musical score of *Things Remembered*. Katie gasped in embarrassment at the peignoir set her mother had selected for her. Adrian winked at Katie, and everyone else laughed, as the women admired the elegance of the beautiful silk nightwear. Cara's gift was a gold necklace with a stunning gold crucifix attached, which she immediately asked her mother to fasten around her neck. Roxie was remembered, also, with a porcelain Nativity angel Rilla had discovered at an art show.

After the delicious meal was eaten, Rilla announced that the serving dishes, desserts, and clean plates and silverware would remain on the table throughout the evening, so anyone could snack whenever they wanted to. A cheer went up from everyone, and they immediately moved to the music room to gather around the piano. Rilla and Adrian took turns playing familiar Christmas carols.

After Adrian finished a rousing chorus of "Jingle Bells," Cara slipped up to his side. "Uncle Adrian, I know Christmas is long over, but since we're having a Christmas celebration, do you know the music to 'Joy to the World?'" she asked. "That's my favorite carol."

"Certainly." Adrian's long fingers glided over the ivory piano keys. "Will you sing it for us, Cara?"

"I can try." Cara sat down beside her uncle on the piano bench.

Imagining what those lovely eyes had seen, what this child had endured, made Katie wonder how Cara could face the world. How could she open her mouth and sing so beautifully?

There was not a dry eye in the room. Love of family, friends, home, and the belated holiday encircled each one in happiness at Grill's Ranch that day.

Thirty-Four

The next morning, after a warm ranch breakfast of blueberry muffins, sausages, orange juice, coffee, and tea, Roxie asked Cara to go horseback riding with her. Riding in the woods behind the ranch would be delightful for both of them. Cara, as sweet and accepting as always, seemed to adjust to everything as it came her way. Outwardly there were no visible signs of strain due to her experience.

With the awful kidnapping behind them now, Roxie felt it was time to talk to Cara about things she had avoided previously. There were so many things she wanted to say to Cara, to explain, to apologize for.

As they dismounted the horses on a path near a frozen stream, Roxie said, "Cara, have you ever resented me for leaving you so often in your Uncle Adrian's care?"

"I knew you were busy, Roxie ... Mother ... sorry, I forgot. I called you Roxie for so long, it's hard to remember to call you Mother. But it really feels good when I say it. It really does."

"I'm glad, dear. Let's walk for awhile." Hand-in-hand they walked along the bridle path. "I haven't really been a good mother."

Cara put her fingers over Roxie's lips before she could say more. "Mother, I want to forget all that. I love you, and I know you love me. Whatever happened before is over and done with, but I want to know you'll be there for me in the future."

"I promise, Cara. I promise with all my heart."

"There is something I'd like to know."

"What's that, dear?"

"I want to know about my father, and I don't want a made-up story. I want the truth."

Cara looked directly into her mother's eyes.

"Cara, that was a long time ago." Roxie stopped walking and let out a deep sigh.

"Mother, I need to know."

"I loved him very much, Cara. In fact, he was the only man I ever really loved." Roxie's voice took on a soft mellow tone, and she stared in the distance as though she were suddenly transported back in time. "He was handsome, tall, had blond hair and blue eyes like you, and he was a doctor."

"Really? My father was a doctor?"

"Yes, dear. A doctor."

"That's so totally weird. I want to be a doctor."

"I know. Every time you say it, it brings memories of Marc back to me."

"Marc? My father's name was Marc Landry?"

"It is, Cara. As far as I know, your father's still alive. He runs a hospital in Kenya, Africa. He's been there almost seventeen years now. Well, I suppose he's still there."

Cara let the words slide slowly through her lips. "Marc Landry. Isn't it strange that he never contacted me? I guess he didn't want me, huh?"

"No, Cara. It isn't strange. Your father doesn't know about you."

Cara's eyes widened in surprise. "Why not? Why didn't you tell him?"

Roxie went on, "We were married after a whirlwind courtship of only a few weeks. It wasn't until he was about to leave for Africa that I found out you were on the way."

"Why did he leave you? Didn't he love you?"

"He loved me very much, Cara, but he had promised to open a hospital in Kenya before we met. The more I thought about it, the more I knew I could never live in Africa, so I got a divorce immediately after he left."

"But you could have called him, written him."

"Yes, I could have. It's just that, knowing he had commitments in Kenya, I didn't think it was a good idea. He chose Kenya over me. My pleas for him to return to England with me fell on deaf ears. I realized if I told him I was expecting a baby, he would give up Africa for me. I didn't want him to regret his decision later on, so I kept you a secret."

"Did he have a wife? Was he ever married before?"

"No. I'm certain that wasn't the case. He was just very dedicated."

"I guess you were really sad to find out you were pregnant."

"No, Cara. I was thrilled, but overwhelmed. I had never been around babies and didn't know exactly what to do. So as soon as you were born, I took you to Red Oaks. It was the only place I knew I could find help."

"Where did you and my father live before I was born?"

"Mostly here and there. I think I've always been a spoiled brat, Cara, and I thought it was alright just to flitter here and there and not keep myself grounded with my own family. Marc and I were married in London and lived for three months in Canada before he left for Africa. I went back to London for your birth."

"Was he a Canadian?"

"Yes. Yes, Cara, he was. French Canadian."

"Did Uncle Adrian or Maude or Gus know about my father?"

"No. They just never asked. When I arrived with this baby, beautiful beyond description, I was underweight and depressed, and they simply loved me and nursed me back to health and never questioned me. They were thrilled when they saw you, and they loved you without measure from that moment on. My mother was still living, and she took you in her arms immediately and kissed you. She truly loved you until the moment she died."

Roxie slipped her gloved hand inside Cara's, and they continued to walk. "I've made some really bad choices in my life, especially moving to California. But the biggest was leaving you, my beautiful daughter, to the care of others while I ran all over trying to find love. The most satisfying love was right in front of me all the time. You, Cara. I didn't realize until I moved to California how much I missed you and my family. It wasn't a simple matter of hopping in my car and driving to Red Oaks. You were an ocean away from me there. It made me very depressed, and I did a lot of soul searching in California. When Adrian called me and said you were gone, I panicked and went to the airport immediately. You know the rest."

"Someday I'm going to find my father. I need to know him. But then, maybe not. I'm just not sure what I really want to do."

"When you're ready, Cara, I'll do everything to help you find him if that's what you want."

"Thank you, Mother. I appreciate that."

"And no matter what questions come into your mind about me, you must ask me honestly and listen for my honest answer. I don't want to be a mother who's forever shielding her daughter from the facts of her life. I've made mistakes. I'll admit to that. But I was never evil, and there never was a time I thought of you without love in my heart. Another thing I want you to know. My life is no longer driven by all the parties and drinking. If being in California had one good lesson for me, it was to make me realize I have a family, all living at Red Oaks. I don't want to be a drifter anymore. I've already missed too many precious moments of your life, and I don't want to miss anymore."

Roxie pulled a small metal rimmed photograph from her pocket and handed it to Cara. "I have something here that you might like."

"This is my dad? Can I keep it?"

"Yes, Cara. This is Marc and me, taken at a carnival in Montreal a few days after we were married. I brought it with me because I intended to tell you all about him during this time together."

Cara looked down at the picture and at the warm, kind eyes of her father and her mother's bright smile. It was obvious they were very much in love.

"Mother, we may have missed the 25th of December together, but you've just given me the best Christmas present I could ever receive. I love you."

"And I love you, too, my darling Cara."

Thirty-Five

When Cara and Roxie returned to the house, Rilla was waiting for them. "Cara, Katie said for you to go immediately to the barn." Rilla's message seemed urgent.

"Oh, okay, I'll do that now. Are you coming, Mother?"

"No, dear. I think I'll rest awhile."

Cara put her boots back on and headed out the back door.

"Over here," Katie called from the hay storage area. "There are seven puppies! They were just born. The runt of the litter was the last to come."

Cara gasped. The mother Collie was lying on her side with the puppies nuzzling against her. Cara spotted one that was sable and white with a black patch around one eye. The rest were all tri-color with a golden sheen to their coats. "Why is that one a different color?" she asked.

"It's all a matter of their genes. They can get color from any of their ancestors."

"I like him because of the eye patch. He looks like a tough guy." Cara's voice was soft and full of instant love.

"You can't touch them today, but soon you'll be able to pick them up without causing the mother to fear for their safety," Katie instructed. "Maternal instinct makes the mother very fearful and protective of her babies."

"Do you think I can come out to see them every day? I've never seen puppies so young."

"Sure, and I'll tell you when it's okay to play with them. They're so cute when they're first toddling around."

Cara visited the barn faithfully to watch the progress of the new pups and the behavior of the mother. She favored the puppy with the eye patch more each day. When the pups were old enough to pick up, she sat in the midst of them and let them crawl over her.

Katie decided to let Adrian in on Cara's new love, hoping he would let Cara have what she had always wanted—a dog. "You should have seen her today, Adrian. The puppies were licking her all over, and she was laughing so merrily it brought tears to my eyes. She has even named one Reggie. He's the runt of the litter and has a patch of dark fur around his eyes."

"What kind of puppy?"

"They're Collies. Very protective and very loyal to their owner."

"You know, a Collie would adjust easily to life at Red Oaks. Collies are very popular in England."

"Oh, Adrian, what a wonderful idea! Cara will be thrilled."

"Will the timing be right to take one back with us? Maybe the little one with the black patch?"

"Let me think." She paused for an instant. "Yes, when we leave for England they'll be about six weeks old. Old enough to leave their mother."

A bright smile crossed Adrian's face before he spoke. "I think we should ask Roxie her feelings on this."

Katie laughed, happy her plan had worked. "Oh, Roxie already knows all about Reggie."

"You sneaky woman," he laughed. "I'm going to have to question your motives in the future. What about Cara? Should we surprise her?"

"Sure. She needs a good surprise in her life. I think the love of a dog will be excellent therapy for her. We could tell her the morning we leave."

When Cara and her family had been at the ranch for three weeks, Rilla felt it was time for them to meet some of the neighbors. She invited their closest neighbors for dinner and told them Cara would sing for them while they were there.

That evening, Cara heard voices in the foyer and walked down the stairway, her heart beating very fast. Suppose she lost her voice in front of the guests who had been invited to hear her sing? She stood a moment on the stair landing, trying to gather courage. She could hear the ponderous ticking of the grandfather clock which was standing on the landing beside her. She walked on down the stairway, her hand on the railing for support, praying she would not stumble in the new patent pumps Katie had bought her.

Cara noticed her mother and Uncle Adrian standing in the group, but her eyes were drawn to a very attractive, tall young man who apparently was the neighbors' grandson. She had been told a young man was coming for dinner, but no one told her he was close to her age or this good looking. A smile touched his lips, but his eyes, behind dark rimmed glasses, were somewhat startled.

"Cara, this is Charles Ray McGuire and his grandparents, Cody Ray and Clarise McGuire, who live next door." Katie looked at Clarise and Cody Ray. "Cara and her family have been visiting us for a few weeks."

"Howdy, ma'am," the young man said as he removed his cowboy hat.

Cara supposed she spoke a greeting to his grandparents, but she could not remember it later. She just stood there, frozen, staring at the young man. He had to be the hottest guy ever to draw a breath. He was wildly good-looking in a dark, brooding Elvis Presley sort of way. He also seemed down-to-earth and unpretentious. At least, that was what she thought at the moment.

"Hello," Cara said, wondering how a pair of blue jeans could look so good.

"So, you're from England," Charles Ray said. "Never met anyone from England before."

"Yes. Yes, I am."

After that Cara could not have told what happened. She dimly remembered dinner at the long table, where she sat between her mother and Katie. She remembered the candles and the silver and the flickering of light through crystal glasses. She remembered Charles Ray's face across the table, his dark eyes searching her own. Of the food, she remembered nothing at all.

After dinner, family and guests moved into the music room as Rilla walked to the piano and motioned Cara to join her. All the nervousness left the moment she stood by the piano with the blur of faces turned receptively toward her, and she knew she would sing well.

She stood straight and slim in her yellow sweater dress, quiet until the opening bars of her song. The full rich tones fell caressingly into the hushed room. She was one with the music; her phrasing and pure tones were so natural they became a part of her.

Forgotten for the moment were all the things, ugly, distressing, and wearying, which had marred the previous months. Her voice filled with beauty and understanding and compassion. In fact, Cara sang as she never had sung before.

When it was over, Adrian came to her first, then Katie and the others. Roxie stood nearby openly shedding tears. Cara stood happy and a little shy in the midst of their kindness.

The adults drifted into the drawing room, but Cara and Charles Ray sat on the sofa in the music room and talked for hours after her song. Then somehow everything changed in the blink of an eye. She knew he would kiss her, and he did. He put his arm around her shoulder and leaned toward her. His lips touched hers, first lightly and then pressing a little harder. Cara kissed him back. For the first time, she understood that a kiss was not something you did with your lips, but with your whole self. She could not believe how wonderful it made her feel.

They came apart slowly. He was red to the tips of his ears, and Cara imagined she probably was, too. She pulled back and said, "That's the first time I've ever been kissed."

"Are you serious?"

"Quite serious."

"Well," he said, adjusting his glasses, "I guess you're my girlfriend now."

Cara began to chuckle. It could have been a very awkward moment, but he was laughing, also.

"It will be difficult for me to have a boyfriend who lives in the United States, don't you think, Charles Ray?"

"Yeah, I suppose. But if you lived here, Cara, I would want you to be my girlfriend."

"If I lived here, I would like that."

"You have a beautiful voice. Are you going to be a professional singer?" Charles Ray looked completely sincere in his compliment.

"No, I'm going to be a doctor."

"Gee, you'll be in college forever."

Cara smiled. "Not really. What do you see happening in your life?"

"Well, my parents live in Massachusetts. They have a house on Cape Cod. I've started business courses at Yale, and they want me to find a job there in the East. I suppose I will, but I really want to be a veterinarian and come back here to live and work. I love it in Virginia."

"That's good. It will all happen if you want it to."

"Maybe. I still have time to change my major."

The young couple spent one afternoon with both of their families in the house, yet as alone as though they were long time friends. They sat in the music room and talked about everything they could think of. And just like that, Cara's world shifted, bringing her one step closer to becoming a woman. Her chest felt as though it were about to burst. Love crashed over her, as unexpected and intense as a sudden storm. From a place in her heart she did not know existed, she welcomed him into her life, and it felt good. She wondered if he even knew.

Cara did not see Charles Ray Cody again during her holiday at the ranch. He went back to his parents' home on the east coast. If nothing else, he had shown her what love was and that, in itself, was worth it all. Cara was more mature now, no longer a giddy teenager. She did not feel sad, but looked forward to getting back to her life in England and fulfilling her dream of becoming a doctor.

Thirty-Six

The morning of February 20th arrived, and Katie, Adrian, Roxie, and Cara were preparing to fly back to England. Katie had gotten a two-week extension of her vacation in exchange for several personal appearances on behalf of Hudson Ballet Company once she returned to New York.

Cara packed the last of her clothing. In spite of wanting to get home again, she was a little melancholy, knowing she would have to leave the ranch and all the new experiences she had enjoyed there.

Adrian walked in. "Are you ready, Cara?"

"Yes, Uncle Adrian, I'm ready, but I'm not anxious to go. It was so great here with the dogs and the horses and the friends we made while we were here."

"Yes, this was a wonderful holiday for all of us. Well, come out in the hall and see what Katie's parents have given you to take home."

Cara walked out the bedroom door and looked down. For a moment, it didn't register, and then reality set in. "A puppy!" Cara squealed.

She bent down and removed the tiny puppy from the carrier. "It's Reggie, it's Reggie." She nuzzled him in her arms, and he licked her face. "I can take him home with me? Back to England?"

"Yes. Katie made sure he has all his required shots, and he's now weaned from his mother's milk. He will take some extra training when we get home so that he doesn't drive Maude crazy."

"I'll take care of him, Uncle Adrian. Honest, I will. I have three weeks until school starts, and I won't leave him for a moment."

Back at Red Oaks, Roxie was a changed person. She settled cheerfully into her new life and happily accepted her role in the family and her responsibility as Cara's mother. Cara enrolled at UCL Medical School in March. She had fully rested in Virginia and had no trouble making the transition to college.

In the next months, Katie rose to fame quickly, and in May she became prima ballerina for the Hudson Ballet Company. After that, more foreign countries were included in the ballet tour. Katie started considering how long she should put off leaving her wonderful career to start a family. She was frequently tired as time passed, which made her doubt her stamina, but she constantly flew between London and New York and enjoyed both her fame with the ballet and the happiness of her home life with Adrian.

In August, Madame Bettencourt received an invitation for Hudson Ballet Company to perform in Monaco for Princess Grace. The performance, if convenient for the ballet company, would be scheduled for December 10th. There was an envelope addressed to Katie with the official seal of Princess Grace. Katie's hands shook as she opened the note, which read,

My dear Kaitlyn Rose,

Please consider being my guest for a private reception after the ballet. I have been a fan of yours for some time and would like to get acquainted with you.

Her Serene Highness, Princess Grace of the Monarchy of Monaco

As the time drew near for the trip to Monaco, Katie tried to convince Adrian to join her, but he consistently responded with an unusual stubbornness. In the library one day, she decided to try again.

"Are you sure you don't want to take off work a few days and join me on this trip?" Katie looked at Adrian demurely. She was trying her best to flirt with her husband since she had sworn to herself never to nag at him in a harsh way. She needed him with her, to share her excitement, to give them both a bit of holiday which they badly needed.

"I'm sorry, Katie. You know my feelings about royalty. While you and Her Serene Highness are chatting, I would be left to wander among the pomp and circumstance of the Monte-Carlo Casino royalty and all those shallow rich and famous gamblers. It's a very uncomfortable evening you're asking me to join in. Besides, I've promised Cara a visit. She wants to show Roxie and me some of the labs she's been working in. She's very excited about it." As he spoke, Adrian continued to shift papers into his briefcase.

"But, Adrian," Katie said to him petulantly, "you could have that visit anytime. I know how much our presence in Cara's life means to her, and if it were possible to get her away from her classes, I would ask her and Roxie to go to Monaco also." She added, "I doubt there will ever again be such a grand occasion for me. Won't you reconsider, my darling?"

He moved closer to her and lifted a strand of her rich black hair from her forehead. When he spoke, his voice was soft and full of love and pride. "Of course there will be other times. You are a star, and this is the life you've always wanted, the life you've dreamed of since childhood. You go, my little one, and enjoy every minute of it. Then, when you're home again, we'll have a special romantic dinner, and you can tell me every detail of it."

Katie bit her lip to keep more words from spilling from her, to stop herself from begging her husband to put his plans aside and fly to Monaco with her. He was right. This was the difficult part of being a famous dancer. It was her fame and her career, which Adrian only shared from the sidelines. They loved each other even more passionately than they had on their wedding day, if that were possible, but they were still apart much of the time. There had been no talk of starting a family, the children they both longed for. It was harder each time now for her to leave him and travel alone. She would focus on that during her flight.

The private jet landed at Nice-Cote d'Azur International Airport, a thirty minute drive from Monaco. The original cast of *Moonglow*

Fascination had been gathered for this very special performance. As Katie stepped off the plane with the rest of the troupe, she gasped at the immensity of the two silver Rolls Royce limousines awaiting them on the tarmac. I suppose, she thought, when your hostess is Princess Grace, even performers are treated like royalty.

Followed by a large truck which transported their sets and costumes, they traveled along a high winding road from France to the Monagasque principality. All the dancers were fascinated by the beauty of the sparkling water of the Mediterranean below them and the lush greenery of the surrounding countryside. Traveling this route, the fairy tale palace of Monaco, sitting on the shore of the Mediterranean, could easily be seen in all its medieval splendor before they arrived in the city. It was, indeed, a feast for the eyes, and Katie tried to memorize the outlines and colors all around her to include in her description for Adrian.

The ballet was to be performed at the auditorium of the century-old opera house, the Salle Garnier, located in the Monte-Carlo Casino. The limousine took the dancers directly there, where a concierge awaited to acquaint them with the stage and the casino itself. The troupe had danced on many celebrated stages, but none could recall seeing an interior as magnificently beautiful as this, with its rich red and gold, its frescoes and sculptures all around the auditorium, and the superb paintings on the ceiling.

Dimitri Petrov, who was again conducting for this ballet, turned to the principal male dancer, Jon Poulevit, and waved toward the various directions from which dancers would enter onto the stage. "Kaitlyn Rose will have a perfect backdrop for the aerial entrance."

Nearby, Ned Blanchent carefully studied the score for the new music that had been added in Act Three. He motioned for Katie to join him. "Are you completely comfortable with the choreography for the new song?"

"Yes. Completely. Don't worry about me on that one." She smiled gaily, recalling the first time she had danced to Adrian's dream music. "It affects me the same way each time I dance to it, Ned. It's one of my favorite songs for my personal rehearsals at home. I don't know exactly how to explain it, but the music lends me an air of freedom with my movements. And the fact that Mother wrote the final score for it as a special gift for me is just thrilling. She swears she is now retired."

They laughed lightly, and Ned patted her on the shoulder, displaying his confidence in the Hudson Ballet Company's prima ballerina. "I'm sure you'll be fine then. I'm glad Adrian dreamed this song. You might just make it famous in this performance."

Katie and several of the other troupe members gave interviews to the press for an hour that day and worked at promoting the ballet. It wasn't a simple matter for her to engage in the business of the dance while missing Adrian so much. But this was the life she had chosen, and the days they did spend together were memorable, making the sacrifice less cruel.

The conductor had called for a 10:00 a.m. rehearsal of the entire cast at the auditorium the next morning. He first gave technical instructions to the stage crew and general reminders to the entire troupe, including the fact that this was a sell-out performance. Then the rehearsal began in earnest.

Arabesque, pirouette, arabesque, pirouette. Katie turned and lifted and bent to the conductor's commands. The rehearsal was rigorous as always, but was more important since it would be the only one on this stage before the performance. Her body, like the bodies of the other dancers, was drenched with sweat.

Practice was as much a part of a professional dancer's life as toe shoes and leotards. The small intimate details were drummed into their minds over and over. Who noticed the two little steps before a jetè? Only a dancer. Muscles must be rigorously tuned. The body must be constantly made to accept the unnatural lines of the dance.

It had been a long week, and this rehearsal was a grueling one. Today Katie was aware of the fatigue in her legs. Her muscles felt overly tense, but the thought of performing for Prince Rainier and Princess Grace was exhilarating enough to make her soon forget her aches and pains.

The crew began arriving at the auditorium again at 4:00 p.m. There were preliminary tasks to attend to, and everyone wanted a perfect ballet this night. The dancers and musicians were there by 6:00 p.m.

Flowers began to arrive, and Katie's private dressing room was soon heavy with scent. On the table near her were a dozen white Calla lilies from Adrian. She reached over and touched one of the fragrant petals. He was so romantic. She knew that at this moment she was very much on her husband's mind. This thought filled her with love, but she was saddened because he would not be in the audience.

Katie sat at her vanity in a pink dance dress adorned with pearls and finished sewing the pink satin ribbons onto her pointe shoes. This simple dancer's chore helped her to relax. She looked at the shoes objectively. They would last two or three more performances, she decided. They were barely a week old. Idly, she wondered how many pairs she had been through already that year. And how many yards of satin? She crossed the ribbon over her ankle and slipped on her shoes as the music in the auditorium flowed, announcing that the ballet would soon begin.

The heat of the bright round bulbs which framed her mirror warmed her skin. Already in stage make-up, she left her hair loose and long. It was to fly around her in the first and third scenes, bold and alluring. Her eyes were darkened, accentuating their shape and size; her lips were painted red.

The other dancers backstage all received final makeup touches and adjusted their costumes. Suddenly there was a hush in the auditorium. Everyone knew that His Highness, Prince Ranier, and Her Serene Highness, Princess Grace, were being escorted to the Royal Box in the first balcony. Katie willed every muscle in her body to relax. I can do it, she thought. I will do it for myself, for my audience, and for Adrian, who always has more faith in me than anyone.

The dancers were called to their entrance positions, and the house lights went down. Katie stood and walked to her door. Because she knew the importance of mastering her skittish nerves before a performance, she continued to take long, deep breaths as she walked onstage toward the other cast members, who she knew were also nervous. Taking her position with the others, there was nothing but cool determination in her eyes. She took her stance with strength and endurance as the curtains opened. She was ready. She could do this.

Thirty-Seven

W hen the orchestra played the introduction to "Dance of the Fairies" and the curtain rose for the first act of *Moonglow Fascination*, there were three dancers positioned on the stage. In less than a heartbeat, they were joined by nine more stardust-sprinkled bodies in beautiful flashes of color and movement. Katie was stunning in her bold steps, her execution perfect, her energy completely revived by her intense discipline and her love of her audience, who gasped at the sheer perfection of leaps and turns. The forest-like backdrop once again added to the mystique of the storyline, as flowers, controlled by unseen electronics, seemed to grow from the floor of the stage in perfect coordination with the dancers' movements. Light dappled onto the performers as if between the leaves of the trees.

There had been rumors about a new dance in the third act, inspired by "The Dream Song," for which Rilla Johnson had written the score. Kaitlyn Rose was to unveil a dance never before seen. The audience applauded at the end of Acts One and Two and wondered how anything could surpass what they had already seen.

Act Three had the same set as Act One, but now it was night, the forest and flowers hidden in the darkness. Blue moonlight glowed from a realistic moon perched at the top of the set. As always, Katie, her hair swinging long and free, made her entrée by gracefully descending onto the stage as if she were gliding down a glass stairway. She wore a beige costume, the skirt of which flowed with sheer scarves of muted pastel colors. The top of her dance dress was beige, also, and layers of gold sequins glittered across the front of it. The same glitter could be seen sparkling in her hair with her every movement.

Danseur Jon Poulevit met her at stage level and, fitting his hands at her small waist, deftly unfastened the invisible nylon cord which had held her, then lifted her and turned her in a perfect pirouette. They danced lightly across the stage together, magnificent in the unison of their movements. As they leaped and turned in graceful steps, the other dancers in the troupe began slowly to appear from within the darkened forest. They formed a complimentary dancing background for Katie's execution of "The Dream Song."

As the crescendo of the music heightened, Jon subtly drifted to join the background dancers. This was Katie's solo. She raised her arms and twirled across the floor as light as a feather, just as she had first done in the practice studio in London over two years ago. In trance-like movements, she let her body go with the tempo of the music. An arabesque ... followed by her grand jeté ... a soubresaut ... a quick, light series of pirouettes. She felt the beauty of her moves, and a familiar inner strength enveloped her as her body arched and swayed to the music as she had never before danced. In the grand Pas de Chat, Katie jumped high while pirouetting, landed, and then looked down, her body dipping low at her waist with the fingers of one hand almost touching the floor. Her long black hair flowed over her shoulders.

The music ended, and the house lights came up. There was a moment of stunned silence in the auditorium, ending with a thunderous burst of applause. Audience members rose almost in unison to signify their honor of this marvelous entertainment, especially the prima ballerina, Kaitlyn Rose. Enormous bouquets of roses and lilies were brought to the stage and presented to Katie and the other troupe members. Thrilling was an inadequate word for the excitement felt before the troupe was ushered backstage for a quick change of clothes.

Back in her dressing room again, Katie was keenly aware that she was about to have a private audience with not just a princess, but the woman the whole world seemed to adore for her beauty, her poise, and her dignity. I'll just have to be myself, Katie thought. I really do admire her and consider it an honor to be given this opportunity. As carefully as she could in the short amount of time, she pulled on a pale yellow linen dress, matching yellow linen shoes, and the diamond bracelet Adrian had given her as a wedding gift. From the dressing room, she was escorted to a private terrace where she would soon be face to face with one of the most famous celebrities in the world. A spokesperson met Katie and reviewed the protocol for meeting a princess.

At the appearance of Her Serene Highness, Katie curtsied, and was acknowledged. The Princess then assumed a more natural, casual role as she led Katie to a glass-topped table laid with linen napkins, fine china dessert plates, and crystal water goblets topped with thin slices of fresh lemon. A delicate bouquet of colorful flowers served as a centerpiece.

Princess Grace lived up to her reputation as a classic beauty in her deep blue shantung dress, with only her famous pearls as adornment. She was truly regal, even in this intimate setting. Katie marveled at her exquisite complexion, which bore only a trace of natural-looking makeup. After all her years in the public eye, the Princess was as beautiful as when she was making movies in Hollywood.

Princess Grace opened the conversation, as was the custom for royalty. "Kaitlyn Rose, I wish to congratulate you on a superior performance in the dance, especially your outstanding movements in Act Three. It was spectacular. You more than live up to your professional reputation."

"Your Highness, I was greatly surprised and honored at the invitation, as were all of our troupe members." Katie noticed a sprinkling of glitter on her hand and arm and blushed, realizing she should have taken more time to be presentable to royalty. "I beg you to forgive the glitter on me. There wasn't time to remove all of it." Then she looked at Princess Grace and smiled her famous smile. "Is there something you require of me?"

As if on cue, one of the casino's culinary maids appeared and presented a plate of sumptuous pastries for the two ladies to choose from. Princess Grace selected two of the small delicacies, and following her lead, Katie did the same. The Princess waited until they were alone again to continue their conversation.

"There's no action I need, but I hope to enjoy your company and get to know more about you. As you may know, I love the ballet. I've funded an endowment for the arts which helps support dancers as well as other creative artists. More to the point, I've followed your career with some amazement. You seem to have risen from the ranks in a relatively short time. At the same time, you're married to British royalty. You have combined career and family in a way I was unable to do."

"Yes, my husband, Adrian, has been completely supportive of my goals with the ballet. But I understand it was the citizens of Monaco who objected to their Princess having an acting career."

"I'm flattered that you have also studied my background." The Princess smiled and hesitated for a moment of quiet reverie. "You are, indeed, correct about that part, but I always knew that marrying Prince Ranier would mean the end of my career."

Katie sighed. "I understand. I put off marrying Adrian for more than a year after I met him because I assumed—wrongly it turned out—he would object to my continuing to dance if I married him. He's related to royalty, even though he avoids the idea of it, and I thought he would adhere to all the royal customs. How little I understood in those early months. He was and is a quiet, dignified man, and I thought he would want his wife to be discreet in her public life. Instead, his love is generous, and he was quite surprised when he learned of my reasons for putting him off."

Princess Grace and Katie spontaneously laughed together for the first time.

"It hasn't been easy to leave Adrian when I go on tour. I miss him terribly when we're apart. And, of course, we've postponed starting a family. At least you didn't have to go through that."

"Kaitlyn Rose, I want you to know I'm thoroughly enjoying your company. You are as fresh as a breath of air. There's no guile in you. I've always been shy about my private life, and it has been a challenge to accept my fate of being in the public eye as royalty. It was your apparent innocence that appealed to me as a woman. How have you avoided the tabloid writers and kept your personal privacy in light of the gossip tactics of the paparazzi?"

"That's another area where Adrian has supported me. He has made it difficult for the press to get at me. Our home is in a rural area south of London, and my time there isn't announced in any way. The man hates the tabloids, and he has frightened most of them away with threats of lawsuits. Only my career is public. My private time is for Adrian and me."

"Do you regret not having had children yet? I love my children passionately. They are my central focus of attention, even when I'm attending to royal business."

Katie brushed the side of her face with one hand as she reflected on the question. "It's funny you should ask that. Before I left New York for my flight to Monaco, I realized I'm missing an important part of my life. I love children, and I'm ready for them now. I've decided when to end my career, but I haven't told Adrian yet. Motherhood and being on tour with the ballet just don't mix, in my mind."

Princess Grace reached across the table and laid her hand on top of Katie's. "How sweet and good you are. Too many women today think nothing of leaving their children with a nanny or dragging them off on trains and planes every time they decide they want to travel. I heartily agree with you. As a mother, my place is at home with my children, traveling with them only on vacations to visit my parents in Philadelphia." She withdrew her hand and glanced at a small time piece lying on the table. "Well, I'm afraid I must end our time together. Duty calls, you know. Kaitlyn Rose, it has been my pleasure to have had this chat with you. I believe your ethics are so strong and clear, you must have excellent parents."

"Why, thank you, your Serene Highness. My parents will be thrilled to hear you drew that conclusion. I'm honored to have met you."

Princess Grace's eyes twinkled with mischief. "Well, I have a surprise for you before we part. Let's walk to the door together. I want to see your face when you discover my secret."

"Whatever are you talking about?" Katie asked in anticipation.

Princess Grace knocked on the door discretely, and it was opened by one of her personal security guards.

Standing in the hallway outside the door was Prince Ranier, accompanied by Adrian, Roxie, and Cara. Behind them stood Will, Rilla, Olivia, and Brad. Katie nearly fainted at the shock of seeing them. Her expression of disbelief caused gales of laughter from all present.

She stammered, but her questions finally came out. "How did you get here? Where have you been? This is wonderful."

Prince Ranier stepped forward with a broad smile and a brief nod of his head. "We hid them away with us in the Royal Box. You didn't think your family would miss that wonderful performance, did you?"

As the full realization of what had been accomplished without her knowledge brought a hint of blush to her cheeks and tears to her eyes, Katie rushed forward and threw her arms around Adrian. "Oh, my wonderful husband." She hugged the rest of her family in a mix of tears and laughter. "This is truly the happiest day of my life. Was the 'Dream Song' really as good as I'm hearing? Did you like it? Was it as good as when I practiced at home?"

Adrian looked at her adoringly. "Katie, you were lovely, more beautiful than the woman who used to danced in my dreams. No one else ever could have danced to the 'Dream Song' as you did. It brought tears to my eyes just seeing you there."

"Thank you, darling."

Suddenly Katie stopped her outburst and backed up several steps to curtsy before Prince Ranier. "Forgive me, Your Highness, I think I have just performed a terrible breach of etiquette. I thank you so much for keeping my family company."

"You are welcome. I enjoyed your performance."

"Thank you."

As the royal couple were escorted away, Katie's visit with them ended. Joyous voices rang through the hall as she walked away with her proud family. Everyone started talking at the same time as questions flew all around the small group. "Mom and Dad, I'm more surprised to see you than anyone. I never imagined you coming so far to see me dance." Katie hugged them again.

Rilla looked at her with a grin and a raised eyebrow. "Well, my darling daughter, if you'll remember, I did write the score for the 'Dream Song.'"

This brought a fresh outburst of chuckles from everyone.

Katie turned to Adrian. "How long can all of you stay? Can I travel back home with you?"

"Well, as long as we're here, I think we can do better than that. Your mother and father have to return to Virginia this evening, but how would you like to stay here overnight and just relax? I know that was not included in the troupe's schedule, but it seems a shame to waste this opportunity."

Even before he finished speaking, Katie was in his arms again. "I love you so much. Oh, I love all of you so much. I know I have the best family in the world."

"Before we leave, I think we have time to join you for a late supper. How does that sound?" Will asked.

Adrian spoke so quickly, his answer overlapped the question. "You might not believe this, but Prince Ranier has taken care of our meal, also. We all have guest reservations in the Salle Empire, located on the Place du Casino here in Monte Carlo. Now, you know I'm not one to hobnob with socialites, but I guess if I want to have supper with you, I'll have to make an exception tonight."

Will patted Adrian firmly on the shoulder. "Think of it this way, son. If an old cowboy from Orlanger can make the Prince of Monaco happy by eating the best food around, why, you just have to follow suit." He gave Will a broad grin.

Thirty-Eight

Katie had been too tired to react to her ballet friends hugging her, the audience cheering her on. The intimate reception with Princess Grace, meeting Prince Ranier, the surprise of having her family present for her triumph, and afterward the celebration were all exhausting. They had run together in a blur of color, sound, and endless interviews. She could remember the glare of flashbulbs in her face and the barrage of questions from the media, which she had forced herself to answer before she all but collapsed.

Too many faces, handshakes, and hugs. Too many reporters, even as she and her family attempted to have supper. While moonlight spilled over the Bay of Monaco, Katie simply dropped into bed in her and Adrian's hotel room and fell into a deep sleep.

She had little time to savor the thrill of her royal visit as the flight took off from Monaco for London the next morning. Adrian, in the seat beside her, his face to the window, was entranced by the magnificent view of buildings and the scenes of Monaco far below. Cara and Roxie sat across the aisle and were deep in conversation. Brad and Olivia sat in front of them with their heads together.

Now, as the plane leveled toward the rising sun, reaction set in. Katie knew she had done it. For all of her dancing career, the need to be her best had driven her on. At last, she had proven herself beyond her wildest dreams, but the elation she thought she would feel was not there. She knew what she must do.

"Adrian?"

"Yes, my love." Adrian leaned back and stretched his legs under the seat in front of him.

"What do you think of children?"

"Children?" Adrian sat up straight in his seat and turned toward her. "I love children, you know that."

"No. I mean our children. How many children shall we have, Adrian?"

"I would love nothing more than to have many children with you, Katie, but this has been a taboo subject. Why do you want to discuss it now?" He was smiling broadly as if he already knew what Katie would say next.

"Adrian, I'm leaving the ballet. My performance in Monaco was the last. I'm ready to start our family," she said softly. "I hope you feel the same way. Princess Grace and I talked about children and careers, and it confirmed what I had already decided."

Adrian leaned over and kissed her "Katie, nothing could make me happier. We'll start as soon as we get home." Then Adrian gave a deep sigh and leaned back in his seat with the broad smile still on his face.

Katie felt her cheeks blush as he took her hand. The plane rose and banked, as happiness flooded over her. She felt the same as when he first touched her: safe, loved and cherished. This wonderful man was really her prince.

She would never look back on her career in the ballet as one which had brought so much pain. Instead, she would think of it as a victory. Monaco was behind them now. Her career was behind them, also.

Katie did not see an image out the window, but she sensed the presence of her great-grandfather, Hawk. I've made the right decision, Katie reflected. She leaned back in her seat with her eyes closed. I chose *love*.

The End

About the Authors

Shirley G. Webb & Janet Moreland

Since 2002, Shirley G. Webb in Connecticut and Janet Moreland in Nevada have written and published four romance novels for Young Adults and Women. The authors met online and found they have mutual interests in writing and in Cherokee culture. Both authors say their friendship came first and cemented the rapport necessary for the overwhelming task of collaborating on their novels while living a continent apart.

Many hours of emails, phone calls, trips between Connecticut and Las Vegas, research, and revisions culminated in "The Howell Women Saga"—*Cherokee Love, Dance in the Rain, Song of Love*—and now, the first book in the "Choosing Love" series, *Echo of a Dream*. All of these novels were published by iUniverse, Inc. and are available at www.iuniverse.com and online bookstores.

In 2008, Janet and Shirley joined a group of writers in Connecticut via the internet in a children's story project. The story, published by Lulu, Inc., is titled, *Shenandoah, Beautiful Daughter of the Stars*. It is available at www.lulu.com and online bookstores.

Both authors visit high school classes, discussing with teachers and students the craft of writing and their experiences while writing their novels. They are also in demand by professional groups for their presentations on writing and have been key note speakers at two teachers' conventions in the Las Vegas area.

Shirley G. Webb writes wholesome stories for children, young adults, and adults. This author is known nationally for her story readings to children from her book, *Tales from the Keeper of the Myths* (iUniverse, Inc.: Lincoln, NB, 2003). Dressed in Native regalia, she takes the children back in time to her great-grandmother's Cherokee village and then weaves tales from the ancient Cherokee culture. Her readings form an excellent multicultural program for schools, libraries, and other settings such as scout groups and summer camps.

She has presented her craft of writing workshop for the University of Connecticut (UConn) English Department and has been invited to give her craft of writing presentations to writers groups across Connecticut.

Shirley's web site address is www.shirleygwebb.com/home.html. She can be contacted by email at authorswebb@aol.com.

Janet Moreland is a poet, novelist, and short story writer. She has conducted frequent poetry readings and workshops for teenagers and adults at libraries and coffee houses in Boulder City and Las Vegas. Her book of poetry titled *Spilled Words* (Lulu Publishing, 2008) is available at online bookstores.

With Lathan Hudson and Sheryl Paige, Janet edited an anthology of nostalgic poetry, short stories, and essays written by former residents of Sylacauga, Alabama's Mill Village, who attended Comer School during the 50s and 60s. This book, titled *Green Plums, Dye-Ditch Water, and The Trash Pile Road*, was released by Lulu Publishing in 2007.

Her works as a collaborator also include two short stories: *House of Seven Mirrors*, with Lathan Hudson; *The Infamous Whale Saga*, with Lathan Hudson, Roxanna Bain, and Johnny "Chance" Jones; and a book of dark poetry, *Confusion of The One*, with Lawrence T.

Janet's web site is at www.newsfromjan.homestead.com. She can be contacted about her writing and presentations at her email address: justwrite4me@ aol.com.

Printed in the United States
by Baker & Taylor Publisher Services